Click...Kill

S. SNYDER-CARROLL

Dear Helen,
Thank you
so much for your
support. Love ya.
[signature]

ISBN: 1503236587
ISBN 13: 9781503236585
Library of Congress Control Number: 2014921138
CreateSpace Independent Publishing Platform
North Charleston, South Carolina

DEDICATION

"It has become appallingly obvious that our technology has exceeded our humanity."
Albert Einstein

For Russell J. Snyder
Never was there a better father, and to think he actually sold Mr. Einstein his first typewriter. That's my Dad, always on the cutting edge, always a man with a plan. Is it any wonder he came up with *this* fantastic idea?

PROLOGUE

Masuki Shin hadn't thought about the blood, about how it would splatter, ooze from the gaping wound, and saturate that blasted white shag rug. He'd been so engrossed in the task of getting the camera to work, he neglected to think through the aftermath of his startling demonstration.

Damn it! I should've had the custodians put down plastic, Masuki berated himself, but the pressure on him to do the impossible had been intense. If he didn't perfect the half-baked prototype Chief Yamato Yoshio had acquired from some young American engineer, Masuki's career at Noboru Industries would go up in smoke, not to mention the whole damn company might collapse.

Yes, his ass had been in Yamato's vise since way back in the forties when he first laid eyes on the contraption. Now it was 1963. Who could blame him for not remembering to dot all the i's?

Masuki looked from the pooling blood to the young woman's body face-down on the conference room table. A perfect kill. An exotic trophy. If only he could find a taxidermist who would stuff and mount her, he'd put her in his modest apartment and to hell with what his garrulous wife had to say. Soon he'd move into a mansion and be like Yamato, like all the wealthy scions of Tokyo whose estates were decorated with Bengal tigers, Kodiak bears, and bizarre assortments of wild beast heads.

So why not the preserved corpse of his loyal assistant? Adrenalin coursed through his veins at the thought. It would be a rogue move, yes, and a poignant reminder of this triumphant occasion. His demonstration had gone off far better than he expected, the other department chairmen had been stunned, Chief Yamato rendered speechless.

But as Masuki Shin shifted his gaze back to the ruby puddle of blood on the white rug, his heart sank. From the moment it had been installed, Masuki hated that carpet. Blaringly white, impossible to keep clean, and constantly shedding, such a gaudy monstrosity belonged in a sleazy go-go lounge, not on the conference room floor of Tokyo's most prestigious camera company.

However, Chief Yamato, himself, had selected it.

So what could he, a lowly chairman, say to his idiot boss? You have worse taste than a whore!

Well, that would've been one way for Masuki to get his balls handed to him on a silver platter.

No, Masuki had to rein in his virile proclivities, put his judgment aside, and force himself to cater to Yamato's every whim.

But how this constant subjugation weighed on him! Indeed, he feared he was going mad, caught up in a web of daydreams about finding the old, capricious pain-in-the-ass slumped over in his chair, dead as a fucking doornail.

Ah, then, I take over. Then, I change everything, he'd think with delight until he walked past the conference room; and reality, in the form of the hated rug, would slap him in the face.

What a potent reminder of his utter impotency!

And, as luck would have it, the conference room was in the wing of the building under his jurisdiction, making it his responsibility to see that it was kept in pristine condition, another obsession of the Chief's, and no easy task.

Masuki Shin cracked the whip on his custodians as hard and as often as he had to. He would not let his success in the company be thwarted by a shag carpet, a carpet that at the moment was slowly being ruined.

Ah, his dead assistant...he took a step closer and looked at the part of her face visible to him. Her yellow skin was growing pale, turning white, almost as white as the rug. A shiver ran through Masuki. He shrugged off the feeling of doom creeping up on him. He had much to be grateful for today, much to celebrate.

Concentrate on the future...forget what it is taking to get there.

A tributary of blood streamed across the granite table top and plop, plop, plopped over the edge. Even a carpet this thick couldn't absorb it all.

He turned away, but couldn't stop worrying...*how does one begin to clean-up such an awful mess?*

PART One

1

Howard Russo was dreaming of Sylvia, naked, of the milky whiteness of her breasts. He kissed one and swirled his tongue around her nipple like he was licking ice cream off a cone. But unlike ice cream her body was hot, and he wanted desperately to bury himself in her, suffocate himself in her warm flesh.

What a way to die, he thought as he awakened.

He kept his eyes closed wanting to fall back into the dream, stay in the dream forever, but already his mind was buzzing. He had a shitload to do and the proverbial hoops to jump through before he'd be able to go home to the U.S. of A. and be with his gorgeous wife Sylvia for real.

He dragged himself from his bed, made a cup of tea, and sat down with the London Times. He shouldn't have bothered. Splashed across the front page was another hastily snapped post-mortem photograph of dozens of dead soldiers, their bodies strewn about like rag dolls.

Goddamn fucking war....

One minute he's blissfully dreaming of making love to his wife, and the next he's staring down at yet another gut-wrenching reminder of the hell the Continent was turning into. Looking at the photo, he could almost smell the stench of death and hear the last rattling breaths of those who hadn't died instantly. How young the dead men were. Not men really, just boys, younger even than himself. An ambush, a barrage of artillery, grenades. Limbs ripped apart, heads half-blown off, legs buckling. Boom, boom, boom. One by one they drop, then whole brigades at a time. They're gone and their blood gushes from their wounds and turns the dirt in the trenches to black mud.

It disgusted and tormented Howard. He wouldn't read the article. He didn't need the words. The photograph was gruesome enough. He put his cup down and angrily shoved the paper off the table. The pages flew apart and settled helter-skelter on the floor. He left them there, went to his dresser, and looked at himself in the mirror.

How can I sit here sipping a damn cup of tea when those poor bastards are...dying?

He was exhausted, rarely sleeping through the night, constantly worrying about Sylvia and the work he had to do before his term at Oxford was over and, though he tried not to, the war.

It was all so fucking hopeless.

He grabbed his shaving kit and headed down the hall of the boarding house to the water closet.

Get it together, you idiot, he told himself. He had to set up his graduate exhibition in Ashmolean Hall by noon, or else.

Or else what? What could the dean possibly do to him if he didn't show-up? Withhold his diploma?

Maybe.

Howard really didn't feel like going, but if he wanted to get out of England and back home to Sylvia, he had to get the goddamn diploma or being away from her like this would've all been a waste.

An hour before sunrise Howard let himself into Ashmolean. No one was around which suited him fine; but fires were blazing in the hearths, and the large easels he needed had been left in the foyer. He set to work moving them into the hall where the light was best. By the time he arranged his photographs on them, he had sweated through his already rumbled dress shirt. He lifted an arm and saw the wet perspiration ring under his pit.

*Damn it. Now I look like a bum...*he caught himself. What did it matter how he looked? All those poor, dead guys. Dead as doornails, and him worrying about his ruined shirt, about which photograph to put where, about what people would think about what he'd done?

Never before had he felt this impotent, out of control, and befuddled. He'd been born with a sharp mind, a high IQ, and he'd worked to develop those gifts. Never had he encountered a problem he couldn't solve. It was what he did, find answers. But this was different, this was big, this was war. How to stop it was beyond the reach of calculation. His utter uselessness angered him to no end, and this rage had found his lower back and was manifesting itself in excruciating spasms.

He didn't want to think about the war now, or for that matter, ever again. He wanted to turn back time, wanted the world to be the way it had been when he was a happy boy in his hometown, Trenton, New Jersey, and too little to know what a war was.

Concentrate on the task at hand, you stupid bastard.

Talking to himself did little to spur Howard forward; and at eleven o'clock when the servers brought out the silver trays of cucumber sandwiches, the copper samovar, the Wedgewood tea cups, and the gargantuan arrangement of white gladioli—their buds jutting out like barbs on spears—everything was ready, except Howard.

Months ago, when the dean approached him about having an exhibition as his final project, he was flattered by the invitation and thought, why not? His interest in the camera as a powerful tool and technical wonder was only surpassed by his passion for what the camera could produce, the art of photography. The exhibition would give him an opportunity to see what strangers thought of his work, and it wouldn't hurt to promote his engineering skills either. At twenty-two, he'd already invented a lens with a high speed aperture for the Kodak Company in Rochester, New York. He also held a substantial number of patents on all sorts of camera parts. These patents were what paid the bills so Howard got some fliers printed, posted them in the local pubs and shops, and even mailed one to the London Times. But all this was before the war had worsened and before the work on his new prototype had come to a standstill.

Here was another thing that had him on edge. He'd spent almost every minute of his free time for the past year working on this prototype for a new kind of camera. When the idea first came to him, it had crystallized clearly and immediately in his mind. He knew, as bizarre as it sounded, he could create a camera that could capture the very essence of its subject, and somehow he could attach the camera to a computer and use the "brain" of the computer to manipulate the superfine photographs.

He'd been so confident he was on the right track; and then suddenly nothing seemed to fit together, to even make sense to him anymore. It had to be something with the lens or the connection or the program? If he had more time, if he wasn't distracted by this sorry-assed exhibition, he could concentrate. Yes, alone in the lab with no distractions, he'd be able to figure out where he'd gone wrong.

Annoyed, Howard hurried through the hall to the WC, splashed cold water on his face, and watched through the blur as it dripped off his long nose. He took out his pocket comb and combed his black hair back trying to tame the waves a bit. In the mirror he ruefully studied his whiskers—he never could look clean-shaven for long. His father Carmen had the same problem. Together they'd spent a small fortune with Gillette Safety Razors. He smoothed his eyebrows with a wet forefinger and checked between his teeth. He closed his lips and smiled a close-mouthed smile at himself without feeling the smile at all.

Fake it, Russo. Fake it.

He looked into his eyes at the infinity of small receding images of his face.

Who the hell am I, really? And what in the hell am I doing here?

He stared at himself for a long time, but he hadn't an answer.

2

Masuki Shin liked going to the baths and taking his clothes off. Small penis aside, he approved of his body, its hairless, clear skin, its bulk. His stomach protruded, but he had muscular arms and hard buttocks, full thighs, strong calves. Even his feet, he thought, were well-shaped.

Shedding his suit and tie felt to him like shedding his problems. Naked and alone among the men—he never initiated conversations in the bath house, or anywhere else for that matter—he could for an hour be content with himself and get away from the awful pressures he constantly had to endure.

Working for the slave-driver Yamato Yoshio was not easy, but Masuki knew there were hundreds of men his age eager to change places with him.

That day, only six months ago, when he went for his interview, he waited four hours in the outer offices of Noboru Industries for his turn. The following week when Yamato, himself, telephoned Shin at home to tell him that he was the chosen one, he hung up quickly so the older man, now his boss, wouldn't hear him sniveling as he wept with joy.

His mother had wanted to invite his aunt and uncle and cousins over for a celebration, but Shin, knowing how little money they had and knowing exactly how he wanted to spend it, firmly said to his mother, "We'll celebrate when I am the one who runs Noboru Industries. So save up, Mother, for that happy day. Now I must prepare myself for the challenges ahead. I'm going for a walk to clear my head and make my plans."

Shin took the last of the yen from the box by his mother's mat and left the one room apartment he shared with her. It was dark, but he knew his way through the narrow alleys of Roppongi to his destination. He'd been past the small, dimly-lit bar many times and many times dreamt of the day he'd have enough money to go in and buy cigarettes and drinks the way other men in suits did. Up until now every penny his mother made at the tailors in the Ginza was spent on rent and food and Shin's education. She'd been thrifty and crafty, salvaging fabric from old clothes discarded by rich men to make Shin's business suit. She'd behaved as though she were sure of her only son's potential and knew her sacrifices now would pay off later when she would live with him in the lap of luxury.

Shin knew how disappointed his mother had been with his father, the lazy man content to unload fish at the market, then sit in a rundown bar drinking cheap shochu till he was too drunk to walk. Shin could see on her face, though he knew she tried to hide it, how happy she was when one night he never came home. His mother did send young Shin out before dawn to search for his father at the market, but the people Shin spoke to were surprised to learn that old Masuki had a son; and, no, they hadn't seen him for days because, didn't his family know, he'd been fired.

Shin thought of that day as he sat down at the fancy bar and looked around at the small, but opulent room. Red silk curtains covered the walls and crystal sconces with pleated shades shaped like sails cast a kaleidoscope of colors on the glass that covered the mahogany bar. The bottles of liquor were so free of dust they gleamed even in the dim light. Two other well-dressed men sat in the high-backed leather stools to the left of Shin engrossed in quiet conversation. No, this was not the kind of place his father had ever been in.

The bartender stood in front of the young Mr. Masuki waiting.

"A scotch whiskey, please." Shin had no idea what brand to ask for so he added, "Good quality, please."

But as soon as he said it, he was sorry he did. Would he have enough yen? Now, how could he enjoy himself, how could he savor the golden liquid, celebrate his first opportunity to move up and away from his pitiful beginnings, when he had to worry about whether he had enough money or not?

Shin pulled his heavy wet body out of the steaming pool of water and headed for the cold tub.

No more will I have to worry about how many yen I have, he thought. For now he'd been receiving a decent pay check from Noboru Industries and could afford the "good quality" single malt Sendai at his favorite bar in the better section of the Roppongi Hills. Now he seldom went home to eat. He found that the bartender would send a boy out to bring a meal back. He could sit at the bar and sip his drink and enjoy a solitary meal all at the same time.

Better visit mother before I go tonight, he thought. *If not, she'll be waiting to harass me when I need to sleep, when I'm exhausted, and the golden liquor is working its magic. She'll ruin the night.*

He really must move out, get his own place. He was twenty years old now, an engineer already at such a young age. He'd applied himself diligently at the university, and his exemplary performance kept him from being conscripted into the service. Trouble with China was escalating, Japan was building up forces; but they needed engineers and high-powered surveillance equipment. He was ahead of all the men his age, working for the most progressive camera company in all of Japan, if not the world.

So why was he still living in a dump with his mother, who reveled in pointing out every one of his faults? How she'd turned on him! Before she could not say enough times how smart he was, how clever he was, how wonderful he was. And now that he was showing her how smart and clever and wonderful he was, all she did was put him down.

"Why don't you come home?" "Where do you go?" "How can you leave me alone like this night after night?" She badgered him. Didn't she realize how hard he had to work? How Yamato Yoshio worked him to the bone every day? How he never left the laboratory until very, very late? Like tonight, it was after 11:00 p.m., and he was only just finishing his bath. What did she expect?

As he dried himself and dressed, he remembered overhearing one of the older business men, Ishikawa Daiki, telling another man about his daughter. "She is my daughter and I love her; but unfortunately she looks like me and not my beautiful wife so, of course, I have saved up a war chest of a dowry for her. Any man who marries this poor daughter of mine, who has, honestly, been hit with the ugly stick, will be richly rewarded."

Daiki's horsey laugh offended Shin's ears so he moved with his drink to a table in the corner by the door. But now as he headed out of the bath house, and the thought of going home to his mother weighed on him, the man's words rang in his head, *"a war chest of a dowry…."*

A difficult temptation to resist, indeed.

3

By noon, Ashmolean Hall was packed. Howard put on a happy face and politely greeted his guests.

A short, plump, young woman with curly red hair hurried through the main foyer. As she struggled with pulling her arms out of her overcoat, her breasts pushed against the soft pink wool of her sweater. This young woman didn't look a thing like his wife Sylvia, but when he spied the points of her bra, his dream came back to him. Hell, he never should've left Sylvia behind. He should've insisted she take off from Rensselaer and come abroad with him. What difference would a semester's delay have meant to her?

God, he'd been so awful lonely. In a matter of days, if all went well with today's exhibition and the university granted him his credentials, he might be able to leave for home. Yet, this did little at the moment to assuage his gnawing discontent.

The redhead was coming through the foyer in his direction. She'd linked arms with her friend, a striking, raven-haired beauty, her severe bob cut at the jawline leaving the white flesh of her swanlike neck completely naked. Her posture was ramrod straight, her waist incredibly small. The redhead chattered away, and the other woman leaned in to listen. Mismatched as the two of them were, the thought of spending a night with either of them, or better yet, both of them popped into Howard's brain.

"Oh, sandwiches! How lovely! Mr. Russo...you are Mr. Russo, aren't you? Tell me you made them yourself!" The taller one laughed more huskily than Howard would've expected as her eyes swept over the long table of food before she looked into his.

"Oh, Constance, of course he didn't make them." The corkscrews of red curls bounced as the other woman giggled. "Well, I, for one, am glad for the tea. There's a dreadful chill outside that seems to have followed us in."

"Nan, I was just teasing Mr. Russo," Constance said and extended her hand toward Howard. "So pleased to meet you. We saw your picture in the Bulldog. Nan's brother is a grad student here. Stewart Longstreet? Perhaps, you know him?"

"He's ever so handsome. I do think so even if he is my brother," Nan interrupted.

Howard tried to interject that he didn't have a clue who this Stewart guy was, but then Constance looked directly at Howard and said, "But Nan's Stewart's not nearly as handsome as you, Mr. Russo."

And Nan babbled on, "We were so thrilled about the exhibition. Such a marvelous opportunity to be able to actually meet you and take a look at your work. You know you have quite a reputation."

For what? Howard was tempted to ask. He didn't think anyone knew of him except the people at Kodak, but he liked the way Constance wasn't the least bit shy. On another day, what she'd said about him being handsome might've made him blush, but today all it did was put crazy ideas in his head. Her deep voice, the gap between the buttons of her blouse, the way she didn't seem to notice that a bit of her cleavage was visible to him, it was all coming together in his head and he started playing an old game of his. Would he like to fuck her? But he was married now, happily. Maybe, if he were a single man, he'd ask her out for a pint or two and then take her back to his flat. Yes, if he were single, he would've taken this Constance back to his room.

When he wasn't studying or working on his prototype or hanging out with Lytton at the Lion's Gate, he was thinking of Sylvia, of the ripe, juicy apples of her breasts and the thick curly dark hair between her legs and the wet place he put his tongue every time she let him. There were times he was so hungry for her he could taste her. And then he'd start thinking about the last time they made love before he left for Oxford. He took one of her breasts in his mouth, the whole thing, and his lips were pulled back, his teeth bared. He felt a bizarre desire to bite it off.

Nan was giggling again. Her giggles sounded like cackles to Howard and dashed any possibility he might include her in the fictitious invitation he was already fantasizing about offering to Constance. How would he, if he were going to take Constance out for a drink, get Constance away from Nan?

Howard was almost six feet tall and towered a good five inches above even Constance. He looked down. The women were looking up at him with their mouths open like baby birds waiting for worms. He felt like feeding them, like dropping crumbs down into their cherry red, little beaks.

An older man pushed by them almost knocking Howard into Nan. Howard turned in expectation of an apology, but the hefty man was already talking to someone else. His face was ruddy and mottled with liver spots. He had a rather ugly bulbous sausage of a nose.

Too much sun or too much whiskey, thought Howard. *Must not be a local. Can't get that kind of sunburn around here with all the goddamn fog.*

The man wore a black, slightly wrinkled suit, a pinstriped shirt whose collar was ever so slightly frayed, and a loud paisley ascot, mostly purples and pinks. He had a double chin and the second one was fleshy like a pelican's empty gullet. His thin hair, the color of pine needles, was slicked back in flat strips that did little to hide his baldness. Behind shiny gold wire-rimmed glasses, his dark eyes sank into their puffy sockets. It looked as though he had no eyelashes, yet his eyebrows were long, brown, and swept up into wings.

Howard watched as the fellow moved away from the person with whom he'd been conversing and plowed through the crowd determinedly, his head swiveling back and forth as though he were searching for someone. He stopped in front of one of the photographs. It was of an artist painting a nude man who stood with his legs spread and his arms folded across his chest like the famous Colossus. Howard had taken the shot from behind the artist so the artist and his painting were in the foreground, the naked man in the background. The model was not well-endowed, but in the painting the artist altered this reality. The enlarged penis in the painting was eye-catching and beautifully shaped and clearly a thing any man would love to have. Howard thought the photograph was funny. When he looked at it, it made him laugh every single time.

The disheveled stranger stared at the picture.

What's he thinking? Howard couldn't read his expression.

"I beg your pardon." Howard moved away from the two birds and headed toward the man. By the time he caught up to him, though, the man had moved to a landscape of Innisfree and was examining it through a small magnifying glass. He was so close to the photograph the nob of his inflamed nose almost touched it.

"So vivid, so blasted vivid." Howard overheard the man was talking to himself.

"I take it you like it?" Howard leaned forward. Together they stared at the picture of a cottage by a lake.

"Brilliant! What's not to like? It's capital work! Capital!" He stepped back and tucked the small instrument into his breast pocket. "I've been there many times, but looking at this is more powerful than seeing it with my own eyes. Are you the young man responsible for all of this?"

Howard nodded, and the stranger gave him the once over and stuck out his large lower lip before he said, "You don't say."

He moved on to the next photograph. It was of a woman dressed in sooty old clothes trying to paint the glass transom over the door of her small house. The brush was too full. Globs of black paint oozed down over her hand and most of her forearm and dripped onto her face and shoulder. She seemed in a hurry and not to care about the mess. Her face was only partially visible, but from what could be seen, she seemed to be frowning.

"What's your secret, chap?" The man turned to look Howard in the eye. Sweat dotted his forehead and a dark rim of perspiration lined the edge of his ascot where it touched his throat.

"Patience." Howard had no clue why he said that. He had little patience, especially for failure or imperfection. He invented things in a mad rush, took his photos with barely a moment's hesitation.

"Why, I'll say, and your patience has paid off. You must've taken this one in London. Why it really captures the filthy black mess we've gotten ourselves into, eh? With the blackouts and all. I, myself, think they're useless. Why the bloody Nazis can find us by following the Thames. You know you can see the water at night from the sky. Why sure they can, it reflects the moon, or the stars, that is if there isn't a moon. It's a bloody silver path on a black slate." His tone was argumentative as though he expected Howard would disagree.

The man's voice rose an octave higher as he talked and walked to the next picture. Howard followed not wanting to be rude, though by now he found the man annoying and his bloated opinions of the photos patronizing.

"But it, this bloody awful war, isn't your problem. I see you're a Yank." He waved a flyer in Howard's face. "You'll graduate in a couple of weeks, and it'll be off across the pond for you. Back to safety, back to new inventions." He smacked the paper into the palm of his hand and stopped to look accusingly up at Howard. "And what new great thing might you be working on at the moment, Mr. Russo?"

"A new camera." Howard paused not wanting to go into any details, but the man steadied his gaze on Howard and waited. Howard reluctantly added, "A camera that can be hooked up to a computer."

"A what? What in bloody hell? A computer? Why do they even genuinely exist, man? I, myself, think they're simply figments of an overactive imagination. Come now, Mr. Russo, you must admit that talk of a machine that can think, that can outsmart a real living, breathing human being, well, that kind of talk must be poppycock. Wouldn't you say, old chap!" The stranger leaned back and rose up slightly on his toes.

"Oh, sir, it's not just talk. Computers are real." Howard felt the urge to set the old man straight. Here was his opportunity to put the blowhard in his place. "We have one right here on campus, and I've worked on it, and I can tell you, Mr.?"

"Um...Bailey."

"Mr. Bailey, I can tell you that one day these figments of an overactive imagination, as you call them, will run the world."

Enough said, thought Howard as he started to look over the man's head in anticipation of moving on to talk to someone else, someone less tedious than this old hoot.

But Bailey persisted, "How? Tell me how, young man, you and your generation think machines will be able to run the world?"

His incredulity was infuriating.

"Damn it, sir," Howard said impatiently, "don't you realize computers can already add and subtract? I'm looking to the future. There will be millions of things machines will be able to do so I thought down the road there will be some way to hook a camera up to...oh, it's very complicated. If you were an engineer, I might be able to explain it to you."

"Admit it. You can't explain it because all a computer is, is a glorified abacus. So I don't see where you're going with your idea about the camera, but don't mind me. It's a jolly new world out there, and tots like yourself certainly do hold the future in the palm of your little pink hands." The stranger drew in his breath, and after a gravelly cough added, "Old and stupid, out-of-touch, that's what I am, that's just what I am. Guess I don't understand much anymore, but..." he paused again as if reconsidering something, "it wouldn't hurt none for me to try to understand what you're talking about. Right, old chap?"

Bailey rocked back on his heels. Howard looked down at him. A crumb clung to the corner of his mouth and between that and the dumbfounded expression on his face, he looked pretty stupid indeed. The last thing Howard wanted to do was talk to this man about his idea. True, at this point it was nothing more than far-fetched science fiction, but Howard knew there had to be some way to connect a camera to a computer and program the computer to manipulate the photographs. It could work, and if it did, it would be powerful. He just shouldn't have said anything. It was none of this fellow's business, whoever he was.

By now Howard was sorry he ever left the two women, especially Constance. He felt shaky and tired. It was wearing him down, thinking about his bizarre and fantastical idea, trying to explain it when he couldn't get it to work. When he heard himself talk about it, it sounded crazy, absolutely crazy; yet when it was in his head, it made perfect sense, beautifully perfect sense.

The hall was filled to capacity. People jostled about trying to balance their tea cups while eating their scones. The cacophony of voices rose and echoed from the high ceilings. A swirling haze of cigarette smoke hung overhead. The fires in the two hearths at opposite ends of the hall flared as the caretaker walked from one to the other prodding each with the poker and throwing on new logs. The air turned stuffy, the room hot.

"Look," Howard said, "I am not even sure what I'm talking about. It's just a crazy idea. That's it. Just a crazy fantasy of mine, that's all. Sorry, excuse me, but I think I need some fresh air."

He turned quickly almost knocking down a middle-aged woman who was heading toward Mr. Bailey and shouting at him above the din, "Sir Astin! Sir Tyler Astin! Over here! It's me! Over here, Sir Astin!"

"But, Madam, that's Mr. Bailey," Howard interrupted.

"Oh no, my dear, that's Sir Astin. Why, I've known him nearly my whole life."

"But, but..." Howard was going to argue, going to turn back and ask the man why he'd lied, but he didn't. He shrugged his shoulders. *Sir, my foot. If he's been knighted, then I sure wouldn't want to be — the damn liar.*

As Howard neared the doorway, he saw two of his professors standing in front of his largest photograph, a cow from the herd that grazed in the field adjacent to the hall.

"...never quite understood cows before. This one appears to have feelings. I hadn't thought they'd had any." A fragment of their conversation drifted toward Howard just as he passed by them.

"Howard Russo." The other one spotted him and called out, "Join us!"

Howard reluctantly stopped and stepped backward to face them.

"Well, young Mr. Russo, I don't think I'll be able to eat a good roast beef again without feeling rather badly about it, at least not for a good long while. You've bloody spoiled it for me with this image here. It's so realistic, like I'm looking into the soul of the poor beast. Yes, young man, you just plain spoiled my love affair with braised meat."

"Sorry, sir," Howard mumbled and smiled so half-heartedly he feared he'd offend his teachers, but he had to get out of there. Without explaining he moved away, pushed past the human herd grazing at the table, side-stepped the throngs milling around near the heavy wooden doors, and went out into the grey morning.

4

Ishikawa Kenta wasn't as ugly as her father Ishikawa Daiki had claimed. She, in fact, had a rather pleasant plainness about her that Masuki Shin found tolerable. Besides, the grandness of her bridal attire more than made up for the reality of what lay beneath the thick white face make-up applied by the Geisha from Kyoto who had been hired by her father at no small expense. And the voluptuous wig, fashioned from a real human mane, hid Kenta's own limp, sparse hair and completely distracted one from noticing her pea eyes, fat cheeks, and pointy nose. The Geisha tried to diminish the impact of her double chin by brushing a dark shadow over it. It only worked from a distance. At close range the attempt at deception was embarrassingly obvious. But Kenta waddled down the garden path on her yukata beneath her giant parasol as though she were a princess.

It took Shin a minute to take in the spectacle of his bride in her shiro-maku and tsuno kabushi. She looked like a sumo wrestler decked out in a white sheet with a white pillowcase for a hat. He joined her at the entrance to the central sanctuary and walked beside her with a stoic look on his face.

This is all for the best, he told himself as he glanced around scanning the crowd for his in-laws. The parade through the garden of the Meiji Shrine seemed to take forever, but then again Kenta wasn't hurrying and kept annoyingly checking her hakosiko to make sure the sheathed sword was in it. She needed all the good luck she could get on such an auspicious day. When Shin spied his future father-in-law, his face lit up.

Soon the promised dowry will be in my hands.

He would buy a beautiful apartment on the highest Roppongi Hill, near enough to his favorite bar so he could still stop there frequently. And there would be three separate rooms for his future children. He could see that his new wealthy family would be more than generous to any offspring he and Kenta would produce. Thinking of such a bright future led him to become excited about having sex with his huge bride. He imagined her full breasts and the deep cleft of her large ass. It would be fine. He would force himself to be content with her while helping himself to her father's bounty.

The ceremony went off without a hitch. Shin's mother wept at the heartfelt words her son spoke to her future daughter-in-law as he made his commitment vows.

"My love for you, Kenta," he said, his voice shaking with emotion as he glanced at his new father-in-law, the great and famous business man, Ishikawa Daiki, "will outlive even the life of Fujisan." Many shook their heads approvingly, and Shin was sure he saw a tear in Daiki's eye.

Kenta was escorted from the front of the temple by her attendants to a side room. Moments passed before she emerged in a bright green uchikake. Woven into the silk fabric were hundreds of images of Mount Fuji. Such a fortuitous coincidence! But all Shin could see were the dozen or so gold kanzashi that dotted the massive black wig.

All of that gold is mine! Truly, there has never been a better day in my life.

The wedding party and guests walked across the courtyard to the reception hall. The women sat at the tables. The men gathered around the bar. Many rounds of food were served in rapid succession, and the whiskey flowed so freely that it wasn't long before the women were full and the men drunk.

Soon, Masuki, thought, *Ishikawa Daiki will hand me the dowry.*

So anxious was Masuki that when his father-in-law approached him, his heart beat so rapidly he thought he might faint. His palms were sweaty. He wiped his hand on his kimono before he shook Ishikawa's. But instead of an envelope filled with money, the business man handed him a key.

5

A few feeble rays of sun pierced the cloud cover and slashed a narrow yellow path on the hay-strewn lawn. In the cold air Howard's breath condensed into white vapor. He shoved his hands in his jacket pockets and began pacing the length of the fence. The air reeked of manure. Smoke swirled down from the chimney and stung his eyes.

I tried not to look. Howard was thinking of the front page photograph in the Times of the bloody trench. One boy sprawled atop two others, skull half gone, legs open, crotch soaked with urine. *Peed his damn pants. Probably shit himself too. His arms outstretched. Christ on the cross. And that rifle almost as long as he was. Just out of reach.*

Beneath that photograph was another of hundreds of children marching behind a boy carrying a red flag embellished with a black swastika. The children thrust their thin arms out like daggers and their beautiful faces had scowls on them and their eyes looked like holes in the barrels of guns. If you looked quickly at the picture, it was like you were looking at one giant, rolling, war machine.

There were rumors, horrible whispered rumors, about how people were being rounded up and taken away on trains to areas outside cities where no one was allowed to go. Smoke bellowed day and night from distant stacks; and when the wind blew in a particular direction, the stench made the farmers sick, forcing them from their fields and into their homes. What was burning? No one dared to say.

But they know. And I know. Howard stopped walking and fought hard against the feelings sweeping over him. Anger welled up in him. His fist was in the air. He pounded it down on the top of a fence post. Again and again and again, harder, harder, harder. There was a pop. Howard knew he'd broken a bone and he was glad. The pain calmed him. He watched as his hand swelled and the throbbing began.

I deserve to be in pain. All hell is breaking loose, and I'm wasting time taking photographs of goddamn cows.

He rested his head on the post and imagined himself in a uniform, the cold barrel of a rifle in his hand. He imagined the screams of children, not the marching children but the dying children who were being gassed and whose corpses were being burned in the ovens. It was the dead children that the farmers smelled. That's what was making them sick.

The thought of violence revolted Howard, but now hot blood was rising up inside him. Whoever did such things had to be stopped. The thought of going to war, of leaving Sylvia again was hateful to him, yet he could no longer avoid this moral imperative. If he was a good man, which he did believe himself to be, then it was up to him to stop such evil from spreading or at least die trying.

All of his dreams of a camera that could produce great art, the kind of art that was full of truth and beauty and could reveal it to those who hadn't found it in the world or each other, might have made a difference. Such a tool might have helped make the world a better place by giving everyone the chance to see everything more clearly, but under the circumstances he couldn't waste any more time on his prototype or on the mainframe computer. Not now. Maybe not ever.

Starry-eyed bullshit, that's all it is, really. Where'd I get such stupid ideas from to start with? That stupid anthropology class. So what if the Masai thought the camera had captured their very souls. So what? How could I have extrapolated that out to dream up a camera that can really capture someone's soul, mind, whatever?

Howard was stuck. He knew he would never be able to get the blasted connection between the camera and the computer to work soon enough to do anything to help stop what was going on in the world right now. No, he must fight the enemy like every other able-bodied man. He must join the service. He shook his head, turned, and walked back toward the hall.

At first he heard only a loud din when he came through the foyer, but soon he was able to hear bits and pieces of conversation. Compliments were being uttered everywhere. People were talking about him and his work. The crowd was parting like the goddamn Red Sea to let him pass. All eyes were on him. Everyone was looking at him like he was somebody other than who he was. Then someone started clapping. Then everyone was clapping. This seemed unreal to Howard and made him uncomfortable. He wanted them to stop, to leave. He wanted to take his photographs down, every last one of them, and throw them all away and get on with the real business of his life: war.

It was still early, though, and new people were arriving from as far away as London. Constance found him and stood close to him looking up at him admiringly.

"They love you, Mr. Russo," she whispered, and Howard allowed himself to be distracted by her, to let the breathy alto of her voice carry him away from where he was, from what he had decided.

Constance petted his arm softly and it did calm him. He looked at her and saw her eyes were the color of wet moss. He examined her face and noticed she'd plucked most of her thick dark eyebrows out, but the remaining hair of those two perfect arches promised that he'd probably find the same kind somewhere else on her body, if she gave him the chance.

And he thought, *the way she's looking at me, if I ask her nicely, if we hit it off, she might give me that chance.*

Yes, he definitely would've tried to make it with Constance if he'd met her before. That is in his past life back in Trenton, when he was single and Sylvia was just the pesky kid next door.

No, he'd be better off not thinking the way he was beginning to think about Constance. He would be faithful to Sylvia, his beloved Sylvie, as he liked to call her. He would go to war. He would fight the Nazis.

His mind made up, Howard looked around the room and couldn't help but be a little impressed with what he observed. People seemed to really be taken with his photographs, like the photographs had cast some sort of spell over them. Observing this gave Howard, for lack of a better way to describe it and for the first time in his life, a feeling of the special sort of power he was aiming to achieve with his new invention. It was the power to impress people so deeply that what they saw changed them permanently. Yes, Howard was feeling the power of the artist who has successfully married a vision to a form never to be forgotten.

He took a deep breath and let himself feel good if only for a minute about what he'd accomplished and how far he'd come.

The Russo family had never had an easy time of it. His parents, Carmen and Marie, came to the States right after they were married in Naples. They moved in with relatives in Trenton; and, though they couldn't speak a word of English, they were determined to work hard and make their way in America.

The Russo's started a little restaurant in the downstairs of Carmen's brother's house. When Howard was born, the family was living on the second floor and struggling to keep their restaurant going. They all figured out early on that Howard was smarter in many way than the average kid, but what could they do about it? Having a genius for a kid didn't help pay the rent. Howard was left to his own devices and grew up like a weed, strong and resilient. He thrived in school, and by the time he got to Trenton High, his teachers had already heard of "that little genius, the Russo kid."

Science was not Howard's first love, art was. But, hell, he was good at science, good at mathematics and analysis. He decided to pursue a career in engineering because his counselor talked him into it and helped him get a full scholarship to New York's Rensselaer Polytechnic Institute. No one was surprise when once there he continued to excel. Predictably, upon graduation he was named a Rhodes Scholar; and, despite being just married to Sylvia, he accepted the opportunity to attend Oxford University. How could he turn that down!

Now, it was obvious to Howard that this exhibition proved not just his artistic ability, but also the quality of his patents. He'd taken all these photographs with equipment he'd developed. From now on he wouldn't need Kodak. Kodak would need him.

But, damn it, it was useless for him to relish his success and contemplate his future, wasn't it? Soon, very soon, he'd be completely out of control of everything in his life. Soon, he'd be fighting, perhaps, just to stay alive.

If I live through this goddamn war, he promised himself, *I will finish that goddamn camera, harness it to the goddamn computer, and use it to make this goddamn world a better place. And if by some chance in hell I happen to get rich in the process? Well, good for me...and Sylvia.*

"Why, Mr. Russo, it looks indeed like you've made a fantastic impression today," said Constance, who was still beside him.

"Please, call me Howard."

"Only if you call me Constance."

"Well, Constance, the only person I really hope I made a fantastic impression on today is you." As soon as he'd said it, he knew he shouldn't have. What in the hell was wrong with him? Wasn't he just thinking about Sylvia?

"You most certainly have." Constance smiled so broadly Howard could see that several of her back teeth were missing. It disappointed him, and he berated himself for being so picky as to be put off by a few missing molars. But seeing this flaw in Constance helped him to come back to his senses.

This young woman's presence was flattering, but he felt terrible about having said something to her that he should only have said to Sylvia. He stared over her head at the hubbub.

I don't want to be here, he concluded, *or with her.*

"Congratulations, old chap!" Someone slapped him jovially on the back.

"You've done a bloody fine job, Russo! Why the somber look?" said one of his professors.

Admirers had gathered around him, wanting him to autograph their programs, wanting to buy his photographs.

"What did you do? Hypnotize that cow? I've never seen one look so intelligent, so, well, human. It's fantastic."

"How about photographing me? I'd love to sit for you and see what you could do with me in one click."

"My word, young man, I'm over the moon about what you've done here. Why you're so talented that if you took a photo of a gun and I looked at it, why it might actually shoot me."

6

A week after the exhibition Howard Russo found an envelope embossed with the Royal Crest and addressed to him in his mail slot.

An invitation to be honored along with other outstanding Oxford graduates. A reception at Buckingham Palace? With the Princess? Right...the Princess and the guinea from Trenton in the same room!

Seemed ludicrous to him, but he had to admit the invitation did give him a momentary lift, and he could sorely use one right about now. How could he have done what he'd done? Talk about losing your mind. But now, at least, this invitation gave him something to write to Sylvia about, something other than the prototype, complaints about the war, or what he should confess to her that he never would.

And Momma and Pop'd get a kick out of it, something to brag about to the neighbors.

Howard sat down grateful he had something positive to write:

Honey,
Wait till you hear this one, and wait till you tell my parents...I've been invited to Buckingham Palace! What do think about your husband clinking teacups with the Royal Princess herself? Proud of me, huh?
Please tell Momma and Pop. They'll probably get a good laugh out of it. I hope.
Now for the less important news. Make sure you look over my notes on the prototype.

Yes, Sylvie, I'm still having some problems, but I am so close I can smell success. If only I had more time. The exhibition was a big distraction, and so is what's going on across the Channel. Even here things are getting a little scary, but I don't want to go into that now. No, I want you to be proud of me and to miss me as much as I miss you. Do you? I pray that you do.

But I just can't get the prototype out of my mind. When I get it to work, I know it will be something that will help people see the world differently, clearly, like how it should be.

I'll be home for Thanksgiving with diploma in hand. I cannot wait to wrap my arms around you and hold you close again. When we are together, I'll....

He hesitated. Better not tell her about his decision to enlist. No, that could wait. Better to keep things light-hearted.

...hug you till you burst. Till then, be good. Keep your big nose (only kidding, I love your nose) to the grindstone. Remember, you are my only love. You and you, alone.

> *Your loving and faithful husband,*
> *Howard*

Why did he put in that last part about being faithful? Was it his guilt talking? He was so disgusted with himself that he almost tore the note up, but he told himself, in my heart I'm faithful. She *is* the one I really love. So he left it alone and put it, along with the notes about his prototype, inside a large envelop.

He mailed Sylvia summaries of his progress every week. She wouldn't understand everything in the notes yet, but a few years down the road when she finished up at Rensselaer, she'd be able to pick-up where he left off, if she needed to, if something happened to him, in the war, the goddamn war. The thought of it hung over him like a bolt of lightning about to strike.

I'm committed now, Howard thought. He knew it wouldn't be long before his country was completely embroiled in Europe's problems too. It was, he saw clearly now, inevitable. Things were deteriorating quickly. It'd become impossible at night to sleep for more than an hour at a time since the bombing had picked-up. London was still the direct target, but it seemed the Luftwaffe were everywhere. Warning sirens blared. Planes flew low overhead. The bombs boomed with varying intensity, gratefully still a safe distance away. In between the bursts of noise, Howard lay in his bed listening to ordinary things like someone humming in the hall, the sound of a taxi door slamming, the couple next door arguing, or making love. And when there were no other sounds, Howard concentrated on his cat Schrödinger's purring.

The cat didn't exactly belong to him. It was more like he belonged to the cat. The white fur ball of a thing was waiting at his door one afternoon. He tried to shoo it away, but it turned around and rubbed its jowl against his leg determinedly. The creature followed him in and never left. After a few days when the cat was stretched out on its back asleep on the window sill, Howard heard the thing purring, but when Howard lifted its little paw it was so limp and lifeless, Howard was afraid it was dead. So he named him Schrödinger because he'd just read the mathematician's brilliant response to the quantum theory EPA article by Einstein, Podolsky, and Rosen. God, this guy Schrödinger really gave that trio something to think about. He argued that because of something called entanglement, a thing could be both living and dead at the same time. He illustrated his theory by describing what would happen if you put a cat, a flask of poison, and a source of radioactivity in a box. The radioactive source would shatter the flask and the poison would kill the cat, but there would be a point at which the cat could be both alive and dead.

He hoped his Schrödinger liked to travel. He'd take him back to the States with him and leave him with Sylvia to keep her company while he was at war.

It was raining hard again, and Schrödinger's purring was punctuated by the pelting rain. These normal sounds comforted Howard, helped him to stop thinking about what was happening somewhere not all that far away between the normal sounds, buildings collapsing, windows being blasted out, glass shattering, people screaming. And then the things he couldn't hear but knew had happened because people, pets, wild animals were all being hit, their blood splattering then quietly leaking out of their blown-apart bodies.

Howard's shades were down so he turned the lamp on and looked where the yellow circle of light met the darkness. It was like looking at the edge of world. A small island of hope lost in an ocean of despair.

I'm drowning in that ocean.

God, he hated himself for what he'd done, hated to even think about it.

The night after the exhibition he invited Constance out. He took her to the pub for dinner, and it was a pleasant, innocent evening.

But, no, he couldn't leave it at that. No, after a few pints, he had to convince her to come back to his room. She declined politely at first, but after his persistent claim that all he wanted was to continue their conversation in a more comfortable place, she agreed.

When they got there, he took the flask of gin he kept for an emergency out and offered it to her. She took a cautious sip, he a hearty gulp. It started out nicely with kissing. She seemed loose and easy in his arms, and he guided her from a chair to his bed. While he was kissing her, he gingerly worked on the buttons to her blouse. She didn't pull back. He grew bolder. Her bra was made of lace, a beautiful, delicate thing that made him want to weep. The pure whiteness of it made her skin look darker than he expected, but her large breasts filled the cups and met in a deep V. Howard grew hard just looking at them, at the deep cleft between them. He kissed her again, forcefully, until she opened her mouth enough for him to jab his tongue into it. He felt her stiffen, but ignored her hesitation.

He pulled her blouse apart, grabbed her wrists, pinned her down, and straddled her. He ran his tongue down her long neck, her breast bone, into the cleft, and licked the deep cleft. He was so excited, his penis so engorged, he failed to notice that Constance was struggling to get out from under him. His hands were still on her wrists. He didn't hear her begging him to get off her and leave her alone, let her go…

"Please! Please! Let me go!"

"What?" He pulled back and looked down at her, and in what little light there was he saw the fear and anger in her face.

"Get off of me!" She was screaming now, loud enough for the whole apartment building to hear.

Not knowing what to do, only wanting her to stop screaming, he clamped his hand over her mouth to muffle her cries.

He was so close to coming, he wanted to hump her until he did. Instead of stopping him in his tracks, her twisting, struggling body only excited him more.

Let her go. Let her go. He remembered thinking that. He remembered thinking that he'd never done anything like this to any woman. Never forced himself on anyone. Yes, he was a married man. A good man. A good man who should stop what he was doing immediately.

But already Howard feared he'd gone too far, knew he wanted to stay where he was and satisfy himself whether this woman wanted him to or not.

"I won't hurt you. Calm down...." He said it like he was talking to wild dog. "Calm the hell down."

Constance stopped wriggling, but she was weeping profusely. He was about to take his hand off her mouth and kiss her and press into until he felt the relief he so desperately needed when, out of the corner of his eye, he spied Schrödinger staring at him, and he stopped.

He moved off the woman.

"I'm so sorry, Constance. I thought you wanted to...."

She turned her head away from him and said nothing. It was over. His penis ached. Suddenly embarrassed, he stood up and put his hands over it so Constance wouldn't see.

She rolled over and sat on the edge of the bed silently buttoning her blouse. Mascara and rouge mixed with her tears and ran down her cheeks. He could see the dark red blotches on her breasts where he'd sucked so hard he'd brought blood to the surface. She would have bruises, deep purple bruises.

"I am so sorry, Constance," he said again. "Can you forgive me?"

She stood up and took her purse from his dresser.

"Please, I never meant to...be so rough, to hurt you. I thought... Oh hell, please, won't you forgive me?"

"Never," she said it softly. She looked at him, her face full of hatred, the face of a woman who was scared and disappointed and angry. She seemed fully a woman, but she was crying like a little girl, like Sylvia used to cry when they were young and growing up together in the neighborhood and he had teased her.

"Never, you brute." And she left.

Now, beside the sickening realization that he had taken a woman other than Sylvie to dinner and had tried to fuck her, his ruthless behavior gave him even more to feel guilty about.

He'd been like a monster, a selfish pig, the lowest of the low.

But at first it had seemed like Constance wanted him? Hadn't it? Had he been wrong about her? Had he become that insensitive to other people, to a nice woman like Constance?

They'd met for dinner at the pub so he didn't know where she lived. If he did, he would go there right now and get down on his knees and beg her to forgive him.

Every time he thought of that night and what he tried to do, of how carried away he'd gotten, it filled him with shame.

So what if he had all the brains in the world, he wasn't smart enough to undo the terrible thing he had done. Now, even between the air raids, he wasn't sleeping. He tried to rationalize his behavior, find some reason for it. He wasn't himself anymore. Something was happening to him that he didn't want or like.

Blame it on the war, he thought. *It's turning us all into animals.*

But if that were his excuse, then it was the excuse of a coward. Control others so they can't control you. Defeat others so they can't defeat you. But Constance wasn't a threat to him. Constance wouldn't have hurt him.

Then the invitation to the palace arrived. After the initial effect of the flattery wore off, Howard hadn't the least inclination to go to the reception. If he hadn't already mailed the news of it to Sylvia and his parents, he would have forgotten about the whole thing. But now he felt obligated not to disappoint them, not to make them look like fools in front of the whole community he knew they'd brag to about it. So he borrowed his friend Lytton's most expensive suit and got a haircut and a shave.

On the morning of the reception Lytton came by to wish him well.

"So off you go, you bloody American, to enchant our own young Princess. You know, they don't often let foreigners like you in on something as downright British as an invitation to the hallowed halls of Buckingham Palace. Why I, myself, have never so much as seen the interior of the foyer, but far be it from me to put a damper on your day. Go, go, gaze into her Royal Highness's eyes, you rogue, and make her fall in love with you," Lytton chuckled at his own jealousy.

"Goddamn it, Ly, you go if it's such a goddamn honor. Here take the damn invitation and pretend you're me," Howard thrust the fancy envelop at his friend.

"Whoa, calm down, old man. Just kidding you, of course. I couldn't be happier for my good friend. I mean it, chap. You deserve to go. So go on now and give Elizabeth a kiss on the cheek for old Lytton would you?"

Howard smiled and shook his head. Lytton's light-heartedness and teasing only made Howard feel even less like wasting his afternoon sipping tea with any royal highness. He'd rather go to the pub with Lytton and down enough pints to make the world go away.

How am I going to get through this? Howard thought as he wiped the mud off his wingtips with a dishtowel.

He looked at Lytton sitting on the edge of the bed where Constance had been. It made feel like slitting his throat. He swallowed hard, chucked the dirty rag at his friend, and left.

7

Her gleaming light brown hair was parted on one side and held in place with a diamond-studded barrette. She had entered the large opulent room by a side door and stood calmly in front of the young men who formed an orderly semi-circle twenty feet away. Even from that distance Howard eyed the pearl buttons that ran down the front of her ivory silk dress.

Shit, he thought, *goddamn real pearl buttons.*

She cleared her throat and began her speech, but Howard could barely stand to listen to her stilted diction, to her voice that seemed to come out of her nostrils not her mouth. He hated the way her intonation rose on the subject and fell on the object, how in between she held onto the verb wringing the meaning out it like it were a sopping wet rag.

"Indeed, in this troubling year of nineteen hundred and forty, you have g-i-v-e-n the whole of the British Empire reason to hope," or "The Royal Family and I a-p-p-l-a-u-d your fantastic accomplishments," or "The very future of our great sovereignty d-e-p-e-n-d-s so on your continued hard work."

Blah, blah, blah.

Howard was not concentrating. He was looking down at his hands and growing angrier by the minute with himself for ever agreeing to come.

Then the Princess stopped talking. He looked up to discover she was smiling at him. He noticed the pearl buttons again; and against his better judgment, he found himself wondering what would be revealed to him if he could unbutton those buttons. He thought about her breasts. No way as big as Constance's, but they might have the kind of deep ruby-colored nipples Sylvia's had.

Yes, ruby colored, like two large and perfect gems. If only he could see this young woman naked, except for that intricate lace collar that lay on her shoulders like a mantle of snow crystals. No, she would look lovely naked except for the collar.

Snap out of it, Russo, he berated himself. What the hell! He was standing in Buckingham Palace fixated on conjuring up breasts and nipples and...how could he ever think about Constance at all ever again? He was a sorry bastard for sure.

The Princess stepped forward to where the men were standing and beginning at one end greeted each of them by extending her gloved hand and limply shaking theirs.

It was Howard's turn. She stepped very close to him. He liked her clear pale skin, pink cheeks, and full lips. She smelled like the lavender his mother grew around the edges of her small city garden. In spite of himself, he smiled as rakishly as could.

She took his hand and looked him in the eye and waited, it seemed, for him to say something.

"You look nice," he said like he'd just knocked on her door to take her out for a milkshake or something.

"Thank you, Mr. Russo." She lowered eyes without smiling. Howard saw how quickly she blushed. Witnessing the heat rise in her like that did something to him.

*I'd fuck her, fuck the Royal Princess, go wild with her like...*This was going through his mind, and he was holding her hand, squeezing it too tightly. She tried to pull her hand away. Her eyes met his again and for a minute Howard believed he saw something there, something significant. He let go. She took a step toward the next fellow but abruptly turned back toward Howard. Her features hardened, the pupils of her eyes constricted, gone was her enthusiasm. Each word dropped from her lips like a heavy stone. "Rarely does the Royal Family p-a-y tribute to an American student such as yourself. However, Mr. Russo, you a-r-e a genius with a gift we a-r-e in desperate need of. Soon the very future of the Crown may r-e-s-t in your hands."

A chill ran up Howard's spine. She sounded like she was a hundred years old, not some cute young woman who was still just a girl, whose hand he had held onto too long. Howard hadn't a clue what she meant, but the sound of her voice reverberated in his head like the sound of a gong at sunset, lonely and ominous. She was serious, dead serious.

When the reception was over and the Princess left, Howard exited with the other men; but just beyond the double doors he was pulled aside by a butler of some sort in a black morning coat and asked to follow him down a golden corridor and into another room. Smaller than the reception hall but significantly more opulent, the space was dominated by a marble table three times the size of the wooden one in Ashmolean. Pacing in the cramped space between the massive table and a plush velvet armchair was a stout, balding man who Howard thought for a second was the new Prime Minister.

But what in Hades would the Prime Minister of England want with him?

To the left side of the table a much older man wearing a pinstriped suit, a white shirt with a stiff French collar, and large round tortoise shell glasses stood watching Howard.

"We've been following your performance at Oxford closely," this older man said as soon as Howard was close enough to hear him. "We haven't much time, so I will present the facts briefly. The British Empire and our allies are in desperate trouble. We must fortify our position worldwide in light of the current…"

Howard's head was spinning. He wanted to say, *excuse me, Sir whoever-you-are? I beg your pardon, but what in the hell does what you're saying have to do with me? Me? Howard Russo from Trenton, New Jersey, in the United States of America?*

But the old man just kept talking. "…tensions. Your abilities have not gone unnoticed. You know more about cameras than anyone in the world. On top of your obvious scientific expertise, you are also extraordinarily creative. Let me get right to the point, Mr. Russo. We need you for an important mission. I am not at liberty to reveal much else beyond this declaration of our need at the moment, but rest assured the Prime Minister and your own President are in agreement concerning this endeavor."

Howard's eyes shifted to the portly man who stopped moving for a moment to look at Howard and nod.

"Your success," the elderly man continued, "could directly impact on the freedom of both of our countries. We have not acted decisively enough until now, and the Prime Minister is about to change that. The Germans must be stopped. It is the responsibility of every man to do his part to stop such an evil onslaught. We are counting on you to answer the call to duty."

Howard's mouth went dry. He tried to say something, but his throat constricted. He swallowed hard to try to relax it. He had the odd sensation that he'd known all along this was going to happen. The two men watched him as he glanced around at the silk carpet, the gilt-framed portraits, the silver sconces, the velvet, the gem-encrusted candelabra...the immaculate, dustless, glowing room. Both men stared at Howard and waited while Howard seemed to lose himself in the sparkling light of the chandeliers that splashed riotous confetti colors over everything.

Oh, yes, the thought passed like a bullet through his mind, *things are a mess, but not here. Everything here is precious and safe.*

Perspiration dampened his armpits. He feared he might smell. He wished he had bought his camera along. He desperately wanted to take a snapshot of the Prime Minister––it was indeed the Prime Minister. Howard wanted to capture him on film in profile with his cigar between his fat lips and the ash about to drop off.

The elderly gentleman was talking again and spreading a map out. Something about the Bermuda Triangle. Tortola. The Caribbean. U-boats spotted off the coast of Florida near the Boyton Inlet. Aerial photos necessary for the operation to begin. His voice was a crisp staccato as he pointed here and there on the map, and the Prime Minister continued his solemn march in the background grinding his trail of ashes deeper and deeper into the lush carpet.

There was no time for questions and somehow something was settled. Howard would be reporting for duty immediately. His belongings would be packed up and sent on to his new location. The university and his friends would be notified of his "emergency" at home. His wife and family would be notified of his deployment. He would be briefed when he arrived at his destination.

Howard wiped his sweaty palm on his pant leg before shaking the hand of the Prime Minister. The same small man who had shown him in met him at the door. He led Howard directly out of the Palace and into a waiting limousine.

The driver, invisible due to the opaque glass that divided the back seat from the front, steered away from Buckingham Palace. Howard watched the city speed by in a grey blur. *Damn foggy out for May,* he thought trying to distract himself from thinking too much about where he was headed.

At the airport Howard was escorted by a pair of airmen to a small plane with two engines the size of beer kegs suspended from each wing.

"Not to worry," said one of the men who watched him buckle himself into the seat, but the sudden sound of the engines jolted Howard. They were deafening. The man handed Howard a headset, and then he backed out of the small door, closed it, and secured it with a thud from the outside.

Next to Howard there was an empty seat and two more along the other side of the cabin. A small door separated the cabin from the cockpit. Howard was alone.

Damn, I've still got Ly's suit on, thought Howard as the small craft accelerated to a frightening speed, shuddered, and lifted off the runway.

Howard watched through the tiny window as the coast of England grew smaller and smaller, then disappeared from view. He'd never flown before. When he crossed the Atlantic to get to Oxford, he boarded a steamer in New York; and, though he was seasick frequently during the two week journey, he felt relatively safe the whole time.

Now, the plane soared up into thick grey clouds. Raindrops skidded across the glass before being sucked out of view. Dark thunderheads rose up like angry elephants; lightening exploded between them. The craft seemed fragile as it bucked at each strike.

The whole of nature——now that Howard had this new vantage point, now that he could see what had been unseeable before, now that he was riding in a pathetically small plane through the eye of a large storm——seemed full of fury. He thought of how hard he tried to compartmentalize things in his life, how he put his photography in the this-is-what-I-really-want-to-do box, his work on the prototype in the this-is-how-I-can-do-it-better box, his tedious and slow development of camera parts in the this-is-how-I-make-money box, his wife in the this-is-me-as-the-good-husband box, Constance in the this-isn't-really-me box.

I am not me, he thought. *I am not the me who hurt Constance, who cheated on Sylvia, who held on too long to the Princess's hand, who wanted to make her blush, who goddamn loved it when she did.*

The plane plummeted into a deep pocket of nothingness. Howard's stomach was in his throat. His whole body flew upwards. Were it not for the way he was strapped in he would've broken his neck on the ceiling of the cabin. For the first time in his adult life, Howard Russo believed he was in imminent danger. He believed his life was about to end. He willed himself not to panic, not to start screaming like a scared little boy.

Get a grip, Russo. You can't get off the plane. It's not going to turn around, take you back to land, back to Oxford, back to graduation, back to where you belong.

Oh, he wanted to scream; but he knew if he did, no one would hear him. Instead of screaming, though, he found himself beginning to cry. He knew no one could see him. Still, he felt pathetic.

In minutes they were through the storm and into bright sunlight that blinded him. He shaded his eyes from the glare and stared out at the majestic white fields of clouds. He was looking at the tops of the clouds and above them was the crystal clear blue dome of the sky. It struck him that what he'd just been through was probably what dying would be like––the terrible, frightening passage through the dark; and then, just when you've given up hope, you burst into the white light of your new beginning. For a while he sat there shielding his eyes and looking at the clouds, thinking maybe he had died and now everything that happened would be beautiful and pure because, obviously, he'd made it to heaven. But he didn't believe in heaven. He would never tell Momma, Pop, or even Sylvia. He'd been raised strict Catholic. You didn't question doctrine. You lived, you died, you went to heaven––whatever it was––if you were good. Of course, according to the Church, heaven was a great place where you were with God and the angels and all of the other good people who had, along with you, been forgiven for their sins.

Howard didn't buy it. He preferred the idea of reincarnation. He'd studied Eastern religions in undergrad school. It made sense. Energy can be neither created nor destroyed. Electricity kept people alive. Where'd that energy go when you died? Into another person. He liked the logic of it.

He was starting to relax, to think more clearly and feel better about his situation.

What happens, happens. I'll write to Sylvia as soon as I get to wherever they're taking me. I'll make it up to her. She'll never know, but I always will. Damn it, I always will.

Then he looked down. The heavy dark clouds of the storm were traveling in the same direction the plane was and were just below them. They seemed almost close enough to touch.

Howard tried to concentrate on other things. He noticed how cold it was, how a moldy odor from a stack of parachutes next to the cockpit door pervaded the tight cabin space and made him want to gag. He had the weird taste of metal in his mouth. He ran his tongue over his teeth trying to get rid of the scum that had accumulated on them.

The engines whirred and pinged rapidly like machine gun fire. It felt to Howard like someone was sinking rivets into his skull. The bulky headset was heavy and useless and made his neck ache.

He looked through the window again. The sky was grey now, and the clouds below were an impenetrable barrier denying him the albatross's view, denying him a decent look at the great Atlantic Ocean. As the plane gained more altitude, Howard's despondency sank to a new low. He could think of nothing––not even the fact that he was, so he'd been told, serving his country––to avert the downward spiral of his emotions.

He wanted to cry, again, and berated himself for such childishness. He hadn't cried since he was boy, since he fell out of a tree and knocked the wind out of himself. When he came to, his neighbor Sylvia was staring down at him, weeping. A few of her tears dropped into his open mouth and he tasted them and he began to cry too. His mother got to him; and when she saw he was alright, she shook him till he stopped crying. He could feel her shaking him now, "Stop. I knowa you want to a cry, but don't. Bigga boys don't cry."

He shifted his weight and pulled the collar of his jacket up around his neck. He squeezed his eyes shut and tried to block everything out, to stop his thoughts from looping around and around, but he couldn't. He was too mad at himself.

It was the damned exhibition, Howard thought. *That's what got me into this. That's where I met Constance and look what I did with her. And look how I talked to the Princess, the goddamn Princess of the goddamn British Empire, and I'm talking to her like she's nobody. What the hell was wrong with me? I should've never agreed to it. What in the hell did I care if anyone ever saw my photos?*

He was bitter now about how easily he'd been sucked into the quagmire of one-upmanship. He wanted notoriety, even tried hard to promote himself. Now, he regretted wasting such precious energy. Within a week's time, thanks to his ego, he was here instead of in the lab working on his camera. Oh, he wished he were there instead of where he was. And where was he anyway?

In the middle of nowhere, that's where.

He listened to the engines and kept checking outside through the window, but the darkness below and the nothingness inside of him persisted.

He must have dozed off and slept for a long while until the plane dropped into another air-pocket jolting him awake. The harness yanked him back as his body tried to take flight. He gripped the armrests as the turbulence tossed the small craft wildly about.

In seconds it was over, but Howard was shaking.

The plane dipped downward. The clouds were gone, and he could see they were approaching an island set in the middle of a ring of teal blue sea. Darker blue water stretched unbroken to the horizon. The sky was golden.

The airstrip was a small patch of land between two mountains. The palm trees blew outward as the plane touched ground, bounced across the potholes in the runway, and slowed to a halt by a shack. Outside the window, Howard saw a bit of cleared ground and then a tangle of vegetation so thick light didn't penetrate it. The small door of the cockpit opened. The pilot peeked in, said nothing, and slammed it shut again.

What the hell? Howard thought, but he was so grateful to be on the ground, he let it go and sat where he was without complaining.

Through the window all he could see was a forest of emerald and chartreuse foliage. As he looked upward he saw the giant fronds of the palms shivering against the turquoise sky. He had never seen a real palm tree, only photographs; and now he knew how inadequate those images were. He watched the feathered tops sway in the breeze like giant dusters. A strong gust twirled through them, made them dance.

The longer he sat there, the hotter it got. He removed his tie and loosened the collar of his dress shirt. He unbuckled his seat belt and struggled out of Lytton's suit jacket, folding it carefully and putting it next to him on the empty seat. It must've been a hundred degrees in the cabin.

Hell, I've gotten myself into hell. The sobering thought and the rising temperature distracted him from his study of the palms. Sweat ran down the sides of his neck. He took off the headset and wondered why he hadn't done that first. His head felt lighter, better; but his heart was pounding wildly. He pressed his fist against his chest until it hurt. The pressure was reassuring.

Maybe all they might want is for me to take some pictures.

The cockpit door opened. This time the pilot hunched over and moved through the cabin to the side door. He unlatched it and swung it inward and to the side.

"Where are we?" Howard grabbed Lytton's jacket and crouching followed the pilot out of the small exit.

"Tortola, British Virgin Islands. Good luck, chap." The pilot disappeared to the other side of the plane.

Howard stood there dumbfounded. Heat blurred the air above the dry dirt of the runway and road. He'd felt humidity in New Jersey before, but nothing like this. His shirt was drench and sticking to him.

It had been just past noon in England when they'd left; and it seemed, by the position of the sun overhead, to be about that time here.

So it's still only the twenty-third of September. One goddamn long day so far.

The rattle of the palms, the screech of unseen birds, the constant rushing of the surf to the shore. Howard's ears throbbed from the pressure in the plane and now all of this was building up into a nasty headache.

A dusty old Jeep pulled up alongside the plane. The driver was a teenager with gleaming black hair. Beads of sweat the size of large pearls hung on his forehead. He wore a shirt that was frayed at the collar and cuffs, the cloth as thin as tissue. Howard climbed in the back seat, and the kid swung the car around in a dusty circle and headed up a steep dirt road. At the apex there was a break in the foliage. Howard saw the sea ruffled with white foam between the bands of blue-green sea. The kid sitting stiffly behind the wheel jerked it so hard to the right that Howard nearly fell out. They'd made a hairpin turn and were going down a straightaway incredibly fast, too fast.

The car skidded on another tight curve then the grade of the road dropped even more. The foliage threw grotesque shadows across their path. The jeep flickered through them at break-neck speed tempting Howard to close his eyes, but he didn't want to miss one bit of this alien landscape.

When the descent was complete, they slid to a stop facing the ocean. The kid said nothing. Howard, grateful they'd stop, wanted to smack the kid, but he didn't. After a minute or two, they started moving again and turned right onto a level gravel road that ran directly alongside the beach. The sand came up to the gravel. There were some men fishing at the edge of the surf. They were shirtless but wore hats woven from strips of palmetto leaves, and their baggy cotton pants were cuffed to just below their knees. It was breezy and pleasant along the beach, and Howard felt almost happy to be there.

Maybe it's all for the best. How else would I ever get to see such a beautiful place?

Then the kid pressed hard on the accelerator and started speeding again. He turned onto another dirt road. Branches and vines met and formed a dark tunnel over the road that suddenly became steep. The jeep strained to make it up what seemed to be a mountain. Slowly they went up, up, up. The whole time the kid impatiently rammed the pedal into the floor of the jeep again, again, again. It was useless, the vehicle refused to go any faster. Howard had time to look around, to see hundreds of bananas growing out of crimson beaks, leaves as big as doors, trees strangling other trees, wild roosters pecking their way through the gullies on either side of the road.

The car stopped in the driveway of a disheveled bungalow, weathered yellow paint, sticks propping open the shutters, a bunch of old boards hammered together for a door. Coconuts as large as snapping turtles littered the ground. The weary traveler, carrying only his friend's jacket over his forearm, was barely out of the jeep before it backed up, turned, and was gone.

Now what?

Howard took a deep breath, inhaled the scent of jasmine mingled with the fetid odor of rotting vegetation and headed for the bungalow.

The door creaked.

No time to get spooked, he told himself. He was anxious to get out of his hot clothes, take a shower, relax. Opposite him was a wall of open French doors. Sheer drapes billowed in the wind. Beyond the deck gargantuan flat-bottomed clouds formed a sort valance along the horizon. The sea was silver where the sun hit it and bright turquoise everywhere else.

The rickety bungalow was built on the edge of a steep cliff. Howard felt as though if he walked across the room and went out on the deck, his weight might tip the precarious balance of the place and send it crashing down into the sea. He stood motionless for several minutes transfixed by this notion and the magnificent view.

I should take a picture. Get this on film. The drapes in the foreground just as they're lifting on a breeze, those clouds before they move away. Wouldn't Sylvia love this?

Large boxes were lined up along the wall near the kitchen. He saw his port-folios leaning against them. Several small boxes were on the table to the right. The inside of the bungalow was much nicer than the outside. Potted plants sat on the counter and on the windowsills. A bamboo couch and chair were covered in bright floral fabric.

Howard experienced another moment of calm, of trust.

Whatever it is that they want me to do for them, at least they're trying to make me comfortable. In a place like this what could be so bad.

He looked again out at the stunning blueness of it all and gingerly walked across the room out onto the deck and leaned over the side. The deck cantilevered out from the bungalow and was, as he had suspected, half-suspended in air. Far below, a small beach. Then nothing but the blue water. He could see the tops of the hats of the fishermen they'd driven past. From this distance they looked like small tan circles.

If only my goddamn prototype worked, it could capture it all exactly as it is. My prototype?

Howard was seized with a moment of panic because he didn't remember seeing the distinctive metal case anywhere when he had come through the room. He remembered seeing all of the boxes, the clock on the wall. He even remembered noticing that it was thirty-two minutes past noon. He was about to turn and go back inside to look for it when he felt someone push him hard from behind.

He lost his balance and felt himself begin to go over the railing. He tried to stop himself, but his body was in motion. He grabbed the railing with one hand

and hung there struggling to turn himself into a position where he could grab on with the other hand and pull himself back up onto the deck, back to safety, but he couldn't. He just couldn't. The weight of his body became unbearable. He hung on and prayed and screamed. He looked up at his hand. It ached. He felt himself weakening. He saw his hand let go.

No. This can't be happening.

Time stopped as he thought this stupid thought, as he saw himself still standing on the deck. But he wasn't on the deck. He was falling feet first, and the razor-sharp foliage he was careening through ripped his skin open. His arms and legs flailed, desperate to grab onto something, anything. Rocks, roots, branches, anything, but everything broke and bent and gave way.

He rolled in the air. He was on his back and saw his own blood spurt upward, red beads against white clouds. His legs were pumping. He rolled again. Beach. Sea. Then clouds. Bright white clouds. He clawed at the air. The bottom of the deck was a black rectangle far above him.

Heavy and dark like the lid of a coffin.

The men who had been fishing heard the thrashing, the thud, and found the dead man sprawled on his side as a shallow wave swirled over his wounds and turned the sea foam pink. His eyes were open. His hair floated like a short black halo above his head. His arms, legs, and torso were twisted to one side and his head to other. He looked almost as though he were turning to look back to see who was chasing him as he tried, uselessly, to run away.

8

Jake Dwyer wasn't supposed to be born for another month. His mother Lizzy was hanging the new curtains she'd made in the nursery—not a nursery really but an alcove in their cramped efficiency on 83rd Street in Manhattan. She'd set up the basinet near the window. Her first baby would get the sunlight it needed.

When she reached up to adjust the pleats, she experienced a sharp twinge above her pelvis. *Ouch*, she thought as she paused. She was so pregnant and so huge she was always in some kind of pain. The heartburn had been the worst. Second worst had been the itching. The skin of her abdomen was stretched to its limit and gauged with deep marks like a tiger had clawed her near to death. How she wanted to scratch at them, but fearing they might split open and start bleeding, she sat on her hands and cried when it got really bad. There were other symptoms too. Her brain, it seemed, had turned to mush. Her nerves, fragile as blown glass. Nightmares plagued her sleep, the war in Europe had spread to New York, bombing raids, her baby buried under rubble. She'd awaken in a sweat. *Yes, it could happen and then what?* she thought. *If Eddie has to go? If he leaves me? Us?*

How would she manage alone with an infant? Who would take care of them? Protect them?

Another sharp pain. Lower this time, more intense, a knife stabbing her groin from the inside out. It was a terrible feeling that held on and made her gasp. She knelt and pressed both her hands between her legs until the awful sensation stopped. When it did, she tried to get up; but another stronger ache rippled through her. She laid on her side, pulled her legs to her chest, and screamed.

Too soon. Something's wrong.

The pain flared again, and she writhed every which way trying to get it to subside. It made her shudder and groan as it consumed her. She feared she wouldn't be able to stand it if it got any worse; and when she was on the verge of passing out, it again stopped.

She took a deep breath and waited. Nothing.

Indigestion was all, maybe. She got to her feet. She felt okay. Maybe that would be that. She stepped back and looked at the small blue periwinkles printed on the pale green cotton curtains. *Even if our baby's a boy, how could he not like....*

Then the pain was back. And much worse. She eased herself onto the sofa and bent over the dome of her stomach and cried out, "Help!"

She rocked back and forth and shouted for help again. She was afraid. Nothing in her life had ever hurt so much. She didn't want to be alone. The baby might die. She might die.

She attempted to stand up, but was too dizzy and sweating profusely and frightened out of her mind. She willed herself not to pass out and sat back down and prayed for the contraction——it had to be a contraction, *please, be a contraction*—— to pass. Women friends had warned her, tried to describe the incredible pain. It was better to go under the anesthesia and sleep through the ordeal.

But look where she was. No one was around. No one. God, what was she going to do? Hadn't the doctor figured it all out? Hadn't he said she wasn't due until the middle of next month?

Again, the pain dissipated. Lizzy pushed herself up off the sofa and hurried into the hall. She banged on her neighbor's door. No one answered. She was about to go further down the hall, but another contraction gripped her and she slumped to the floor.

"Help me! Please, somebody help me!" she screamed at the top of her lungs.

No one came. When the pain subsided, she got to her feet and made it back into the apartment. She left the door open. Maybe someone would come by and look in and find her. The important thing was to remain calm. She laid on the couch and waited and fought through each contraction. But when she lost count and one barely ended before the next began, she crawled on the floor to her bed and pulled her aching body up onto it. Her child was not going to be born on a couch.

She took her clothes off and stretched out naked on her back. Instinctively, she grabbed her knees and pulled them toward her chest. The door was open. She didn't care. Something broke inside of her. Her inside seem to be running out of her. The mattress was soaked. It didn't matter. The pressure of the baby trying to come out forced her to urinate in the bed. It didn't matter. Nothing mattered except getting the pain to stop. She grunted and strained and held onto her knees. It wasn't working. How much more could she take? Lizzy was sure now she was about to die.

In a last valiant effort to save herself and her baby, she stood up, pulled the wet linens off the bed, and threw them on the floor at the foot of the bed. She worked her way around to the footboard and held onto it while she squatted on top of the pile of linens and pushed with ounce of strength she had.

It's coming. My baby's coming.

She stared at the church calendar on the wall above the headboard, at the picture of Our Lady of Knock, at the date, 1940, September 23.

She looked at the clock next to the calendar. It was thirty-three minutes past noon.

To be exact.

9

The train clanked noisily over the rails. The normally soothing repetitive sound did nothing now but jangle Sylvia Russo's already frayed nerves. Each stop seemed to last an infinity, each stretch between them, was interminable. For the first two hours of her journey from Troy, New York, to Trenton, New Jersey, she had stared blankly over the heads of the passengers fearing the worst until she thought she'd go mad. Then she tried reading Burton Holmes' 1890 travelogue. It was a first edition, a wedding gift from Howard, though she suspected a rather selfish one since he was clearly more interested in photography and Burton Holmes than she. Her mind wandered, the words ran together, so she paged through and looked at the photos. Even the shocking depictions of the naked Hairy Ainu tribe of Shiraoi going about their daily chores couldn't hold her attention. She closed the book and leaned her head against the window. Through the oaks that obscured the cornfields, she watched sunlight flicker. It made her dizzy. She closed her eyes and prayed for sleep she knew wouldn't come.

The dean at Rensselaer said a Mr. Salvatore Russo telephoned, asked him rather abruptly to tell Sylvia to get home fast and hung up. Just like Howard's uncle to make no explanation. Sylvia surmised Uncle Sal must've used the phone at the rectory because a telephone was a luxury no one in the Russo family could afford. Hastily, Sylvia threw a few necessities in her suitcase, grabbed the Holmes tome, and got on the next train.

Now she opened her eyes and looked down at her hands not knowing where else to look or what else to do to keep from falling apart from worry. She pressed her cuticles down one by one till pale half-moons rose from the beds of her nails, and her skin reddened from the pressure.

It took forever to get to Grand Central Station, shuffle behind the crowd into the enormous hall of the terminal, push her way outside, walk the eleven blocks to Penn Station, wait for the Southbound to Trenton, and press forward with the other passengers down into the dark cavern to board the train. She watched the black underground girders impatiently as they slowly peeled off behind the train before it picked up speed.

As they passed Edison, the Raritan River was invisible in the fog that had descended. Sylvia could see only the hedge of honeysuckle growing along the tracks. She was chilly despite the car being overcrowded. Then as the train neared New Brunswick, the fog dissipated, and the sun beat in through the dirty window. She swiveled in her seat, put her back to the sun, and let it warm her through the thin wool of her coat. Her mind was reeling.

What could be wrong? Howard's mother? His father? Could she handle whatever it was without Howard?

How could she ever do anything in this world without Howard? God, how she loved him. In her mind's eye, she saw his eyes, the color of hickory leaves in autumn was the way he described them. She liked to compare them to the color of corn husks, not yellow but almost colorless. And his large Roman nose. And his perfect olive skin, broad hairy chest, slim waist, and lower…just picturing it made her want him. She shifted uncomfortably in her seat. How much longer could she take being away from him? If she had any money, anything of value she could sell, she'd go to him tomorrow, and once again feel the miracle—because it was a miracle—of him loving her.

Awkward, plain, orphaned, and yet, though she never believed he would, he'd come to love her. The very thought of him made her heart race. Her longing was a deep well of emptiness into which she'd tumbled and been freefalling through for months.

She had to snap out of this painful reverie, though. Something was wrong with someone in Howard's family, her family, the only family, except for her aunt, she had.

She forced herself to think about less troublesome things. Mr. Alan Turing's diagrams. He'd given her ten diagrams to study, and she'd committed them to memory. Methodically, and to distract herself, she now visualized each one, searching for imperfections, weaknesses, looking for short cuts. She took out her pencil and on the inside flap of the Holmes book she redrew them. Looking at them she admired Turing's concepts. He was a genius, but intuitively she knew he'd missed something. She wasn't sure what yet, but she'd figure it out, somehow.

The efficiency could be improved, the size scaled down. A seminar was scheduled for tomorrow, and she wanted so to be there, to be the one to fix things, and impress Turing.

This could ruin everything, she thought. *If it's really bad news, if something horrible happened, I might never be able to go back. I couldn't leave Mom alone, or Pop alone. There's no one else. Howard's so close to finishing. It wouldn't make sense for him to come back from England now.*

She understood all of this, but she couldn't help feeling stuck. She was trying to get an education too. Howard already had one degree. This degree from Oxford was just some icing on his cake. She didn't even have hers in the oven yet. But she was the one who would have to give up going back to school. She was the one who would get stuck running the old rundown family restaurant. And Howard? Well, Howard would stay at Oxford. Howard was the lucky one.

She could hear her mother-in-law's broken English, "Sylvia, honey, I can'ta ask my son to a help me."

It would be her way of saying, in other words, "You're the woman. You're the one, Sylvia, whose job it is to help us."

The sun was too hot now, and Sylvia felt like she was burning up. She ran her fingers through her brittle hair, like straw so dry it might ignite. Sweat gathered at her hairline and under her arms, but she didn't move or take off her jacket. She sat there and suffered and offered it up to the Virgin in hopes that the emergency wouldn't be much of an emergency at all.

The train slowed. She noticed through the window the New Brunswick Station sign was peeling. When she'd ridden back to Rensselaer after Christmas break, the blue paint still had some shine, the letters only a little faded. It seemed the longer she was away from home and the closer she got to returning to it, the more decrepit everything appeared.

It's not that I begrudge Howard anything. I love him so, how could I not want the best for him? She ran her hand lightly over the embossed cover of the book on her lap. *It's just that they aren't even my parents, not really.*

Her parents died in a fire at the Scammell factory when she was six years old. Her Aunt Louise, who lived next door to the Russos, had taken her in and raised her like a daughter. The Russo clan had helped too. They'd been good to her. No, not good, great! What was she thinking? How could she resent them? She owed them everything for their love and kindness.

God, she hated herself when she started with the self-pity. *Nobody likes a martyr,* she reminded herself.

For that matter nobody cares much for a critic either, and the more knowledge she acquired the more she questioned her young husband's bizarre and fantastic hypothesis.

Right, Howard, a camera connected to a computing machine, when only one in the entire world, the Colossus, exists? And how had he put it? It can capture the spirit? The soul? The essence of someone? What do want me to believe next? Buck Rogers is real?

The train was picking up speed. The bare birches north of Princeton Junction became a dizzying blur. Sylvia closed her eyes.

She'd felt like the village idiot growing up next door to Howard Russo. Geez, how she looked up to him. He knew everything, and he was so pretty for a boy with his dark wiry Italian hair and unusual yellow eyes. She had a mad crush on him and lost plenty of sleep imagining what it'd be like to hold his hand, or maybe even kiss his lips; but the only interest Howard took in her was to taunt her and tease her and do whatever he could to make her miserable. He treated her like she was his little sister or something.

You want a little sister, I'll give you one, Sylvia concluded around the time she entered her sophomore year in high school. If she couldn't be the object of his affection, then she might as well become his stiff competition.

As soon as handsome Howard left for Rensselaer Polytechnic Institute, Sylvia threw herself into her studies. She'd do as well as that blasted boy...no, damn it, she'd do better. So what if she wasn't as intellectually gifted, she'd put her nose to the grindstone and conquer all that impossible math and science if it was the last thing she did.

Within months her grades skyrocketed, and over the next two years she moved to the head of her class. By senior year Sylvia had decided to apply to Rensselaer too. Why not? She might just qualify for a scholarship, and what would Howard think? Yeah, what would the young man who never even wrote her so much as a short note, though she regularly sent him "friendly" letters filled with neighborhood gossip, think about her showing up on *his* campus?

Taunt me, tease me, but don't ignore me, she thought as her decision to attend the Polytechnic Institute solidified.

There was a problem, a rather big problem Sylvia wasn't going to let stop her. Rensselaer was an all-male institution. Oh well, she'd have to pretend. She applied as S. Bolton and convinced her guidance counselor, Mrs. Anderson, to use the first initial of her first name on her transcript. The gender box?

"Please, Mrs. A., leave it blank?" Sylvia pleaded.

"Only because I know you can compete with every smarty pants up there, am I doing this. So when you get in, don't let me down," said Mrs. Anderson.

Sylvia got an interview! What was she going to do now? She stripped down and stood naked in front of the mirror. She had curves and long ebony hair and what she now realized were stunningly feminine facial features. She was, she had to admit, relatively attractive.

This would not do. In a panic, she went to the thrift store and purchased a man's suit that somewhat fit her. She borrowed a white men's shirt from Howard's father and a black pair of spectators from her aunt. Then, with shaking hands, she chopped off her hair until barely two inches remained. When she greased it back, she did look like a small chinned, slender nosed boy, whose lips and eyes were too big for his face. And she'd have to stop plucking her eyebrows.

Now for her ample breasts. She pinned a medal of Saint Rita to the inside of her bra, took a long, wide strip of cloth, and bound her chest until it was as flat as she could get it.

Okay, she stood in front of the mirror again.

Not really like a man, but not like a woman either.

Would the ambiguity be enough to tempt the admission board into making an exception?

Six men held Sylvia's fate in their hands; and when they first laid eyes on her, they collectively did a poor job of hiding their confusion. Their faces were easy to read, whoever was standing in front of them was certainly different. Boldly they examined her from top to bottom. Were they wondering where in the hell her breasts were? She hoped not. She stood her ground and tried not to break into a sweat.

But why couldn't they stop staring at her? What difference did it make what kind of body her mind was inhabiting? Weren't these men, above all men, supposed to be interested in what was in her brain, not what was between her legs?

Do not start crying, she steeled herself against her rising emotions and prayed.

Then, finally, mercifully, one of them asked her a question. Her mind whirred. Did she hear him correctly? Did she know the answer?

This was not the time to hesitate. She blurted out something, and it was, thank God, right! Then another question followed. Another man asked her something, and another, and another, and Sylvia had no problem answering.

After a barrage that lasted the better part of an hour, the six men leaned forward into a huddle. Sylvia could hear only snippets of their whispers. They wanted to stump her, had tried hard to, and what was this androgynous "it" in front of them, a hermaphrodite? A homosexual? How did "it," or whatever "it" is, possibly know all that "it" did? But "it" did? "It" is a woman. No. Yes. No. Yes.

By the end of the inquisition, though, the men were arguing among themselves about which of them first suggested they waive tradition, rules, whatever it was they had to waive, and welcome the anatomically puzzling whiz kid into their midst, even if "it" was a woman, which they were pretty sure "it" was. When one man asked her directly, Sylvia shrugged her shoulders and smiled.

Since staying in one of the dorms with the male students was out of the question, Sylvia moved into Dean Kessler's house. His wife Anna liked Sylvia and told her more than once, when her husband wasn't around, that she wished she could be as brave as Sylvia was. A bold step for a young woman, yes, but look how it had paid off. Sylvia, Anna Kessler told her a hundred times, was the perfect role model for her own two daughters who were just starting school.

It took the professors and students a much longer time to adjust to having a female in their midst. More than a few were openly hostile, convinced that a beloved, long-standing practice had been abandoned, and the result would be the ruination of the place. Howard remained aloof and avoided running into his pesky neighbor. Sylvia would see him in the distance and head in his direction, but when she was close enough to shout to him, he'd turn his back to her and walk briskly away.

Then one day she almost collided with him in the hallway outside the physics lab.

"What in the hell do you think you're trying to do?" he barked at her.

She'd never seen such annoyance in his face, but she didn't back down. "What in the hell do you think I'm trying to do? I'm trying to live my life the way I want to, that's what!"

"Well, go live it somewhere else far away from me, why don't you?"

Crushed by this confrontation, the harsh words ringing in her ears, Sylvia hurried off without saying another word or listening to anything else big deal Howard Russo might have to say. That night she promised herself she would never talk to her stuck-up, narcissistic neighbor again.

She stopped looking for him, stopped trying to figure out his schedule and "accidentally" run into him. She got good at avoiding him like the plague, but try as she did, she could not stop thinking about him, dreaming about how it might have been between them if only stupid, stubborn Howard could love her the way she loved him, or rather the way she used to love him, which was deeply.

Oh, how useless it all was. She'd thrown herself at him, and he hadn't even tried to catch her. What else was there to do?

Work hard. Keep to herself.

Eventually, some of the Rensselaer men stopped obsessing about the fact that Sylvia was a woman, the only woman on campus, and started noticing how damned smart she was. What a relief for her. They all got on with their lives, even though for Sylvia it was only academically. She had no friends, no social life. True, the staring and whispering behind her back had stopped, but as far as being embraced by her fellow students, well, that hadn't happened. So Sylvia went to class, went to the library, went to the lab, and went to her room at the dean's house. It left plenty of time for her studies, and she devoted herself wholeheartedly to them.

Her efforts didn't go unnoticed. At the close of the first semester just before Christmas break, the renowned Professor Alan Turing—his groundbreaking work at Bletchley Park and his *Turing* machine, the Colossus, already drawing international acclaim—invited Sylvia to be part of an important project. He'd traveled from Princeton University, where he'd collaborated with von Neumann on conceptualizing an electronic discrete variable computer, to assist Rensselaer's mathematicians and logicians in building a Colossus of their own.

Sylvia couldn't get the word, yes, out of her mouth fast enough when the dean informed her of Turing's decision to include some of the brightest students in the project.

Alan Turing, singling her out like this! Well, it was too much. As soon as her classes were over for the day, she hiked two miles into Troy, to Our Lady of Sorrows and lit a gratitude candle to the Virgin.

Sylvia's memories were interrupted by the conductor who lumbered through the car looking for anyone who had gotten on at Princeton Junction. Another hour to Trenton. She sank back into her seat and sighed. Gloom had descended on her. She didn't want her studies or her work on the project to be interrupted, but how could she resent Howard? Was she so small a person that she couldn't sacrifice her dreams so he could follow his? Making such a sacrifice should be easy if she truly loved him, which she did.

The fireworks the first time they kissed, well, truthfully, not the first time, maybe the second time, nearly sent her through the roof. It was the first day of winter break soon after Mr. Turing had selected her to help with the main frame. Howard and she had ridden home on the same train, but in different cars. Sylvia, true to her word, hadn't spoken to Howard since he'd been so cruel to her. She didn't want to care about Howard anymore, she didn't need to. She was consumed by the thought of working with Turing on *the* project, so she was wandering around the house humming Christmas carols to herself, waiting for Aunt Louise to come home from the factory so she could surprise her with the good news.

There was a knock at the back door. It was Howard, hunched over in the wind, snow clumping up on his thick hair.

Put a hat on, stupid. She wanted to yell at him through the door and not open it, but she saw the tray of pignoli nut cookies not wrapped in anything and getting wet from the snow. She opened the door.

"Hey, old buddy, how's this for a peace-offering?"

Old buddy? Peace-offering? He's got to be kidding. She almost slammed the door in his face, but he was smiling at her so earnestly it took the wind out of her sails.

"Damn it, Howard, how could you?"

"You mean how could I be mean to you? Honestly, I didn't mean to be mean to you."

"But you were. You really were."

"I'm sorry, really sorry, Sylvie; but when you showed up on campus and it was this big deal, I got angry. Hell, it was like my little sister following me around and embarrassing me."

"Well, in case you haven't noticed, I'm not your little sister. And if all you're worried about is being embarrassed by me, then take your cookies home and eat them by yourself."

"All I'm worried about now is you...us."

"Us?"

"Look, can we talk?"

Howard followed her into the kitchen and sat at the narrow table while she poured two glasses of milk. She sat opposite him and waited.

"I'm sorry, Sylvia." He laid his hand on her arm.

Never had he touched her like this. They'd chased each other around, tousled and tagged each other, but never a gentle touch like this.

"You don't have to repeat yourself. Apology accepted." She shrugged and looked down at his hand on her arm. Why wasn't he moving it? Then he did move it down over her hand.

"I never should have treated you like I did," he said.

"Don't worry, Howard. It's over. I got over it." She hadn't, and saying she had, trying to lie about it, made her voice tremble. She tried to pull her hand out from under his, but he held onto it, and tears welled up in her eyes.

"See it's not alright. I did hurt you. I was so stupid to act like that when I really do care about you."

He tried to wipe her tears away.

"Sylvia, I care a whole lot about you. These past weeks I've done nothing but think about you, about how brave you were to go to Rensselaer and stand up for yourself. You always were a spunky, little kid, and now I guess I'm realizing you've turned into a spunky, young woman."

Spunky? For God's sake, it sounded like he was talking about a dog. Suddenly, she wanted to crawl under the table. Maybe the way she looked made him use a word like "spunky" to describe her. After all, she could still be mistaken for a man. She kept chopping away at her hair every time it grew a little. Her unplucked eyebrows and naked lips did nothing to soften her sharp nose, her prominent cheekbones, and her chin with the slight cleft.

Howard ran his thumb over that cleft and then over her lips. His eyes on her made her squirm at first; but then she looked up at him, and they fell into a trance staring at each other. Minutes passed, the only sound the ticking of the clock. Then Howard leaned across the small table and kissed her.

And to her utter surprise, Sylvia felt…nothing. No tingling sensation. No goose bumps. Nothing. If she had a brother or a father, this is what kissing them would've felt like.

So, she thought, *I've wasted most of my life mooning over Howard Russo, waiting for a kiss from Howard Russo, and this is all it is. Great, now I can move on.*

She went to take a sip of her milk; but before she could, Howard stood up and pulled her out of the chair. He put his arms around her and held her close.

"What are you trying…?" She couldn't get the words out. He kissed her again, only longer and more forcefully. She was stunned by the feel of his lips on hers, of the pressure of his hands on her body. She felt very warm like she was standing with her back to the sun, the heat of it penetrating her clothes, the warmth melting something in her. She thought of the earth after the last snow, of the sun melting the snow, warming the earth into spring, into the season of starting. Her body was the earth. Howard the sun, the scorching, hot sun.

He began kissing her neck. She felt his fingers in her hair. He was holding her head gently as though it were fragile porcelain. She went soft in his arms for a second before something came alive in her and took her breath away. Her body was air, his kisses lightning bolts coursing through it.

His mouth went back to hers, and she opened it and felt his tongue for the first time, the sweet tongue of a benevolent god. His penis was hard against her pelvis. She pulled back and put her hands on his chest. His heart was pounding.

For me? For me.

She looked up at him as if to say, we better quit while we're ahead, but his face was dark and distorted like he was in pain. Sylvia didn't know what to do, then slowly he smiled and all his features fell back into that pleasant, familiar alignment she so cherished. Looking at him was like looking at the brightest constellation in the sky, looking at a "noumena."

When she was much younger, he taught her that word "noumena." He told her that the Italian poets created the word to describe a thing able to exist in its own light. That was how Sylvia saw him now, had always seen him—a brilliant man with a head full of brilliant thoughts that became brilliant ideas that became brilliant inventions. If ever there was a human being who could exist in his own light, it was Howard Russo.

That afternoon changed everything between them, and the memory of it made Sylvia long for her husband more than ever. How she wished he would be waiting for her at the station in Trenton, but he wouldn't be, and that made her even weaker with longing.

From the window she could see they were getting close to the Clinton Street Station and her thoughts went back to the emergency at hand. She placed the Holmes book back in her suitcase, adjusted her scarf, and listened to the train creak to a stop.

10

The key Mr. Ishikawa gave to his new son-in-law Masuki Shin did open the door to an apartment, just not to one in the plush Roppongi Hills above the beaten-down Roppongi alleyways. No, this key opened the door to the one bedroom apartment directly across the narrow hall from his mother's. Shin could've laughed at the irony of his "dowry" were he not so consumed with anger.

"I know how devoted you are to your mother, how difficult it would be for you to leave her so I have seen to it that you will never have to. The three of you will get along splendidly. I'm sure my lovely daughter will honor your mother in the same way that I know she will honor you," Ishikawa put his hand on Shin's shoulder. It made Shin shudder with disgust. Ishikawa kept talking, "It was expensive to buy in at a time like this. September is seeing some of the highest real estate prices in a decade, but I did promise you a generous dowry and I have kept my word. Have I not?"

How dare he trick me like this!

Masuki Shin wanted to turn to the selfish, cruel man and spit in his face. He would have if Ishikawa hadn't walked away toward the exit to the reception hall. Masuki would have followed him and shouted obscenities at him if he hadn't had his cronies around him and if his mother hadn't been standing by his new wife looking happier than he'd ever seen her in her entire life.

Why couldn't he, especially after so much whiskey, smile too?

Maybe it will all work out. It is my duty, after all, to take care of my mother. Having Kenta there will take the burden off of me.

That thought did comfort him a bit. He went to the bar and despite the fact that the bartender was cleaning up he demanded a double.

The next morning, Masuki, hung-over and nauseous, dragged himself to Noboru and sat at his desk trying to get some work done. He must've fallen asleep because when he felt a sharp jab in the shoulder, it jolted him awake so quickly he almost vomited.

Chief Yamato stood behind him with his index finger still extended in Masuki's direction.

"Seeing you like this almost makes me want to change my mind."

Masuki jumped to his feet. He and the older man stood eye to eye, though the skinny, bird-boned Chief seemed so much smaller than Masuki.

"Sir, it was my wedding night last night. The party lasted until late, and then, well, you understand, there were things that had to be taken care of like, well, you know..." Masuki tried to gather his thoughts and stop sounding like an idiot.

"Stop mumbling like an idiot and come with me." Yamato turned and left. Masuki grabbed his notepad and tried to catch up.

Walking into Yamato's office was like walking into a meat locker. It was so cold Masuki exhaled to check if he could see his breath. A man sat in one of the two taupe-colored leather chairs angled in front of the Chief's massive tiger maple desk. The man had on expensive clothes that were in less than pristine condition. His silk ascot was speckled with grease; the elbows of his jacket were shiny from wear; his white shirt was on the verge of turning yellow.

"Mr. Astin, this is one of my more gifted, though sometimes lackadaisical, research engineers. He is the one I've selected to work exclusively on the development of the prototype."

"Yamato, do you think I give a rat's ass what you do now? That's your problem, old chap..." The oily looking fellow paused to light his cigar. "...and yours alone. I got you the poor young man's camera. And I had to do things I generally refuse to do to get it. So now don't make me wait one damned minute longer for my money."

Masuki was stunned by the way this stranger talked to Yamato, not a hint of respect or fear.

"Mr. Astin, supposedly, you have done what I commissioned you to do, but do you think me foolish enough to take you at your word? I, with the assistance of Masuki Shin, will determine the authenticity of the camera. You'll get some of your payment now; and when the prototype is functioning and our mission accomplished, you'll get the rest."

"Bloody hell, I'll get the rest! I want it all now! You've got the camera, now bloody stick to your word, man!"

"What? Pay you everything now so you can tell our competitors and they can rob the camera from us. Do you take me for a fool? You have no choice but to wait and keep your mouth shut while you do."

Mr. Astin blew a cloud of smoke in Yamato's direction, but it dissipated before reaching the Chief's face. "So you've got me by the bloody balls. Maybe? But don't think I'm not going to be on top of you and whatever this mission is. I'll be such a pain in your ass you'll wish you had paid me off. And you, young man," he paused and blew another puff of smoke in Masuki's direction, "better not fuck this up." He pushed himself up out of his chair, flicked the ashes from his cigar on the fluffy egg-shell blue carpet, and lumbered toward the door.

11

"Howard is a dead!" Pop Russo shouted as Sylvia walked through the door.

"What are you saying, Pop?" The words made no sense to Sylvia; but the old man's face was as white as a sheet, and he was crying. She put her bag down. Was her father-in-law having a breakdown? Had he been drinking?

"Pop, calm down, you don't know what you're talking about." Sylvia put her hands on her hips. She'd get to the bottom of this. Then her mother-in-law came in from the hall and stood next to her husband. She was weeping like a baby, her narrow shoulders heaving with each wave of grief.

Damn, thought Sylvia, *I've got to calm these people down and get to the facts.*

"Sylvia, preggo," Pop said. "Howard was on some isle, some a where. He fell off a deck, broke his neck. That's what'a they told..."

"Who told you? Who is 'they'? Look, Pop, it's all a mistake. Howard is in Oxford, England, not...where did you say it was?"

"A isle, a island, what'a was nomen?" Pop Russo ran his hands through his graying hair and tugged at it.

"Howard, your son, my husband, was not on a little island somewhere!" Sylvia was emphatic. "He was in England which is a big island! Can't you see? It can't be Howard! It's somebody else."

"No! No! They brought'a his body back!" The distraught man yelled back at his daughter-in-law, then pleaded, "Don't'a you see? Momma and me went down'a to Guiardio's, down'a stairs where the bodies are and we seen him. Sylvia, we seen him. We seen Howard, dead." He sunk into a kitchen chair and banged his fist on the table top. Momma sat across from him and put her hands over his fist to hold it down. He let her. They both closed their eyes and sat there and cried even harder.

Sylvia paced around the small table. Her mind was racing in pursuit of an alternate truth. Sylvia hadn't once thought that something might've happened to Howard. She stopped and sat down at the table, too.

"Who, exactly, brought Howard's body back and what exactly did they say? I need to know all of the details." She still didn't believe them, but they were so upset she decided to try to humor them and get some facts and find out how they could have been so mistaken.

Momma opened her eyes, lifted her chin, and sighed. "Alright, Sylvia, now you listen," she said as she clasped her hands together on her lap. "This is just'a how it happened. Your father and me were to go down'a to the market, and we were in the alley when he seen a man in a dark suit, a nice'a one, looking in the window of the bar. 'Hey, you, what'a ya want? We ain't open yet!' your father-in-law yells. 'Mr. Russo? Mrs. Russo? I have to talk to you in private.' Well, your father gets'a red in the face and starts to argue with the man thinking we gonna have to pay for something, but this guy look different. All dressed up nice, you know, and has a funny accent. So I tell Pop, we better let'a him come in and talk to'a us. Your father is mad, but I lead the man into the house. We sit at the table. He'a looks your father in the eye and says, 'Your son Howard is dead. We have delivered his body to the undertaker, Guiardio's and Sons. We will drive you there for you to identify the corpse. I am so very sorry for your loss.' He said just like'a that, and then we leave and two soldiers drive us to Guiardio's. Howard look'a so calm and....still alive except he too grey...I don't'a touch him. Pop kiss his forehead and say, 'He hard as marble.' Uncle Sal call your school and thats'a everything."

"Mom, didn't you ask the man who he was or where he came from or how it happened?"

"It was accident, he fell'a off a deck, broke his neck."

"And where was he?"

"On a island. Pop already tell you."

"What else did he say? Did you ask him who he was?"

"No. You could'a see he was somebody important. Right, Pop?" Sylvia's mother-in-law's shoulders slumped. Sylvia took a deep breath and stood up.

"Never mind, Mom. It's alright."

"Sylvia," her father-in-law whispered, "you could go see Guiardio, old Antonio. Aska him."

"Good idea, Pop."

Sylvia kissed them both and left them sitting at the table. She took her suitcase into the living room, opened it up, and grabbed her camera. Howard had given it to her at her high school graduation back when they were only friends. Her heart pounding, she slipped the strap over her shoulder and went out through the front door.

I'll take a picture of the dead body. When I develop it they'll see clearly that it isn't Howard. That it can't be Howard.

Antonio Guiardio showed Sylvia the paperwork the British official had given him. It stated that Howard Russo's death was accidental. It occurred on the island of Tortola one week ago.

Paperwork can be incorrect. Lots of people make mistakes on paperwork. And who knows? There's got to be more than one Howard Russo in the world.

"Mr. Guiardio, is it really Howard?"

"Mrs. Russo, you know I haven't seen Howard in a few years. Not since he was here for his Aunt Theresa's funeral back in, oh, maybe back in '37. A young man can change a lot in three years. But, and I'm so sorry to have to say this, I'm sure this is your Howard."

Sylvia's mouth went dry.

While old Antonio was leading her down the well-lit staircase, he said, "We're not done working on him yet so don't be upset when you see him."

You mean when I see him and when you find out how mistaken you are.

The mortician opened a heavy door that led to a concrete block room. The temperature was close to freezing. On a steel table something lay under a sheet. Mr. Guiardio drew back the sheet and turned it down just below the corpse's chin.

Sylvia gasped. A thick layer of flesh-colored make-up covered the dead person's face, but it did little to hide the fact that this was Howard Russo, her Howard Russo.

The make-up also did little to conceal the dark purple circles under his eyes and the cuts and bruises on both his cheeks. It was obvious Old Antonio had applied rouge and lipstick trying to make her dead husband look more alive, but all it did was make him look like a clown. The only thing left that was really Howard was his gorgeous wavy black hair, longer and more unkempt than she remembered it.

Mr. Guiardio mumbled and left.

Sylvia, alone with her husband's body, petted the beautiful hair. The unfamiliar odor, the extraordinary cold, the stillness closed in on Sylvia. She pulled her hand back. If she could return to college, to her books, to the lab and her work and her important goals, this might go away, seem like it never happened, like it was only a nightmare she could wake up from. But her heart was throbbing with fear and dread, and slowly it sunk in. What she was looking at was not a bad dream. No, it was Howard and he was dead.

She wouldn't let herself cry. She fumbled in her pocket for a tissue and wiped the rouge and lipstick off her husband's cheeks and lips. Then, without actually deciding, she took her camera and advanced the film. The sprockets clicked loudly. She took a deep breath and the vapor from the embalming fluid that permeated the air tasted like tin in her mouth. She swallowed. Her stomach churned. Bile rose in the back of her throat. She raised the camera to her eye, looked through the lens, and made the necessary adjustments exactly as Howard had shown her. The overhead lights were bright enough, no need for the flash. She set the F-stop. As she checked the lens again, she remembered something.

The last photo Howard had taken of her. They'd just been married, and he was scheduled to leave for England. She posed against their neighbor's rusting Nash Ambassador. Howard said, "Come on, Sylvie, a big smile." Click. He snapped the shot. That night he developed it in his basement darkroom and called her down to look at it. She didn't like it. She looked like she had a smirk on her face, not a smile. Her hair, which had begun to grow in, was parted in the middle and pulled back with pink barrettes that made it look like she had two lumps of coal taped to the sides of her head. Her skin was too grey, her eyebrows too dark, her slacks too baggy, her sweater too bulky. She begged her new husband to tear it up.

"It isn't the way I really look," she argued. "I'm not me in that picture!" And she tried to grab it from his hand, but he held it up out of her reach and laughed.

"Too late now, honey. I think you look ravishing, and it's the way I'm always going to remember you." He tucked the photo in his pocket as she again tried to get it; and, as if to add insult to injury, he threw his head back and laughed even harder. She slapped at him and pummeled him and tried to reach in his pocket, but he fought her off as gently as he could and then wrapped his strong arms around her and kissed her until she stopped struggling and kissed him back.

The dark room floor was cold and damp, but that didn't deter Howard. He spread a heavy blanket on the floor. Hurriedly he helped Sylvia out of her clothes and had his off in a flash. He pulled Sylvia down on top of him. She straddled him, and he held her at the waist and kept her just above him so he could suck on her breasts, get her even more excited than she already was. When she was ready and he knew she was, he eased himself into her. Never had it been this good for her. It was like it had taken all of the kissing and fumbling and awkwardness of their physical life together thus far for them to get it right. But they finally had and they were one in joy, in release, in love. They had been so lucky for everything to turn out as it had, so lucky to have their dreams come true?

Sylvia pushed the memory from her mind.

Don't let yourself fall apart.

She studied the corpse now in an almost scientific way thinking how Howard's insides, though slowed by the chemicals, were breaking down right in front of her. The outside was so still, his skin like frosted granite, if there was such thing.

Click.

She snapped a shot, then another, then another. She thought of some photos she'd taken of green peppers and of how dense and solid they looked even though they were hollow.

Click.

Howard's body looked the same way.

Click.

The camera made her brave. She leaned in close to Howard's face and through the lens beneath the make-up cuts and bruises looked even more brutal.

One day when they were just little kids, they were playing in the small yard of the row house. Howard wouldn't get off the old tire that hung from a branch of the only tree. He was swinging on it, and Sylvia was begging for a turn. Howard ignored her, swung higher. Sylvia disappeared for a while, and Howard assumed he had gotten rid of her until she reappeared from the alley way kicking up dust as she shuffled along with one hand behind her back. She seemed disinterested and was looking around humming "Red Red Robin" until she was almost right in front of the swing. She stood a little off to the side but close enough to touch Howard on his way down. He swung forward ignoring Sylvia, then back, pumping his legs harder. Forward, back. Forward. The empty beer bottle flashed in the sunlight for a split second before Sylvia whacked Howard over the top of his head with it. He fell backward and out of the tire and rolled in the dust clutching his head as blood blinded him and muddied the ground. She watched him try to wipe his eyes with his forearm so he could see, but he was bleeding badly and couldn't keep ahead of the gushing blood. Sylvia saw how much pain he was in but let her self-righteous anger keep her from feeling sorry for him.

Serves you right for not giving me a turn, was all she could think.

Then when Howard's mother came to the back door, she ran to her screaming, "Mrs. Russo, Mrs. Russo, he teased me, he should've given me a turn." But Mrs. Russo was already past her and holding Howard who was crying in her arms as she pressed the skirt of her apron into the wound on his skull.

She had hated him at that moment. Maybe if he had died, she might've regretted what she'd done; but he hadn't, so deep down inside she really wasn't sorry. Even when Aunt Louise made her say sorry to him and he had said, "It's okay. I forgive you." She felt neither the apology, nor his acceptance of it, in her heart.

Now this man she'd known almost her whole life, this man who was a boy she fought with and played with and fell in love with, was dead.

She put the camera down on the gurney and again leaned close to Howard's face. If he were breathing, she would've felt it on her chin. She studied his closed eyelids, tried to picture his eyes. The color of wet corn husks was how she always thought of them. Not at all like most Italians, but exactly like hers.

"God, Howard, oh my God," she whispered, "Who did this to you?"

She kissed his lips, and it felt like she was kissing ice.

12

The next morning, the morning of the funeral, a letter of consolation arrived from the Queen of England along with two trunks that bore postmarks from the British Virgin Islands. It stated that there had been an accident resulting in Howard Russo's "untimely and unfortunate death." The young man had apparently fallen from the deck of a cliffside bungalow. It noted that Howard was on an important assignment on behalf of Her Majesty's government, but never revealed what that was. The letter expressed England's gratitude for Howard's sacrifice. Nothing specific was spelled out, but it did leave the impression that Howard had agreed to go to Tortola and do something for the British.

Sylvia read it again and again trying to get something out of it that wasn't there.

Better to concentrate on what happenned, than to curl up in a corner and lose my mind.

She could feel the grief trying to grip her, paralyze her. She fought it with every bit of fortitude she had.

An 'unfortunate accident'? The more she examined the empty rhetoric about duty and honor, the more suspicious she became. She couldn't imagine Howard signing up for a mission to a remote island in the Caribbean, the success of which would supposedly "save the free world."

Howard was too…? Sylvia couldn't quite put her finger on it. Too preoccupied? Too self-centered? Too smart? How could he agree to get involved in the horrible political mess in Europe? He just wasn't the type. For him to "volunteer" for a dangerous mission seemed to Sylvia beyond improbable; and, even if he had agreed to help in some way, Howard wasn't the least bit clumsy. Her well-built husband was far too agile to lean over a deck railing so far that he'd lose his balance and tumble hundreds of feet down the side of a cliff.

She wasn't patient to begin with when it came to not knowing something she felt she should know. She didn't like a mystery; and if she did come up against one, she wanted the answer. And, damn it, this man was her everything, her life. Her frustration was mounting. She thought of Howard's dead face, his closed eyes, closed ears, closed mouth. See no evil, hear no evil, speak no evil.

What really happened, Howard? Please, you can let me know. Send me a sign. I know you can, honey. If anybody can figure out a way to get through to me from heaven, it'd be you.

She threw the royal letter down and watched it fly off the table and float to the floor. Something buried deep inside of her was slowly and methodically clawing its way to the surface.

Howard's prototype for the camera? Impossible, he would've written me if he'd been able to make it work. The last letter she got with any details about it was back in May. The camera was barely half-finished. Howard wrote specifically that no one knew about it, warned her, because of his desire to get patents on it, not to tell a soul about it. I'm the only one who knew about it. The only one. But, if someone did know? If Howard had completed it? There would be lots of people, corporations, competitors that would want to get their hands on it.

Sylvia gave up for now trying to figure things out. It was already 7:00 a.m., and they had to be at Guiardio's by 9:30. She didn't care what she looked like, but for the rest of the family and the neighborhood she'd try to pull herself together.

She'd asked Father Marrazzo if she could say a few words after his sermon. So as he took his seat on the altar, she ascended to the pulpit and began, "I just want to say to all of you who loved Howard that Howard loved you all just as much. He wasn't always one to show it. We all know how hard he worked on all of his inventions. We all know how he would wander away from a family party to be alone. We'd see him scribbling away in his small notebook. God only knows what ideas were racing through his mind, forcing their way to the surface, demanding his attention.

But I didn't understand then what it meant to be so smart. I used to think Howard didn't want to be around me. I'm sure all of you felt that way at one time or another. But as I got to know Howard as a boyfriend and husband, I realized he was doing what he had to do. His mind worked differently. It wouldn't let him rest. I have just received a trunk full of hundreds of computations and drawings. He wanted to change the world for the better, and he could have if he were still here. Howard was the best man any woman could want. He was honest, loyal, and fair. For years all I was to him was a neighborhood brat. Even after we fell in love, I thought he only wanted me because I was a woman who loved him. But I have found out differently because Howard trusted me, and only me, with his vision. I guess what I'm trying to say is, he thought that I was smart too, and up till now, though I loved him anyway, I didn't realize that, and I'm sorry I didn't."

It was the truth. All of the bad things she had ever done or said or felt about Howard when they were young came from jealousy and from being rejected. And now, too late, she realized how much he did love all of her, her body and her brain.

She surveyed the sea of faces in front of her and felt dizzy. Who were these people staring right through her as though the tightly packed molecules that she was were all jumbled up and spread out, and she no longer existed as she was but rather as a faint cloud of her former self? How could they not see her when she was denser than lead?

So discombobulated was she that she thought the marble floor beneath her was melting into liquid and because she was so dense and heavy, so very heavy, it was swallowing her up.

In the rear vestibule the silhouettes of the standing people were a black jagged barricade between her and the bright sunlight beyond the open doors. The stained glass windows on either side of her split the light that came through them into shards of color that spilled over the people in the pews. The black robed choir leaned forward like crows, the brass pipes of the organ glistened like polished canons, the fifteen foot fresco on the ceiling of the Virgin crushing the serpent beneath her foot floated overhead like a ragged flag.

Sylvia was trapped by something she had no way of escaping; and, though she was on the verge of saying something more, she couldn't. All of the words in the world would not be enough to make up for losing Howard. She would never see him again, never hear the sound of his voice again, never look in his eyes again, or feel his sweet breath on her neck, or his hand in hers...

She lowered her head and quickly walked down the altar steps back to her pew without trying the least bit to hide her tears.

The family proceeded down the long aisle behind the pallbearers who carried the wood casket on their shoulders. Father Marrazzo turned at the doorway for the final prayer. He made the sign of the cross in the air above the lowered heads of the congregation and in a firm voice declared, "Thou art dust, and unto dust thou shall return."

Sylvia tried to pray, but what had been regret and grief a minute ago turned to anger. In desperation, she mumbled, "Lord, make me an instrument of your peace...Lord, make me an instrument of your peace," but she couldn't remember what came next; and she felt like she wanted to pound her fists on her husband's coffin or pummel herself with them. Then something in her mind clicked; and an amorphous thought crystallized, Howard was murdered.

Click.

I will find out who murdered my husband.

Click.

And I will make them pay for what they have done.

In that moment any part of her life that had not already been changed by the death of her husband, was inexorably changed as she silently vowed of revenge.

Momma Russo followed Sylvia up to Howard's room scolding her for being in such a rush to get things done, for being disrespectful to her dead husband's memory by rushing around to see what was in the two trunks.

"Shush, Momma, shush! It's got to be done. I have to find out what happened to Howard. It'd be disrespectful of me to just sit around and cry like some baby. Wouldn't it?" Sylvia pushed open the door to the room she and Howard had shared as newly-weds. They'd gotten married in a rush after that first kiss, neither of them wanting to wait. Father Marrazzo tried to talk them out of it; but they wore him down, and he performed a quiet ceremony with the immediate families the day after Christmas. Pop offered them Howard's old room since Howard was set to leave for Oxford for the spring semester. When he came home next winter, they could get their own place.

Howard's mother followed Sylvia in and sat on the bed wringing her hands. Sylvia opened the trunk. Howard's clothes, bed sheets, towels, all of his personal belongings carefully wrapped in packing paper. Obviously not something Howard would've wasted his time on. Sylvia piled his things one by one on the bed. At the bottom was his old Leica. Gently she fingered the cold metal of the well-used camera. No new prototype here.

Sylvia had to use a screwdriver to force the smaller trunk open. A jumble of paperwork and photographs. This too was unlike Howard. He was a bit of a slob when it came to his clothes and toiletries, but he was obsessively neat with his work. But here was a mess. Torn and crinkled pictures, empty folders, pages ripped from notebooks. No, someone had rifled through everything in the trunk. Sylvia wanted to run to the police station and tell them, look what somebody did to my husband's things!

But what would they do? Shrug, pat her on the head, tell her to calm down, it's only notes and photographs, not the end of the world.

She was crying before she realized she was. Momma Russo knelt next to her and put her arm around Sylvia's heaving shoulders. They stayed there that way for a long while. When Momma left, Sylvia buried her face in one of Howard's shirts and vowed, *I will find whoever did this and make them sorry. I swear I will make them sorry.*

13

For the next several days, Sylvia did two things: she ate and she worked on organizing Howard's belongings. She was hell-bent on finding something in his notes or photographs that would help her make sense of his death. She proceeded slowly and methodically, but there didn't seem to be a single clue about who would want to harm Howard or steal his notes. What she did discover, though, was something about her husband she hadn't suspected. He was a lover of the humanities.

She read with great interest his paper on Stern's *Tristram Shandy*. The eighteenth century writer was concerned, according to Howard, with the eternal challenge of waiting for life to begin, and cleverly juxtaposed that consideration against the fear involved in waiting for it to end.

And in a short essay Howard drew a fascinating comparison between the Shinto custom of hanging wooden prayer plaques on temple trees and the Germanic Christmas tree tradition.

A rough draft of another paper attempted to delve into Hardy's and Tolstoy's treatment of women in love, but out of control.

A knock on the door startled Sylvia who was lost in her husband's analysis of the works of Velazquez and Goya. Pop came in, handed her a large envelope, and left.

It was from Howard.

Sylvia reached over and rested her open palm on it. It was cold and smooth, but to her it seemed alive, like a pulsing heart. Howard was in this envelope. He had come to tell her what had gone wrong.

She bowed her head, *please, God, let it be a sign.*

She picked the envelope up with trembling hands, took a deep breath, and ripped it open. The first thing she saw was the handwritten note.

So he was invited to Buckingham Palace? Wow, Buckingham Palace. It took a minute to sink in. Sylvia was puzzled. *Howard? Meeting the princess? By invitation?*

She stopped reading and imagined Howard shaving, brushing his teeth, smoothing his hair back with a glop of hair cream, carefully putting on his best suit, checking the handkerchief in his breast pocket, sucking on a mint, going to the palace, in that palace! Did she know her husband at all, this man who went to a palace and met a princess? She felt sick to her stomach. She'd missed a whole episode, a big important episode in Howard's life by not going to England with him. But she couldn't have gone, there was no money for her to go, and there was her own work, her own education. But the thought of Howard doing such a frivolous and romantic thing as going to Buckingham Palace made her cheeks turn hot, even as she told herself how stupid it was to be jealous now.

Along with the letter were four diagrams. Sylvia recognized the drawings of Howard's prototype immediately. There were ten pages of instructions detailing the materials to be used in the manufacturing and the specs for the copper plate that would be used instead of film. Another sheet of paper had a drawing at the top that showed how the camera could possibly be rigged to a computer. At the bottom were programming notes. Sylvia was baffled. What she knew about computers and what Howard was suggesting seemed worlds apart, yet something inside her glimpsed the tip of the giant iceberg Howard must've imagined.

There were three other documents: an anthropological study of the Masai's fear of photographs, a paper about the Amish which outlined their distrust of the modern gadget called the camera and its potential for spiritual corruption, and an essay whose primary thesis was a contemporary justification of Emerson's concept of the transparent eyeball.

Sylvia took her time and read every word and let it all sink in before she was calm enough to pick up the letter and read the rest.

...Now for the less important news. Make sure you look over my notes on the prototype.

Yes, Sylvie, I'm still having some problems, but I am so close I can smell success. If only I had more time. The exhibition was a big distraction, and so is what's going on across the Channel. Even here things are getting a little scary, but I don't want to go into that now. No, I want you to be proud of me and to miss me as much as I miss you. Do you? I pray that you do.

But I just can't get the prototype out of my mind. When I get it to work, I know it will be something that will help people see the world differently, clearly, like how it should be.

I'll be home for Thanksgiving with diploma in hand. I cannot wait to wrap my arms around you and hold you close again. When we are together, I'll hug you till you burst. Till then, be good. Keep your big nose (only kidding, I love your nose) to the grindstone. Remember, you are my only love. You and you, alone.

> *Your loving and faithful husband,*
> *Howard*

The letter fell from Sylvia's hand and drifted to the carpet.

I love you too.

She sunk to the floor.

Why be alive when my Howard is dead?

She laid on her back. Her tears trickled down her temples into her hair.

It took Sylvia some time to get a grip on herself. *Be a woman, not some sniffling girl,* she told herself and willed herself to go through every single paper again. The diagrams, the drawings of the camera, the depiction of the computer connections, the instructions for the program.

Slowly, she began to understand what Howard was thinking, though she hadn't a clue yet of how he planned to accomplish what he imagined. A camera wielded the power to change things. People took cameras and the pictures they produced for granted because they were becoming so commonplace; but Howard knew, had known better. He realized a machine capable of capturing a person in a moment of time had the potential to be made to do even more. His vision was futuristic and fantastic and profound all at once. How she wished he were alive so she could tell him that she knew...he'd have been so proud.

So where was the prototype? It wasn't in either of the trunks, and yet, in the letter he clearly referred to it as "almost finished." His old worn-out Leica was there, but where was the magnificent invention Howard sketched, described, and claimed he had just about perfected?

Maybe he'd turned it over to the British government? Or the United States? But why wouldn't he have told her that?

Maybe...maybe someone had stolen Howard's prototype?

A disaster. Her husband's dream gone.

She looked at the pile of papers in front of her. Could she figure out a way to recreate it? Was she capable of such a monumental undertaking? Could she, if she did recreate the prototype, be able to develop the program?

She had to try. She couldn't just let it all go to waste. When the new 'giant brain' at Rensselaer was finished, anything might be possible. Then she thought of Mr. Turing, and her heart grew light. Wouldn't he be downright fascinated?

Who the hell was she kidding? Turing would think she'd lost her mind. And it would take years and years for her to get to where Howard was with the whole thing.

No, I've got to find that prototype. Howard never would've left England without it. I've got to go to that island where he breathed his last breath.

She wouldn't go back to college. She'd sell everything she had, work, beg, do whatever she had to do to get to the godforsaken island of Tortola. She'd uncover the truth about what happened to the prototype, and Howard, if it was last thing she did.

14

Sylvia sat in the back of the boat in the scorching sun. Humble tin shacks lined the beach of St. Thomas, but on the steep mountainside brightly painted mansions peeked through the lush foliage.

I'm not in Trenton for sure anymore, thought Sylvia, feeling as though she'd travelled very far to arrive in the middle of nowhere.

The clear water of the Caribbean Sea stretched out around the small vessel like an undulating teal carpet, splotched here and there by the shadows of the clouds. The engine chugged loudly. Gulls squawked. A sailfish leapt up and hung in the air above the crest of a wave like a kite. Sylvia riveted her eyes on the spot where it had disappeared beneath the surface. Maybe the marvel would breach the surface again.

The skin on her face was burning hot so she put her arm over her forehead and shut her eyes trying not to think about what was to come. She was exhausted. For weeks she'd done nothing but work all day in the tavern and all night at the bakery down the street. She saved every dime, and when word got around the neighborhood that she needed money to go find out what happened to Howard, everyone found some way to give her a little something.

The Russos and her aunt were against the whole thing. Momma Russo begged, "It's a God's will, Sylvia. Say your rosary and leave-a things alone. Leave-a a them up to the Blessed Virgin now."

But Sylvia knew she was going to Tortola no matter what anyone said. She phoned Dean Kessler and asked him to apologize for her to Mr. Turing for not returning to work on the project. The dean tried to convince her to come back to the university, "...for your own good."

All that did was make her cry.

Sylvia opened her eyes. The light blinded her for a second, but there it was straight ahead, the island of Tortola, a black speck in the distance. She ran her fingers through her short hair. It was like touching a strange man's head. This time she'd had no compunction about cutting her hair off almost to her scalp. Aunt Louise shrieked, "Not again, Sylvia!" But for Sylvia it was a safety measure. She wore no make-up, no lipstick, and hid her breasts under a baggy man-tailored shirt.

She was, after all, traveling to a strange country alone. Looking like a man had gotten her into Rensselaer hadn't it? The men, young and old, didn't befriend her as they might another man, but they also didn't try to impress her as they might have if she'd looked more like a woman. She was so unattractive they acted, for the most part, like she wasn't there. That was just fine with Sylvia. Anonymity would get her what she wanted, the ability to sneak around and stay out of trouble. The more invisible she was, the better.

The boat slowed in the harbor. A few rickety docks came into view. Beyond were some bungalows, their wood bleached bone white by the sun. On the shore the hulls of dilapidated row boats were scattered about like the discarded teeth of a giant. There was one large clapboard house with a balcony. Philodendron vines ran along the balcony railing and lush palms fanned out above its awning. Sylvia could see it was a place of business, maybe a bar or restaurant. Mounted on the only visible wall was the massive shell of a leatherback sea turtle. Music was playing. A woman was mopping the floor, sort of dancing with the mop to the music.

That's as good as any place to start, thought Sylvia as she gathered her belongings and headed down the gangplank.

God's will be damn, Sylvia thought of her mother-in-laws admonishment as she headed past a small sign nailed to the trunk of a tree that read, "The Inn." She followed the dirt path and climbed the wobbly steps.

"Excuse me, please. Are you open?" Sylvia said.

The place was empty except for the young woman Sylvia had seen from the boat, who stopped, leaned on the handle of the mop, and stared with a perplexed look on her face at the stranger.

"Sorry to bother you," Sylvia apologized.

The girl—Sylvia could see now she was only a teenager—pursed her lips and let out a low whistle before she spoke. "Why yes, we are always open here at The Inn. Sit down, sit down, and I will be right with you." But instead of inquiring about what Sylvia might want, she shook her head, shivered, turned back to her sultry dance with the mop, and began humming to the music.

Sylvia surmised she'd created a dilemma for the young person. The tan men's shirt tucked into a pair of loose-fitting khaki slacks, the sensible Oxfords, the strap of the camera bag across her flattened chest; well, anyone would have been confused about exactly what kind of a human being they were talking to. How drastically Sylvia's appearance contrasted with the appearance of the girl. The mahogany-colored skin of her face glistened with sweat. With each swish of her hips the blue fringe of her skirt brushed her thin calves. Her white cotton blouse with short puffy sleeves was tight and barely covered her midriff. She was almost as tall as Sylvia, but wiry and slender except for her breasts, the size and shape of large ripe mangoes. Sylvia had never seen anyone so stunning and she took advantage of the girl's self-absorption to snap a photo of her.

Her name was Harriet. She was sixteen, three years younger than Sylvia. Sylvia knew she couldn't drink the water on the island so she ordered a beer, and Harriet brought her something lukewarm called Red Stripe. The first sip made her shudder, but after that it went down pretty smoothly and seemed to take the edge off her weariness.

Harriet moved the chairs back around the small tables where she'd mopped, shooed a green parrot away from a bowl of limes, and wiped the moisture off the five bottles of rum that sat on a shelf by the kitchen door before she came back around the bar and said, "Miss? You are a miss aren't you? Where's your husband, miss?"

"He's...I don't have a husband, and yes, I am a miss."

"Well, who did you come here with? Your parents, maybe?"

"No, I'm alone." The fan was whirring overhead. Sylvia was grateful for the breeze. The beer had made her hot and slightly high.

"Alone?"

"Yes."

"Alone here might not be the best for you, miss."

"I had to come."

"Why?"

Sylvia wasn't sure how to answer or how much she should tell anyone on the island.

"May I have another, please?" Sylvia slid the empty bottle toward Harriet, who had her elbows on the bar and her face propped up between the pale palms of her hands. Her eyes met Sylvia's. Sylvia had never seen such black irises that made them almost indistinguishable from the pupils. It was like looking into bottomless wells.

"Miss, where did you come from?"

"New Jersey, the United States."

"Why, miss, if you don't mind me askin', would you want to come all the way from the United States to this island *alone*?" The concept seemed to baffle Harriet who had never been off Tortola. She shrugged and walked into the kitchen shaking her head. The energy in the motion made her long tight curls tremble.

Harriet brought the beer back, gave it to Sylvia, pulled a stool up to her side of the bar, sat down, and began chatting away about all of the crazy people in her large family. Then she went on to bemoan the fact that she couldn't go to the British school in Road Town.

"Not for us. We got our own school, miss, but it's not good like the one the Brits got for themselves. I don't go. I know how to read. I get my own books and reads and reads them."

Sylvia liked Harriet, liked the sound of her voice, her accent. Harriet bragged about how she could dive thirty feet with no tank, how she could beat anyone her age and some older at arm wrestling, and how she had won the limbo contest at the church festival seven times. She hated all of the boys on the island except one, but she would never tell anyone, not even her new friend Sylvia, who he was. But she was sure this boy with golden hair—"there is the clue, miss"—knew.

"At least sometimes, I swear, he looks at me like he is reading my mind. I tell you, miss, it gives me the shivers the way he looks at me, the good shivers. I calls them the love-shivers. You ever have the love-shivers?"

Harriet interrupted her lengthy monologue only once to serve rum punches to a man and woman who had come off a yacht and sat whispering at a table in the corner. She sauntered back, put the tray under the bar, and reached across it to touch Sylvia's arm. Her touch surprised Sylvia, who couldn't help herself from looking down at Harriet's dark hand against her own pale skin.

Maybe it was the beer because when Sylvia looked into Harriet's eyes again, she had the sensation she was about to fall into them and it scared her. Sylvia pulled her arm away.

"Sorry, miss, but I just wanted you to look at those two. See how the mister is rubbing his foot up and down on the ladies leg. Love-shivers, yes?"

"Harriet, you don't have to keep calling me miss."

"Well, you are older, and that is how I was taught, miss, I mean, Sylvia. So back to the love-shivers. Did you or did you not ever have them?"

Sylvia leaned forward. She didn't want the couple to hear. She whispered, "Yes, my husband always gave me the love-shivers, every time I looked at him or even thought of him."

"Your husband? So why is he not here with you? How could he let you come this far without him? I don't understand."

"I don't understand either, Harriet."

"You are making riddles, miss."

"I'm not making riddles, but the whole thing is a riddle because last month my husband died here."

"Here?" Harriet looked from side-to-side, glanced quickly at the couple from the yacht, then back at Sylvia. Her eyes widened, and the black orbs were suddenly circled by white.

"Did he fall from the deck of a bungalow?"

"So I've been told."

The whole island knows. It was a bad..." She held onto the word bad while she shook her head slowly. "...accident."

"But I don't believe it *was* an accident. I don't believe my husband just fell off a deck."

"I tell you, Miss Sylvia. That is exactly what happened."

"And I am telling you, I knew my husband and it could not have been an accident."

Harriet's eyes narrowed and she said, "You think someone here hurt your husband on purpose? Is that what you are saying? Because I tell you, miss, there are no murderers here. And if anyone of us was a murderer, we would only murder each other, not a man we don't even know." Harriet blinked, then averted her gaze to examine the pink palms of her hands.

Sylvia was not completely surprised by Harriet's reaction. She shouldn't have just come out with what sounded like an accusation. She had no evidence, and now she was alienating the first person she met.

"Do you know where I might get a room?" Sylvia switched the subject.

But Harriet wasn't finished yet. "Miss, I am young, only sixteen, but I warn you. If you look for trouble here, you will find it."

Sylvia slid her empty bottle to the side and looked up at Harriet. "I'm sorry. I didn't mean to offend you and the last thing I want is trouble, but I feel like I owe it to my husband to find out the truth."

"Never trouble trouble, or trouble will trouble you."

"Don't mind me, Harriet. I understand what you are saying."

"Okay, miss..."

"My name is Sylvia."

"Okay, Sylvia, you will not forget that I warned you, though."

Harriet, her hand on the bottle, began to move away, but before she did she turned and smiled crookedly.

"Go see my older brother. He will find you a place to stay. You tell him Harriet sent you, and he has to help. Make sure you say the last part so he knows I'm serious. His name is Mark, but everyone calls him La Bomba. You'll find him at the Shack."

15

The Shack was a battered structure on the beach side of the only road that led from the docks toward Road Town. Perched on eroded pylons, the building extended out over the sea. The tin roof was pitted with rust. The front of the building was unpainted and covered in graffiti: "show La Bomba your titties and get free drink," or "come in early, stay all night" or "La Bomba's special drink is a bomb, get ready to explode."

La Bomba, who looked old enough to be Harriet's father, sat on a red cushion on top of a steamer trunk in a small shed near the main entrance. The large, black man in a faded Hawaiian shirt and a pair of frayed shorts bore no resemblance to his willowy sister. However, when Sylvia explained that Harriet had sent her, La Bomba smiled and his deep dark eyes sparkled, their resemblance to Harriet's suddenly uncanny.

He invited her to sit on a nearby stool and as she did, he shifted his weight on the faded cushion and brushed a tiny spider off his hairless thigh. He pulled one huge leg up by the ankle, then the other, crossing them one over the other. The position looked painful until he leaned back calmly and placed both of his large hands on his knees like a regular Buddha.

Sylvia was nervous, but she forced herself to speak slowly and carefully as she tried to explain to this strange-looking man who her husband was and how impossible it was that he could have accidentally killed himself or committed suicide.

La Bomba didn't interrupt or move. He seemed to be listening calmly to the young American woman. When she stopped pleading her case, La Bomba stared down at the sand, cupped one corpulent cheek in his hand, and grunted to himself. After several minutes, he looked up at Sylvia and smiled, his teeth strikingly white like his sister's, his fleshy lips pinker near the inside of his mouth.

"Well, so you are asking for my help? I know much about everything on the island. It is true. But for me to tell you what I know, there is a big price."

A gull squawked as it swooped by. Sylvia, level with La Bomba's bare feet, could not help looking at his toes, the size of small sausages and at his toenails, long, yellow and the texture of coarse sand paper.

"A price? A big price?" Sylvia was crestfallen. She had barely enough money to get to Tortola. It never occurred to her that she'd have to pay for information.

"Look, Mr. La Bomba," she pleaded trying to keep her eyes from going back to the man's enormous toes, "he was my husband. I loved him more than life itself. His parents are sick with grief. He was their only son. We are all sick with grief. Couldn't you just give me something to go on?"

"Well, it goes without saying I am sorry for you, but La Bomba has many people to take care of and money is scarce. I could not let others know that I would do anything for nothing. It would ruin the reputation that I have so carefully established for myself." He paused and stroked his smooth chin with fingers that had nails almost as neglected as those of his toes.

"Perhaps we can barter in the island tradition."

"Barter? I have nothing but a few clothes." Sylvia looked down at her bag, at her camera sitting on top of it. She didn't want to give her camera up, but it was the only thing of value she had. La Bomba looked at the camera too. Sylvia saw it in his face, he was going to be all business.

She stood up.

"Just forget it, Mr. La Bomba. I'll just try to get a ride to Road Town and get in touch with the British authorities there. Maybe they know something. Thanks anyway." Sylvia was about to turn and leave when she remembered the rest of what Harriet had said. She looked back at the large man.

"Oh, and your sister said to tell you that 'you had to help' and not to forget to tell you that part, the part about 'you had to,' but I guess now it doesn't make any difference."

"Now, Miss Sylvia, don't be too hasty." It seemed he'd reconsidered things pretty quickly. "I see you have a camera."

Her heart sunk. So he did want the camera. So she'd have to hand her most prized possession over to him.

"I assume you know how to use such a nice machine."

"Yes."

"You have film?"

"Yes."

"And can you develop pictures here on the island?"

"Yes, I have plenty of film, and I could set up some sort of dark room if you could get me some chemicals and basic equipment."

"Good, well, very good." He began massaging his chin. "That's a start. You can photograph my family, and you can work at the Shack. I always need workers; and, perhaps, in time I will tell you what I know."

"Perhaps? In time? How much time?" Sylvia sank back down on the stool.

"It all depends."

"On what?"

"On what kind of photographer you are and whether or not you know how to cook."

"I can tell you, La Bomba, I'm an excellent photographer; and, as far as cooking goes, I'm Italian by marriage and from New Jersey, so I'll manage."

"What you say about being Italian and from New Jersey means nothing to me so let us wait until you make something and I taste it." He grinned at her.

"It's settled then?" asked Sylvia.

"There is one more condition."

"Now what?" Sylvia tried not to let her impatience show in her face.

"When I tell you, you can tell no one what I tell you." La Bomba stopped smiling and leaned toward her. He got so close to her face she could smell the rum on his breath. "No one. Do you hear me? No one," he whispered and his solemn voice rang in her head like the toll of a funeral bell.

"But what if it was...."

"No what ifs."

La Bomba's mood shifted quickly. He laughed loudly, tilted his head back, and shook out the long coils of his dreadlocks and they cascaded down his back like a black waterfall.

"Now, I'll show you the kitchen," he said as he struggled to his feet and led Sylvia into the Shack, behind the bar and through a rickety door to an open deck that ran along the opposite side of the building. It had a sawed off garbage can for a sink and half a steel drum for a grill. Sylvia stared at the filthy space and then at the back of La Bomba's enormous head wondering what in the devil she'd gotten herself into.

La Bomba offered Sylvia the vacant bungalow where Howard had died. Sylvia was sick at the thought, but what choice did she have. She had to do as she was told, or she'd never get any answers.

She struggled up the mountain road with her bag, full of apprehension; but when she entered the same space where Howard had spent the last moments of his life, the first thing she saw was the view, and it took her breath away. The sky was golden, the sea silver. She stood in the middle of the room in amazement. Never had she seen anything so magnificent.

She watched as the sun dropped below the horizon and the sky blazed with colors she couldn't name. Slowly, she walked out on the deck and over to the railing. She looked down. The beach was so far away. She imagined Howard's body falling, tumbling down the cliff, hitting rocks, bouncing off them, and slamming hard into the sand. Even the softest sand couldn't cushion a fall from this height. His neck broke and too many bones to count. There'd been no autopsy. Mr. Guiardio said little about it except that Howard must've died on impact. Sylvia saw the fishermen still fishing in the dusk. They must have been there and must've tried to help, but it would've been too late.

What terror must have gripped him as he was falling? Knowing he was about to die, knowing there was no way to stop it, no way to sprout wings and fly up and away and live again. Sylvia's head was reeling. She feared death. Despite believing in God, she feared going to Him. *What if He wasn't there? What if there was nothing?* She didn't want to die. Even though she was crazy with grief and anger and loneliness, no, she didn't want to die.

The sky was changing, red to orange, purple to pink. It was so gorgeous that Sylvia's anxiety lessened. *There has to be something, some other beautiful place for us.* She wanted to reach out to it, fly out to it, to her husband, there on the other side of the sunset, there in heaven.

She hurried inside to get her camera. These were the most alive seconds of the day, when the bright orb sank, when the colors started ticking to silver. Soon the sky would be indistinguishable from the sea. Sylvia snapped photo after photo. The camera had to capture it all. Then suddenly the dying beauty of day made her go weak inside, and for a second she felt a weird impulse to put one leg over the railing, then the other, then lean toward the sea, and let herself go. When it was over, maybe she would find Howard. Maybe he'd be in that other place, his arms spread wide to welcome her.

Just to touch him one more time.

Well, she would do anything.

She stood in the growing darkness and looked down at the railing. She wrapped her hand around it and shook it as hard as she could. It didn't wobble an inch. She stepped back and looked at the height of it.

Impossible to accidentally fall over that high, sturdy railing.

Something made a sharp sound in the dark. *A bird?* She couldn't tell; but soon there was a chorus of them, and she figured out they must be frogs. The sound was too close, too loud. She went inside, locked the doors to the deck, and closed all the windows. She slid a large chair against the front door and pushed the sofa against the deck doors. She went into the kitchen and grabbed the biggest knife she could find. The air was growing hot. She was sweltering, but she kept her clothes on. She stretched out on the bare wooden floor. She could feel the heat of Howard's last steps on earth searing right through her skin into her soul.

16

At sunrise, Sylvia walked down the hill to the Shack. The doors to the shed were open, and she heard his snoring before she saw La Bomba sprawled out on some cushions on the floor. The huge black man reminded her of the Cyclops in the Odyssey. If he ever got riled up enough, would he scoop her up and eat her for breakfast?

She banished the image from her mind. She had too much at stake to be a wimp.

As she headed through the Shack toward the kitchen, she noticed a boy, a teenager, perhaps, with long, golden, curly hair fishing off the deck. He wore thin pants rolled up to his calves and no shirt, and the tan skin of his back glistened in the sun. Rough waves were crashing onto the deck, but the boy seemed undaunted; and when the pole jerked, he quickly regained control and began feverishly reeling in whatever unfortunate creature he'd hooked. The sinewy muscles in his back flexed as he brought a bright red fish to the surface. He raised the pole with one hand and the fish flapped furiously in the air. He grabbed it and turned quickly to remove the hook from the fish's mouth. His eyes met Sylvia's. She smiled, and she could see the heat rise in the boy's face. He looked back at the wriggling fish before tossing it in a bucket and turning again to the sea.

Sylvia, though she'd only gotten a glance of him, liked the features of the teen's face. In that one second, she saw how nearly perfect they were and knew he would photograph well. She could, with the right lighting, make him look like a young god, a young Poseidon clutching the wriggling ruby spoils of his kingdom.

La Bomba only wanted her to cook fish, plantains, and rice, or chicken, plantains, and rice, or conch, plantains, and rice. Sylvia got good at all of the above quickly, and since no one ever came to the Shack before noon, the mornings became her time to wander freely and take some photographs.

Everything was new to her, the turquoise sea, the shells, the palm trees, the plants, the birds, the lizards, the insects. She didn't know where to turn her camera next. Soon she had a drawer full of undeveloped film.

She began thinking about where La Bomba's men could build a dark room, and she'd have to get on him about the paper and the chemicals and more film.

Every so often, Sylvia was able to get her hands on a copy of the London Times, thanks to Harriet who "borrowed" it from the owner of The Inn. Hungry for news of what seemed a different world, Sylvia devoured every last depressing word of it. The Allies were in trouble and Germany had advanced into Austria and Poland. The endless meetings between the United States and Great Britain seemed to be going nowhere. Still, she hoped that perhaps she would find some clue in that awful mess that might help her unravel what had happened to her husband.

How had Howard gotten embroiled in the war? Why had the British government flown him to Tortola? What could Howard have done on this spit of a place that would've helped the cause?

And then a worse thought struck her, her husband could have been sent here as a spy. To spy on what or whom she hadn't a clue; but if he was a spy, and the Nazis found out, they would have had to kill him. Yes, the Nazis would have been glad to push him right off that deck.

God, the world's going crazy! It was difficult for her to comprehend all that was going on intellectually, let alone emotionally. Emotionally, she'd all but shut down. She was numb to all things, except two—her mission to avenge her husband's death and what she saw through the lens of her camera. On this island, she could not be the meek bookworm she used to be. Here, in her self-imposed exile, she had to be conniving, ruthless, and hell-bent on finding Howard's killer.

And when she did? Well, would she have it in her to...she wasn't sure. But for now she'd do whatever she had to do, even cook for this strange boss of hers. Her only comfort was the beauty of all that surrounded her, and her only distraction from her painful loneliness was trying to capture it on film. That kept her going, and during the day as long as she was busy, she was fine.

It was only at night in the dark after she barricaded herself in the bungalow and laid on the floor that she couldn't stop the tears from coming. She felt so alone in the world. She'd been here for weeks and she hadn't learned one single thing more about what really happened to her husband than she knew when she left Trenton. So much for being conniving and ruthless.

Oh, it was crazy to think that the Nazis had anything to do with Howard. No one on the island seemed the least bit connected to anything that was going on in Europe, let alone to the Nazi Party. And really, would Hitler send someone to such a remote place to kill someone as unimportant as Howard? How could Howard have been a threat to Germany?

She had no sound hypothesis, no ideas, nothing. She was a complete failure at subterfuge and detective work. She needed to pry more information out of La Bomba, but how? She knew he was the key to finding out what really happen to Howard. She knew he knew everything about everybody on Tortola, but damn if he wasn't like a wall without a chink.

Well, to hell with him, she thought. *If I have to take a pick ax to him, I will.*

The next morning Sylvia went right to the shed and found the giant man listening to the BBC on a short wave radio rigged up to a wire contraption that acted as an antenna.

"It's only me," she hollered to get his attention. "Do you have some time to talk?"

He was next to the radio listening. The human voice was nearly indistinguishable from the loud crackling static. He held up his enormous index finger in an uncharacteristically refined gesture.

"He is not a man. He is a demon!" La Bomba screamed at the radio so loudly it made Sylvia flinch. Obviously he was reacting to what he heard that she couldn't.

"What happened?"

"The Germans have sunk a cargo ship off the coast of Aruba. I hate this man who calls himself the Fuhrer. I hate him for what he is doing, for bringing the war to our Caribbean Sea. Hasn't what he's done in Europe enough for all good people to rise up and say, 'enough'?"

Sylvia was struck silent by the news, but before she could answer, La Bomba turned from the radio and faced her. "I tell you, Sylvia, it is time for serious voodoo. There is the daily ritual my wife Lucinda and I follow to purify our house and protect our children from evil. Lucinda sweeps dust from the corners and burns it and sprinkles cat urine on cobwebs. We chant the secret words and blow smoke from bundles of dried palms across the threshold. But this evil that is coming closer and closer, there may not be a spell strong enough to keep it away."

Sylvia angled herself away from La Bomba, reached into her bra, and un-pinned her St. Rita medal. "Here, you can borrow my favorite saint. Her name is Rita, and she will protect your family."

La Bomba stared at the figure of the saint on the front and then turned the medal over. "And who is this on the back?"

"The Sacred Heart of Mary. She's even more powerful than Rita. She is the Mother of Jesus."

"Oh, I don't know if I like how her heart is on the outside, but her face does look kind. Yes, I suppose she could protect someone."

"I believe she and Rita are with me at all times. I pray to them to take care of me."

"That's good, Sylvia."

"Right now I'm praying that any Nazis in Tortola will leave."

"On my island? Oh, I would kill them if I found out."

"But what about the British in Rock Town?"

"Well, they are on our side——against Hitler."

"What about spies?"

"I have spies all over this island. Trust me, Sylvia, there are no Nazis here and there never will be. I would die killing them."

"Then it must've been the British who killed my...."

"Ah, ah, ah...remember our deal. When the time is right, I will tell you what I know."

"When will the time be right? Please, I can't stay here forever. I miss my family, Howard's family. I miss New Jersey...and school."

La Bomba turned the volume up on the radio and put that same big, fat index finger to his lips, "Ssshhh...."

So much for the pick ax approach.

A few days later, Sylvia was in the kitchen making a list of what she needed from Rock Town when she saw the beautiful young fisherman coming down the beach. He was again shirtless, and he had on the same threadbare pants that hung low on his hips. Behind him the sun was setting, and he looked like he was walking out of a blazing fire. He stopped when he was alongside the deck and stared at Sylvia. She looked down at her list and tried to ignore him, but she could feel his eyes on her.

"I've watched you taking pictures," he shouted loudly as though he were a great distance away. He had a clipped, British accent, and Sylvia liked the sound of his voice instantly. She put her list down, but instead of saying something back to him, she picked up a large conch and began scraping the slimy worm from its shell. If she looked at him, she'd have to say something to him, and suddenly she couldn't think of a thing to say that might be of interest to a boy. Instead, she focused intently on the giant slug undulating on the chopping block. She frowned at the squirming creature, thwacked it hard with the side of her cleaver, and before it had a chance to die, chopped it up into bite-size pieces and threw them in with the rice she had steaming in a big pot on the grill. When she looked up, the young god was gone.

The next evening at around the same time, he returned and climbed over the rail of the deck. This time he wore a pale green shirt that matched his eyes, and he smelled of gardenias and the sea.

"I'll take you around the island if you'd like. I've got a small boat and not much else to do. You can take pictures. La Bomba knows me. My name is Virgil Faultington. He'll tell you I'm alright."

"That would be nice." What was she saying? Did she really want to go out in a boat with this boy? No, she was a married woman. Well, she was a widow. Even thinking of that word made her want to weep. She rubbed her hands on a towel and tossed a handful of plantain peels onto the compost heap, watching as they landed on a wriggling fist of maggots. Without looking at him, she said, "Look, my name is Sylvia Russo, and I'm sorry, but I really can't go...." She raised her head, but he was gone.

That night Sylvia had more trouble than usual falling asleep; and when she finally did, she dreamt she was lying on the beach at sunset. Howard was next to her. He was naked, and she was looking at his penis. She was wet down there, ready to make love to him. She ached for him to be inside her. She moved her eyes up his body and looked in his eyes, but they weren't eyes the color of corn husks, the color of hickory leaves in autumn, they weren't Howard's eyes. They were light green like the sea in the morning when the clouds were thin, they were Virgil Faultington's eyes.

When she woke-up and remembered the dream, she again thought of climbing over the railing on the deck and letting go.

17

Yamato Yoshio wasn't pleased with the lack of progress on the prototype so he had secretly been going into the lab when Masuki wasn't there and trying himself to get the thing to work. He was, after all, not just a business man, but an engineer, an inventor, a photographer who had gotten this fledgling company to where it was. Masuki, he discovered, was right. Noboru Industries needed a new, more powerful mainframe, advanced programs, and a great deal of luck to get the American's camera to do what he thought it could do. And he, or somebody, had to get it to do it.

He hadn't left his beloved hometown in the South where he was born in 1905 for nothing. His family had owned paddy fields there, and he'd grown-up working those fields with his grandparents, parents, siblings, and the rest of his extended family. They were a close-knit clan who lived well thanks to their collective industry and thrift. He would've stay there forever in the small village where he was related to almost everyone, but his life veered off in a different direction after his father bought him a used camera and a large box of film.

In 1918, on Yoshio's thirteen birthday, his father gave him a very rare thing in Japan, a Kodak Brownie. He said, "Son, this is not a plaything. This is a machine that will save us money. Look how many of us there are and how far we travel, all the way to the city to have family photographs taken. Your mother, your aunts, your girl cousins, all they want are the photographs. This is a camera from America. The directions are in English, but you are a smart boy and will figure out how this thing works. When you do, we can stay home and work, and you will record all of the auspicious events of our lives."

"Where did you get such a magnificent thing, father?"

"It took some doing, but I have my ways, Yoshio. Where it came from is not as important as where it will take you."

Young Yoshio didn't understand his father at the time, but his confusing words were never far from his mind.

It took the boy a while to figure the camera out, especially how to develop the pictures; but he did it and everyone in the whole village had new respect for the boy. It was his success with the Brownie that convinced the elders in his family to send him to Tokyo for a proper education. It was by the sweat of their brows that Yamato Yoshio graduated at the top of his class in 1926 from the University of Tokyo.

He never returned permanently to his village because the family invested every last yen they had in his new venture in Tokyo, Noboru Industries, named after his father, Yamato Noboru.

Did he have any choice now, but to push ahead, take any means possible to move the company ahead?

Yoshio wasn't ruthless by nature, but he knew that to make money one had to take things seriously, very seriously, and so he did. Soon he was able to bring his parents and his siblings to Tokyo. He bought a compound of small houses on the hills in the Roppongi section. He married a beautiful woman and had three beautiful children. For many years things went well for Noboru Industries and the Yamato family.

And all would have continued to go well were it not for the conflict with China and now America. 1941 was not turning out to be a good year. The latest model camera was already twelve years old. If they didn't come up with something new and exciting, their customers would start buying from foreign companies like Kodak. He didn't want to be harsh with his employees, but he had to motivate them anyway he could.

And demand was down. Customers all over the world weren't worrying about buying new cameras when their sons were going off to fight.

Yoshio didn't want to disappoint his family. He didn't want them to lose everything they had worked so hard for. He could not let the business go under.

Minute by minute, Yamato Yoshio felt the mounting pressure. Yes, he would have to change, take drastic measures. Being a slave driver was something he never imagined he'd lower himself to become, but now it seemed his only recourse. Well, he would at least pretend to be harsh.

18

The next morning when Sylvia came down the hill, Virgil was waiting for her. She'd been hoping he wouldn't be there and had spent the morning going back and forth trying to decide if she should go on the boat or not. She even rehearsed a polite excuse. "I'm so sorry, but I'm not feeling all that well today. Maybe some other time."

Then she thought about all of the photos she'd be able to take, so she put on her bathing suit. Then she noticed how pasty white her body was, how hairy her legs were, and how she'd lost so much weight that no matter how tightly she knotted the straps of the suit, her breasts didn't begin to fill the cups, so she put on a sweater and pants over the suit, which made her look all lumpy and disheveled. The straps even stuck out above the neckline. Then she thought, *why do I even care what I look like in front of some boy I barely know?* But the truth was, she was embarrassed by the way she looked, the way she'd let herself go. She left the sweater and pants on despite the fact that she was about to swoon from the heat and forced herself to leave the cottage, go down to the beach, and recite her excuse to this Virgil person. She couldn't afford to offend anyone on the island.

When she got close enough to him for her to hear, he hollered, "Follow me," and turned and walked toward the beach.

"But…wait a minute. I can't go. I don't feel that…."

When she caught up to him, he was holding the boat in the shallow water and laughing. "I won't look if you want to take that sweater off before you die of bloody heat stroke," he said.

"Don't worry about me dying of heat stroke because I can't go with...."

Virgil took her hand and pulled her into the knee-deep water. "Yes, you can die of heat stroke around here so trust me and don't be stubborn about it. You can strip down when we get out there."

Before she could argue, she was in the boat and they were moving away from shore.

How could it be even hotter in the middle of the sea! Sylvia was dumbstruck, but it was. The sun was in her face making it feel like her skin was on fire. The boat was churning steadily through the water, but the air was as searing as the sun and offered no relief. She couldn't remember ever being so hot. She felt faint. She had no choice. The clothes had to go. She stripped off the sweater and wriggled carefully out of the pants. Virgil turned the boat parallel to the shore and now there was a breeze. Sylvia began to feel like herself again. She sat in front of Virgil and held on for dear life as he put the boat in high gear.

Finally he slowed the boat near an off-shore reef. Sylvia quickly put her pants and sweater on. They drifted silently, the boat rocking gently in the waves. The wind had stopped, and soon sweat was dripping down Sylvia's temples. She ignored the feeling that she might melt away like some forgotten dish of ice cream and sat as still as possible staring into the water. It was clear enough to see to the bottom, and fish were darting in all directions.

Soon she was engrossed in this unfamiliar universe, a turquoise kingdom of mysterious creatures. She leaned as far over the side as she could to watch the pale anemone bloom and wilt on the coral mesas. A bright yellow eel shot out from between the rocks. Hundreds of silver minnows twirled themselves into a glinting ball. Two groupers the size of border collies slugged along on the sandy bottom. Sylvia, too awestruck to take any photos, sighed in wonder.

"We've got to go back now." Virgil broke the spell. "I've got a few things I've got to take care of for La Bomba."

"Do you work for him?"

"Sometimes."

"You look awfully young, young enough to still be in school."

"I'm not that young, and besides I didn't much care for school when I did go."

"But how could you not like school? How are you going to learn anything?"

"By doing it, is how. Not by babbling on and on about it."

Before Sylvia could come up with a retort, Virgil started the engine, swung the boat around, and headed back to the Shack. As he helped Sylvia out of the boat, he said, "We'll go again."

And they did, the next morning, and many mornings after. They never talked much except for Sylvia's questions about every single thing she photographed. She had to know the name, the life span, what it ate, where it lived. Virgil had all the answers. There seemed to be nothing they encountered in the sea or sky that he didn't know volumes about. Though she was older and better-educated, he was opening her eyes to astonishing new things, things that distracted her from her aching sorrow and filled her heart, at least momentarily, with bliss. How could she look in the eye of a dolphin—passing so close to the boat she could reach out and touch it—and feel anything but joy.

When La Bomba finally gave her a whole day off, Virgil took Sylvia to a small island west of Tortola. He dropped anchor fifty yards off shore in a place called the Baths where hundreds of boulders, some the size of cabooses, littered the beach.

Sylvia, who had given up completely on wearing her baggy bathing suit, had on a thin cotton shirt and pants. She rolled up her sleeves and her pants legs and, holding her camera high, slid over the side of the boat into the thigh high water. Virgil took off his shirt, jumped in, and swam past her to shore where he stretched out on the sand to wait for her.

"I told you so!" he hollered to her.

"I don't have a bathing suit that fits!" she hollered back. "Besides, I have to be careful with my camera."

"Oh, cameras are a bloody pain! You should've left it back at the Shack!"

Virgil was about to lie back and close his eyes, when he saw a swell in the distance. "Sylvia, watch out! Turn around!" He was on his feet and running through the water toward her. As the wave hit, he lifted her up. She was soaked despite his effort, but the camera was safe.

"I told you so," he said again as he carried her to the beach and put her down.

"Oh, leave me alone! Don't look at me!" Sylvia knew Virgil could see her bra and underpants through her wet clothes. She turned away, but not before she saw an odd look in his eyes. She could hear him breathing, he was so close. Then he put his hand on her shoulder and whispered, "Sylvia?"

She shivered when she heard him say her name. The way he said it made her think of what her name really meant, sylvan––of the forest. So what was she doing on this blistering beach, so far from her element? She was "of the forest," the dark and mysterious forest. Up to this moment she'd considered her name an accident, like the accident of birth. She was born, she was named. But, no, she thought now, there is something about me that is dark and mysterious, parts of me in shadow, parts unexplored. *Virgil holding me, lifting me, carrying me. His hand is burning through...*

She brushed his hand away and turned to face him. He looked down at her drenched clothes and frowned. "You look like a bloody drowned rat."

"Thanks! Just what a girl wants to hear."

"Ah, now, seriously, you look amazing. A regular mermaid you are. Trust me." He was only slightly taller than Sylvia; and as he stared at her, his face softened. "The sun will dry you in no time."

He sat in the hot sand, laid back, closed his eyes, and patted the space next to him. She sat down an arm's length away and looked at him. He was a pretty boy, despite the incongruity of his features. His hair was the texture of La Bomba's, yet as golden as the sun. His eyebrows black, his lashes pale. His nose long and straight like that of an aristocrat. His lips as plump as a puffer fish's—he'd caught one with his bare hands the other day and held it up for her to almost kiss.

How old is he? Sylvia thought as she laid back and let the warm sand caress her wet body. She tried to focus on the shushing of the waves, but her thoughts kept drifting back to Virgil, to the way he looked lying there. His hair, his face, his skin...his glimmering skin. She'd dreamt of his eyes. She hadn't meant to, but she had looked into them in her dream and found them beautiful. When Virgil had lifted her up, had carried her across the foaming threshold, she felt light as air, like she was once again a blissful being, capable of feeling...something she hadn't felt in a long time. She felt like the girl she was before she had to grow up, the girl she was before Howard had decided he loved her.

Howard and her life with him, for him, about him, was over. What did she want now?

No, it is too soon. It would be wrong, absolutely wrong...to want Virgil.

When the sun was past its apex and Sylvia's clothes were dry, they waded through the tide pools between the giant rocks. Sylvia was fascinated by the starfish, the urchins, and the shrimp, but the most exquisite creature of all to her was Virgil. He laid in the shallow water crawling around pointing to things and rolling over to check that Sylvia was following. With his slicked-back hair, his silky skin, and his sleek body, he looked more fish than human.

From a different world, she thought.

Then he swam away from the rocks and the beach and into the waves. Sylvia lost sight of him when he dove beneath the surface, and she felt an impulse to dive in and follow him wherever he might lead her.

19

The following week, they arrived at the Shack simultaneously, as though preordained.

Virgil peeled shrimp, gutted snapper, and hauled trash out into the palmettos and buried it. While he worked he was talkative, much more so than he'd ever been on the boat. He had endless questions about life in the United States, and Sylvia was more than happy to describe all of it——snow, traffic, skyscrapers, escalators, movie theaters, street lights, pizza. Virgil wasn't getting paid for helping at the Shack, but he told Sylvia he was getting something better than money, knowledge of the outside world.

"Sylvia, I actually do want to make something of myself," he explained. "I want to get off this island and as far away as I can from everything that happened here."

"You sound bitter, Virgil. What happened here that could be that bad?"

"Nothing…and that is the problem."

"You're not making sense. You just said you want to get away from everything that's happened here, didn't you? And now you say nothing's happened here?"

"Don't mind me, I'm simply tired of this place. This small, poor island, I'm tired of it. You haven't been here long enough to know what it is I am talking about. I'm talking about wanting more, wanting to see the world."

Wanting to see the world, Sylvia could understand that. But getting away from Tortola? Virgil always seemed so enthralled with the flora and fauna of the island, so happy being in his boat and cruising the open sea.

Later, when he left and she was alone, other things he'd said bothered her too.

He wants to "get away" from "everything that happened here." And what the hell happened here was Howard's murder!

Oh, it was all getting too confusing. All she'd been thinking about was Virgil. She had to stop spending time with him. Now he was showing up in her kitchen and hanging around until she gave him something to do, acting like he worked there, like she needed him there. It had to stop. She wouldn't go out on the boat with him or do anything else with him ever again. Yes, Virgil Faultington could drop off the face of the earth for all she cared. She was a woman in mourning and from here on out she'd act like one.

But what if he wants to leave Tortola because he knows something about what happened to Howard? She had to be logical and not cut this teenager out of her life until she was sure he didn't know anything, or hadn't done anything he shouldn't have. But just as quickly as the thought came to her she dismissed it. She could not imagine Virgil the nature lover harming so much as mosquito.

The next night after the customary eating and partying at the Shack, Virgil showed up, snuck a couple of beers out of the bar, and invited Sylvia to join him on the jetty. She went but only with intention of interrogating him.

The sea was as calm as a lake and the air remarkably still. As soon as they sat down on the cool rocks, clouds erased the moon. In the pitch black Virgil popped the caps off the beers with a shell and handed one to Sylvia.

"Thanks, but no thanks. I didn't come here to drink. I came to talk to you about something important." Her voice reverberated in the quiet night. You've got to help me, Virgil."

"Sure, Sylvia. What do you need, a new grill?"

"No, this is serious. I have to tell you why I'm really here."

"Why you're really here? I thought you were here to cook for La Bomba."

"Cook for La Bomba? Are you kidding? I'm only working at the Shack so I can get information about my husband."

"Husband? You're married?"

There was something in Virgil's voice that was suspect...feigned surprise? Was it just her or was Virgil pretending not to know what she was telling him? God, an awful heaviness came over her. Tortola was a small island and not just geographically. Why hadn't she realized that everyone on the entire spit of land probably knew why she was there, knew her whole life's story?

What an idiot she'd been, but what was there for her to do now but act dumb just like everyone else.

"Well, technically I'm not married now because my husband's dead. He died on this island. The British government sent him here and had him taken to the bungalow I'm currently staying in. He fell from the deck and died. I'm sure you heard about it. They claim it was an accident or suicide. I don't believe them. My husband had an important camera with him, a valuable prototype, valuable enough that someone might kill him to get it. I want that camera back. It is my husband's legacy. If I don't get it back, I'll have to try to recreate it which will be damn near impossible because all I have are diagrams and notes.

"Oh, it's all a mess. La Bomba knows something, but he won't tell me. That's why I'm working for him. He said he'll tell me when the time is right. But it's been weeks and my patience is wearing thin. I'm about ready to go to the island authorities in spite of La Bomba."

The clouds moved on and the moonlight afforded Sylvia the chance to see Virgil's face, but as soon as she focused on it, he lowered his head and muttered something to himself she couldn't hear. Then he fell silent.

When he spoke his voice was barely audible. "Don't go to the authorities. They'll do nothing for you." He paused then added, "Trust me."

There was that phrase again. Only this time, though only whispered, sounded more like a threat than an assurance.

So I have struck a nerve, she thought.

No, she wanted to trust Virgil. More than anyone else in the world. But there was no denying how suddenly he seemed distant.

He leaned back and sighed.

That sigh went straight to Sylvia's heart and almost canceled out all her misgivings.

"Why didn't you tell me about your husband before?" Virgil said, his voice heavy as stone with sincerity.

"I told Harriet, La Bomba's sister. She told me not to tell anyone but her brother, and he told me not to tell anyone on the island so I didn't."

He laid down on his back and turned his head away. "Still, you should have told me. As soon as you met me, you should have told me."

Oh hell, Sylvia couldn't bear to see him sullen like this. He was so beautiful. The moonlight gilding his hair and the skin of his face. She bent over him and without thinking about it, without meaning to, she kissed him quickly.

Had she lost her mind? She started to get up. *Hurry back to the bungalow. Barricade yourself in. Get as far away from this young man as you can.*

But Virgil's hand was on her arm.

"Don't go. Please?" He sat up, pulled her close, and kissed her neck. His lips were warm, soft, an invitation to stop thinking, *get away, get away.*

Sylvia looked at Virgil. His lips were open. *To me.* She wanted her tongue to touch his, to be inside his warm, wet, mysterious mouth. She felt his breath on her face.

It had been so long since she'd kissed Howard. She closed her eyes. Could she pretend? Could it be that he was with her in the moonlight in paradise? On the incoming tide the sea had turned rough and was pounding jetty. The wind was back. How her skin tingled. How alive she felt as he undid her bra and held her breasts like they were precious, delicate starfish, his touch so light it made her yearn for him to pull them taunt. But, no, he massaged them slowly. His touch light, persistent, driving her mad with desire. Her insides throbbed. Her tongue in his mouth grew hard and demanding. She pulled back and cried out.

He was beside her, and she could feel his penis against her leg. She moaned as he slid his hand down the front of her pants and put his fingers in her.

"No, don't. Please don't." But she didn't mean what she was saying because when he'd taken her clothes off and climbed on top of her, she lifted her buttocks to open herself up to him. Then the world was spinning around. She opened her eyes, saw the moon and the stars. So this is where she was and this was who she was with.

She lay there motionless and spent.

At first, she had no thoughts, but slowly...*Not Howard, but Virgil.*

She'd let Virgil in. How could she? Oh, she wished she could just be sucked up into the sky and blown away. But that wasn't going to happen so she had to face what she'd done, what she'd let this teenager do to her. She looked over. Virgil was at the edge of the jetty. He lowered himself into the roiling sea.

"Virgil, Virgil, come back," she screamed into the wind.

But he didn't.

20

The weather rarely deviated from its tropical rhythm, and Sylvia couldn't keep track of time, not that time mattered much anymore. Virgil and she had settled on letting nature take its course, and it did. They became lovers, lovely lovers who secretly slipped in and out of each other's arms as easily as one beautiful day slipped in and out of another.

The only day of the week Sylvia was sure of was Thursday, because every Thursday, Harriet rode her bicycle to the Shack and spent hours in the shed talking and laughing with her brother. She'd emerge, shout something funny about his shady dealings at him over her shoulder, get back on her bike, and ride away. She'd leave the London Times with La Bomba, and not even so much as wave to Sylvia.

Then one especially hot day, she walked into the kitchen.

"My old friend Sylvia, why do you not wave to your old friend Harriet?" Her brow furrowed with perplexity.

"I guess I'm always wrangling with some stubborn sea creature who doesn't want to become dinner, or maybe I was waiting for you to wave to me."

"Were we not so very friendly that day when I sent you here to my brother, and now you cannot lift so much as one hand as a hello to me? Well, what am I to do with you?"

She was close now, and Sylvia saw the twinkle in her eyes and smelled the jasmine blossom she'd tucked in her hair and knew all was right between them.

"You know those octopi can really put up a good fight."

"Yes, yes, miss, blame it on the poor little beast who won't hold still so you can chop him up in little pieces. I understand." Harriet leaned across the make-shift counter and smiled. "So things are going well here with my brother?"

"Yes, he's been so kind to me."

"And fair?"

"Yes. Well, he hasn't told me anything about my husband yet, but he says he will."

"He likes you."

"I like him too. Thank you for sending me here."

"How could I not? You had nowhere to go. It could have been terrible for you. At least here you are safe."

"Yes, I feel that way." Sylvia wiped her hands on a rag and thought, *safe from what?* But Harriet was smiling up at her so she leaned on the counter facing her and smiled back.

"So, Harriet, why did it take so long for you to come and talk to me? Every week I've watched you visit your brother, and you didn't bother once to visit me? I'm the one who should be hurt."

"I was waiting," she said slowly and frowned.

"For what?"

"Something." Harriet broke her gaze with Sylvia and looked down at her hands.

Sylvia couldn't ignore the hurt that skittered around inside of her, nor deny that she had worried about why Harriet was ignoring her. She never had any real girlfriends, always feeling so different from the way she imagined they felt. Let's face it, all she had was her aunt, Howard, and his family. That was it. She loved them and they loved her and everybody else was an enigma. But seeing Harriet again, sharing a laugh, made Sylvia ache with homesickness, and she wanted to reach out, take Harriet's hand, and hold onto it forever.

"Sylvia?" It was a whisper.

"Yes, Harriet?"

"I will tell you the truth."

Here it comes again, more "truth," thought Sylvia.

"The truth is, Miss Sylvia, I was afraid of the way you look. You know, like a man. Why do you do it?"

"Well, do you really want to know?"

"I asked didn't I, miss?"

"Look, Harriet, when I was young, I saw this photograph of the famous pilot, Beryl Markham. The photographer captured her picture just as she turned to wave to the crowd before her solo flight to England. She was dressed like a man in a shirt with a collar, pants, and sturdy boots. I thought she looked wonderful in those clothes, clothes that would help her, not hinder her. How could she fly an airplane in a skirt and heels? The right clothes had set Beryl Markham free. That photograph stuck in my head so when I wanted to go to an all-male college, I decided to try to look male. I wore pants and I chopped off my hair and, guess what, it worked!

"And when I decided to come here, I didn't want to attract any attention so I cut my hair again and wore the kind of clothes I needed to, not the kind of clothes that would only cause me trouble." Sylvia paused and laughed. "Harriet, do I really look that bad?"

"No, you look very nice, and that is the problem. Please, do not tell my brother, but that first day, when I thought you were a man, I was attracted to you. Then I realized, no, this is a woman dressed like a man, and I felt upset at myself for thinking strange thoughts about you; but even when I figured it out, it took a while for those feelings to fade. On this island women loving other women that way is not considered a good thing, so I stayed away until my brother told me about you and Virgil. Then I thought, oh I see, you are not really the way you are in my crazy head."

"Oh, Harriet, trust me, I'm not like that. Really, I'm not." But as soon as she said it, her heart dropped. Would loving Harriet, this sweet, smiling being, be so terrible? Sylvia seemed to be shedding all taboos. This island was a place where the rhythms of her body were starting to rule her, where her twenty-one year old body was more alive than it'd ever been. Crashing waves, chattering birds, peeping frogs, laughing humans, and music washing over her every night at the Shack. Everything was bombarding her senses washing away all worry, all sorrow. All the cacophony was silencing her superego and luring her happily into a state of heightened sensuality absolutely foreign for her. She looked into Harriet's huge eyes, and in them she saw her own small face looking back.

Harriet stood up and wagged her finger at Sylvia. "Well, back in that crazy place you come from called America, looking like a man might have worked for you; but on this island a girl must look like a girl, and that is that," Her gruff tone positively wounded Sylvia, but then she winked and Sylvia got the joke and they were giggling again like two school girls.

21

Three months after she had arrived, La Bomba came into the kitchen late one night. He found her scrubbing the cutting surfaces with lemon juice and salt. Virgil was scraping the grill, and they were both humming to the eternal night music.

"Leave us alone." La Bomba looked at Virgil. "Get in that poor excuse-for-a-boat of yours and go home so your father will stop bothering me about why you are always here." He shoved a few pounds into Virgil's hand and patted him heartily on the back. "Go on now. Sylvia and I have private business to discuss."

A large laugh rumbled up out of La Bomba's broad chest, and the beads around his neck jiggled. When he looked at Sylvia, though, his face turned serious. She followed him to a table and they sat down across from each other.

"Here is what I believe happened to Mr. Howard. What I tell you is the truth, or I would not say it. Yes, I do sometimes lie. Yes, sometimes to my wife, and you may have seen me be less than honest with some of my men, but that is personal and business. This is neither of those. This is about your patience and your grief. Believe me I would not lie to you, but remember you can tell no one."

"But, La Bomba, why all the secrecy?"

"Because I must live here. This is my home and I do not ever want to leave."

"Why would you have to leave? If my husband was murdered, we must report it."

"I cannot say if it was murder, but I will tell you that something went wrong."

"What do you mean, wrong?"

"After my young friend dropped Mr. Howard off at the bungalow, another vehicle drove up. It was a limousine. No one around here has a limousine, so I inquired and found out a Brit named Astin had borrowed it from the Governor. So you see the highest British authority on the island is involved. If they know that I know about this, it will be big trouble for me. I survive here because I have learned to work with the Brits. They trust me. I work for them. I even made the arrangements for your husband to stay in that bungalow. In return I don't ask questions. I keep my mouth shut."

"So I will talk to this Astin! You don't have to say a word."

"You can't."

"Why?"

"He left the island soon after the accident."

"Where did he go?"

"I have no idea."

"Please?"

"He is gone. That is all that I know. I told you, I don't ask questions."

"Was he alone? Was there a driver?"

"Most likely."

"Well, you must know who it was. Someone from the island?"

"Whoever it was, was simply someone who Astin or the Governor controlled. Without Astin, this person is harmless. I know this for certain. Trust me."

"Trust you? You are telling me that someone from this island drove Astin up to the bungalow where my husband was pushed off the deck and murdered, and you won't tell me who it was? And you want me to trust you?"

"Yes, yes, and yes. Trust me because I am looking out for you now. The person who drove Astin to the bungalow is a victim, too. Trust me because as much as I didn't want to like you, I find that I do, very much in fact; and I do not want anything bad to happen to you."

"I don't care about myself, La Bomba. I just want whoever killed my husband to be punished for it."

"Punishment doesn't have to be cast like a net over the one who deserves it. No, the guilty one, in time, will swim right into it."

"Then you are not telling the whole truth like you promised. You have a secret that you fully intend to keep, don't you?" Sylvia tried to distance herself from her anger, but her voice trembled like a leaf in the wind.

"Many secrets must be kept on a small island like ours, but, my dear Sylvia, we are not the only ones with secrets. Perhaps Mr. Howard had secrets of his own that were worse than even this one. You said his body was escorted home by the British officials and the soldiers, and that he was given a commendation. How do you know that he was not into some business even worse than murder, worse than one man's death?"

"What could be worse than the death of my husband?"

"The death of many husbands, wives, brothers, sisters, mothers, fathers, and children can be much worse. War is much worse. Living with guilt is much worse. Living with guilt can make one lose one's mind. When a person has done something wrong, the something that he or she did wrong will be all that the mind can think about. It is like a little worm that gets inside a beautiful piece of fruit. On the outside you might not even notice the little pinhole on the skin where it has entered, but when you bite into the flesh of the fruit it is putrid and ruined. Likewise the evil deed rots the spirit of the evil doer. Never mind about revenge. The islander who had the bad luck to be assigned to drive Mr. Astin that awful day, will live each day of the rest of his life with his body in heaven and his mind in hell. The sun bursts above the horizon, a parrot screeches, the banana leaf unfurls, great ships of clouds glide over the sea, and all of this makes the poor reluctant sinner's soul writhe. You see, he will grow to antici-pate death just to stop from thinking about what he has been a part of."

"Still, that person is alive and my husband is dead. Some people will never feel bad about anything they do wrong because they don't have a conscience. On this island it is difficult to have a conscious. Nature takes its course here, and not everyone's nature is good. Oh, it just doesn't seem fair."

"What in life is?"

Sylvia had no answer. It wasn't easy for her to accept that she could do noth-ing to avenge Howard's death. Hearing it from La Bomba made her want to cry.

"Sylvia, stop looking like a wounded bird and do something to honor your husband's memory. You knew him to be a good man, and every good man deserves to be honored when he passes."

She said nothing and let his words sink in.

Was he was right? Was it over? She would never know what happened, never get revenge, but she could do what La Bomba said, she could honor Howard's memory.

La Bomba stood up and pulled the string attached to the bulb in the ceiling. Across the dark sea the moonlight was a silver river. The big man put his heavy arm around Sylvia's shoulders, and she started to cry. "Come, friend, dry your eyes and let's have a drink."

22

Lizzy and Eddie Dwyer didn't have much experience with children, but they were sure what their four-month-old son Jake did was remarkable. Either they had a genuine prodigy on their hands, or it was a fluke, an isolated incident, a single unexplainable phenomenon.

One day after a long nap, Lizzy gave baby Jake a sponge bath. When he was all clean and smelling of powder, she propped him up in his high chair with pillows and gave him an empty baking soda box to play with.

When Eddie came home from his job cleaning floors at the Empire State Building, he kissed his wife and went over to his baby son.

"Hey, young man, your dad missed you today." He bent and kissed little Jake on the top of his long, curly dark hair. He had so much of it, and Lizzy refused to cut it just yet. The baby looked up with big eyes.

"His eyes are the color of corn husks, aren't they, honey?" Eddie smiled at his boy.

"That's a good way of describing them, Eddie. What made you think of that?"

"I don't know. Just popped into my head, is all." He kissed his son again in the same spot, took him out of the high chair, and swung him around in the air. The baby giggled. Eddie watched him laugh.

"I thought for sure they'd be blue like yours and mine, Lizzy. But there ain't a bit of blue in them." He was inspecting his miraculous little creature closely.

"No, they ain't blue," Lizzy agreed. "But they are the prettiest eyes I've seen. That is, next to yours, Eddie."

"Oh, I'm not jealous. I'll never be jealous of our little boy. Why I love him as much as you do."

"I'm sure you do. Now let's sit down and eat while he's not crying."

Eddie put Jake back in the high chair, and he and Lizzy sat down at the table. They bowed their heads, said grace, and started to eat. That's when it happened.

Baby Jake was about to put a handful of mashed potatoes in his mouth. He stopped and looked at his mother, then his father.

"Where's Sylvie?" the baby said.

Lizzy nearly choked. "Who's Sylvie?"

"Is that what he said?" Eddie stared in disbelief at the baby, who was busy stuffing another handful of mashed potatoes in his mouth.

23

Sylvia walked carefully up the road and the sound of the peepers reverberated in the darkness. Tiny fists of blood punched at her eyeballs from behind, and the pounding echoed against the roof of her skull. Her stomach was bloated and queasy. She'd never been drunk before, and by the way she felt now, she knew she never would be again.

So afraid she'd start vomiting, she spent the entire night sitting upright in a canvas chair. Somehow she must've slept because when she opened her eyes, the sun was already above the bungalow. The roosters were rustling around in the brush off the deck, having stopped crowing hours ago. Sylvia forced herself to get up and move around and by the time she made herself some coffee, she was able to think more clearly.

"Honor the memory of your husband..."

What would Howard have wanted her to do? Sylvia put her cup of coffee on the railing of the deck and massaged her throbbing temples. She stared out at the sea and watched dark clouds spread out like the scales on a fish. She thought about what La Bomba said the night before, and then about all of the letters Howard had sent her—not just the one from right before he died, but all of them.

Week by week, he'd been explaining what was in his head to her, slowly formulating his hypothesis about the power of photography to change the world. He thought photographs could alter the negative perceptions people had of one another. If the camera could tap into a subject's spiritual reality and show that to others, then how could hatred for others persist? She couldn't recall at the moment all of Howard's meandering philosophy, but she did remember the passion with which he wrote about it. Sylvia had brought some of the letters with her, and they were still in her bag. Maybe tomorrow when she felt better, she'd get them out. And, yes, she would commit to making Howard's dream come true.

She was watching the western sky turn white as the sun slowly descended through it. She too was slowly descending back into reality.

La Bomba told her about a man named Astin. He'd been seen in a car heading toward the bungalow after Howard had been dropped off.

"Something went wrong."

That's how La Bomba put it. Maybe Astin had gone to the bungalow to talk to Howard. Maybe they got in an argument and fought, and Astin pushed Howard. But what about the camera? Why would Astin take the camera?

Sylvia knew she had to do something, but right now, probably because her head felt like it was stuffed with cotton, she couldn't figure out exactly what. Gloomily, she began to think about leaving. The island had grown on her. She'd become a good cook, and she had a following among the locals. She didn't even mind extracting the stubborn conches from their shells so much anymore. La Bomba doted on her in his teasing way. She didn't exactly trust that he ever really told the truth about anything, but she knew she could trust him completely with her life. It was a feeling deep within her, an intuitiveness that was dark and mysterious, positively sylvan.

And there was Harriet. How she would miss her. Thursdays had become her favorite day because late at night Harriet would go out to the jetty with Virgil and her, and the three of them would drink and joke and stretch out in the sand and dream about fixing the world by making everyone Tortolan.

And Virgil? How could she leave Virgil?

It was a difficult decision, but the next day, clear-headed Sylvia packed her things and spent one last night on the jetty with Virgil and Harriet. It was perfect, the moon a day away from being full, a south wind, and even a shooting star. They stayed there, the three of them talking and dreaming out loud almost till dawn.

Sylvia asked La Bomba to drive her to the dock, which he did so personally. When Sylvia took his hand to say good bye, he pulled her close and kissed her cheek. His dreadlocks swung forward and hit her like knotted cords. Then he reached over and shoved something in her bag.

"No one will come to the Shack now that you are gone. No one, I tell you, on the whole island can cook as well as you. I will be ruined, Sylvia Russo."

"Don't tease me, La Bomba. You will do just fine without me."

"No, I won't. You will be missed." And he was gone.

Sylvia boarded the ferry without looking back until she went up to the top deck and stood by the starboard railing. The boat eased past the Inn on its way out of the narrow harbor. She saw the giant turtle's shell and felt as hollow and empty as it was—bereft of everything and everyone that had made her feel alive again. She looked for Harriet, but the bar was empty. Soon the ferry glided out to the open sea toward St. Thomas.

Later, as she waited in the airport Quonset for her plane to leave, she looked in her bag and discovered a large wad of money tightly wrapped in a rubber band. *That man*, she thought, *he shouldn't have*. She wanted to count it, but dared not in public. She was sure from the size of the bundle there was enough there for a lot of things, but, most importantly, there was enough to buy her the time she needed to recreate Howard's prototype.

24

Sylvia loaded a new roll of film into the Fluke, flung the strap across her chest, put on her camel hair coat, and headed out into the cold night air toward the fraternity house. Her shadow against the white drifts of snow looked deformed, the lens of the camera sticking out under her coat like a huge nose attached to her chest. The wind was whipping across the quad at around thirty miles per hour, stinging her face; but Sylvia was hell-bent on testing her program one more time. She'd become skeptical of success to the point of nicknaming the new prototype, the Fluke. If, by some miracle it ever did work, it wouldn't be because she'd adhered to some logical progression of ideas, but simply because she'd stumbled on the solution.

The farewell party was in full swing. For so many of her fellow students, this was their last party at Rensselaer, maybe, their last party for a long time. War against Germany had just been declared and that had changed everything. They'd enlisted in droves and were now trying to forget what tomorrow would surely bring.

Smoke and noise overtook Sylvia as she pushed the heavy wooden door open and entered the foyer of the frat house. She wove her way through a crowd trying desperately to keep anyone from bumping into the camera. In the cavernous dining hall all of the furniture was pushed against the walls. A band had set themselves up in a corner and were doing their best to make what could pass for music. Couples were swinging each other around the make-shift dance floor.

Somebody had unscrewed most of the ceiling light bulbs. The room was so dim and smoky, it was difficult to make out faces. In the darker shadows around the perimeter of the room, lovers in each other's arms looked like clumps of shrubs in a midnight garden. Several kegs of beer lined up along one side of the room were barely visible over the shoulders of the young men pressing in to fill their mugs.

Sylvia hesitated near the entrance into the dining hall. She unbuttoned her coat and began adjusting the settings on the camera. The music was growing louder. Someone had put a record on the phonograph and the band was playing along. It all sounded better, but much louder. Sylvia didn't know where to look next. It wasn't as though she had anything against drinking and partying. La Bomba would've loved this scene, even though it was so different from the parties at the Shack. On Tortola the people didn't seem any different when they partied from when they didn't. But here, all of these classmates of hers were always so reserved, so holier-than-thou. But look at them now, she thought, they're acting like complete idiots. She shrugged off her rising disgust for her American contemporaries and tried to feel kindly toward them since most of them would be at war before too long. Sylvia began snapping shots of whoever passed by.

"Hey, Russo, what are you doing in a place like this?" It was her most recent lab partner, Jacob Carruthers, who, because his body was extremely round and his head extremely small, reminded her of Twiddledee. He was one of only a handful of students at Rensselaer who ever talked to her outside of the classroom, so she liked him despite his somewhat repugnant appearance and his tendency to constantly verbally spar with her.

"What's it to you, Carruthers?" she shouted.

He stood less than a foot away and puckered up his lips when he saw Sylvia aim her camera at him.

"Sorry I asked, Russo, I guess you don't want me to worry about you."

Sylvia knew Jacob didn't understand her. How could he when she kept him at arm's length? Just like she kept everyone at arm's length. The last thing she wanted was anyone finding out what she was really up to. She watched as the homely man in front of her took a drag on his cigarette and blew a ring of smoke right in her face.

"Stop that! I hate smoke and you know it," Sylvia said as she leaned close to his face as she always did when she was going to give him a piece of her mind. "And you are right, Jacob. I don't want you to worry about me. I don't want anyone to worry about me, and, furthermore, I don't want anyone period!"

Jacob laughed, "Come on, Russo, you lie, you know you want me." He lifted his half-empty mug in the air in mock tribute to himself. It was obvious that he didn't care that most of the men on campus considered Sylvia Russo a genderless oddity. This fraternity's pledge master had even promised automatic brotherhood to any freshman who could verify, beyond a doubt, "that Russo person's" gender. So one clever freshman paid the maid at the dean's house to use his Brownie to get a shot of her in her underwear. However, when he went to the camera shop to pick up the photographs, the proprietor told him he wasn't going to ruin his reputation by developing pictures of half-naked people. This incident only fueled the already-passionate debate over Sylvia's true gender.

So, though she had no intention of being anything other than Jacob's friend and though she'd never admit it to anyone, Sylvia was grateful for his attention. He was staring at her now, and she could see the admiration in his eyes; and, while it warmed her heart, it also made her stomach churn. Too bad he wasn't better looking. She smiled at him, then turned her back just in time to take a picture of the pledge master vomiting into a wastebasket. She hurried over and stood so close to him she could smell his foul breath. He was sliding his tongue slowly along his bottom lip.

"Are you alright?" she asked.

"Wha? You talkin' to me?" He slurred his words. "Ga away, whate'er you are...." His face was a ghostly white. He tilted his head and stared blankly at Sylvia. She raised the camera until it was right in front of his face, opened the aperture to its maximum width, and snapped a shot. That was exactly the kind of close-up she'd been hoping for. Satisfied she had what she needed, she slung her camera over her shoulder, walked back past Jacob, and blew him a kiss. She saw him lower his head and turn in the direction of the kegs.

Buttoning her coat, Sylvia hurried out the door into the cold night. She fumbled in her pockets for the lab key as she rounded the frat house and began to cut across the field to the Troy Building. The large brick building was the newest on campus and housed the wonder machine Turing had almost completed during her absence.

Alan Turing maintained an office adjacent to the massive EDVAC, though he was seldom there, returning only periodically from England to tweak his creation and give Sylvia new insights into the possibilities the computing machine presented. Since Sylvia's return, she'd barely left the place and felt like she'd become a disembodied extension of her genius mentor, an extra appendage like a third arm or leg. She was grateful to have had the opportunity to learn from such a man, though parts of the experience had been trying, especially during the first few months when they were together in the lab for hours on end. Mr. Turing sucked his teeth obsessively, twisted his pinky finger in his ear every few minutes, talked to himself incessantly, and paced about the cramped space like the frustrated marathoner he was.

But she couldn't deny it, as annoying as all these little habits were, she was ecstatic when and if he agreed with one of her ideas. Then he'd lean forward and look into her eyes with his flinty ones. She could sense his mind speeding up, churning out one logical hypothesis after another. One time he got so excited about something she'd said, he wrote it down on a small scrap of paper, balled it up, and playfully tossed at her.

"You are the bloodiest, smartest young thing in this whole blasted institution. I knew I'd chosen well!" In this sudden burst of enthusiasm he reached over, squeezed her thigh, ran his hand almost up to her crotch. All that did was make her clam up. He, on the other hand, laughed his brainy head off, and added, "Do love that haircut. A bit chopped up, but rather flattering the way you always grease it back, my dear."

Now that Turing was away most of the time, Sylvia worked feverishly on installing relays she knew she would need to develop the computing code according to Howard's notes. Today, Turing had flown back to London. She had the chance to get this right. She would try one last time to get the program up and running. She locked the door to the Troy Building behind her. She didn't have to rush now. No one else had a key.

She took her coat off then carefully took her camera and one thin wire from her bag. She slowly wrapped the wire around the spool of film which was still in the camera. The other end she attached to the panel nearest the central controls of the computer. After flipping a combination of switches, the screen of the prototype television RCA had loaned Turing lit up. It was full of static, though they'd rigged and re-rigged it a hundred times. Sylvia pushed the download button on the Fluke and held her breath. Slowly, the static moved up the screen and the contorted, vomit-smeared face of the fraternity pledge master stared at her. She typed her command on the typewriter also wired to the panel. "COME TO THE TROY BUILDING."

She took a deep breath and pushed the red button on the control panel. The screen went dark. She removed the wire. She got up, unlocked the door to the Troy Building, and stood staring at the round clock above it for fifteen minutes.

Nothing.

She sat down in front of the computer and stared at the clock next it for another fifteen minutes.

Nothing. Damn it.

She leaned her arm against the cold metal of the panel and lowered her head onto it.

Damn it, Howard. Damn it. So much for success. She felt stupid and lonely. She was wasting her time, her life.

Damn you, Howard. Yes, she was furious with a dead man, furious that he'd died, that he'd left her alone, that he expected her to do something he couldn't do!

She thought of Tortola, Virgil, Harriet, the jetty, beer, moonlight, waves lapping against stone like the longing lapping against her heart. She felt weak with desire, not for Howard, no, she was too angry with him.

No, it's Virgil, his golden hair, golden skin, his warm hands on my...

Sylvia began to hum "In the Mood." Why not go back to the party, get drunk, find Jacob and go into the shadows with him? Why not let him have her? Why not let someone have her? This was it. She would let her hair grow back, wear dresses, lipstick, even perfume. She would let herself be...

What? A quitter?

She took the lens off the heavily modified Leica and looked at it. "You are nothing but a flop," she said as she stuffed it into her bag.

She put her coat on, turned off the lights, and slammed the door to the building behind her. She again cut across the field. She was in a hurry to get to her room in the dean's house, get undressed, and lose herself in sleep. It was snowing now and getting deeper in the gullies and getting into her boots as she trudged along. Her head was down against the driving wind, though it didn't sting her half as much as her disappointment.

She was a failure. She'd failed at avenging her husband's death. She'd failed at getting his prototype to work. He'd dreamt of his camera helping to bring understanding and tolerance to world that was spinning out of control. Things were worse now than ever, and there was nothing one young woman like herself could do about it. She'd been foolish to think that she could compete in a man's world, that she could fix what was broken on planet Earth through technology. Developing a new technology, she was discovering, was no easy task.

Why not escape everything? She thought of those couples in the shadows, of how good it felt to let your body become a part of someone else's, of how two bodies coming together like that was something…natural, something that made you know you were alive. She thought of Virgil…of Turing's hand on her thigh…of Jacob's puckered lips.

Sylvia walked out of the dark field into the light coming from the frat house window. The music reached her through the howling wind. She hurried away, her head tucked into her shoulders; but had she turned to look back, she would've seen the door open and pledge master walk down the steps and head toward the Troy Building.

25

Yamato Yoshio was worried about two things: his company and his family. The bombing raids had turned into a nightly occurrence. How long before Noboru Industries was hit? How long before his whole family might be wiped out?

He called a special meeting with the chairmen to announce his decision. Masuki was to pack up his prototype and all of his paperwork, and depart for Nara tomorrow. Yamato had rented a small house near the main temple for Shin and his wife.

"And, naturally, you can take your mother," Yamato said. "It is not a big place, but you will be safe. Continue what work you can. When things are safe here, you will be called back."

"But I need the computer, Chief Yamato. And I have other commitments here in Tokyo."

"You try my nerves, Shin. The computer cannot be moved. Whatever other commitments you have here are not as important as your commitment to this company. You will follow my orders and go to Nara. Go and make new commitments to the deer."

The other chairmen laughed at the cleverness of the Chief. There were more tame deer in Nara then wild women.

Other chairmen were being dispersed to other small villages throughout Japan. This way Noboru's staff would not be depleted when the company could resume business as normal. All who were involved, except for Masuki, agreed that Chief Yamato's plan was an excellent one.

That night, Yamato arrived home with enough food for a feast, a case of sake, and bags of sweets. He gathered his family around him. There were his aging parents, his old aunt, his wife's mother, her sister, his wife, his smart young son, his two beautiful daughters.

"This feast will be our last in Tokyo for some time. Tomorrow, you will pack up the houses, and the following day you will travel back to our old hometown. Things are getting worse here. The bombing is escalating; and, though we are in the hills above the city, we have no assurance we will be safe."

"You will come with us," said his wife.

"No, my dear, I must stay and look out for the company."

"Then I will stay too," she insisted. The children had their heads down, and Yoshio could feel their resentment at being sent away.

"There will be no arguments. I am head of this household. My mind is made up. You will all go, and with smiles on your faces. I will come to visit as often as I can. And let us all pray this madness is over soon. Now eat up and drink to better days ahead!"

So, it happened as Yamato decreed. His family hurriedly packed their things, and the next day they left for Hiroshima.

26

Sylvia let her hair grow long and concentrated on her studies—the least she could do was get her engineering degree and get on with her life. She even stopped sparring with Jacob Carruthers. In fact, she started being nice to him, so nice that they went on what actually might be called dates.

On Saturdays in the spring they'd get into Jacob's new jalopy and drive out to Vermont, Sylvia hollering along the way at poor Jacob to pull over so she could photograph the farmers tapping maples or women hanging quilts. When they got to Bennington, they turned north and headed to Manchester for lunch. The trout at the Main Street Diner was served in small cast iron pans and so delicious they never dreamt of going anywhere else.

Then as the semester was nearing the end, Sylvia, who had had her aunt ship her a few of her dresses and wore them brilliantly, seemed to be attracting all sorts of attention. The pledge master seemed to always be hovering around her. He'd stand as close as he could get to her and take deep breaths like he was trying to breath in the air she exhaled. At first it bothered her, but as time went on she began to think of him more as a pet, a large cute puppy dog who couldn't get enough of its master. Other men followed her around campus asking if they could carry her books or if she wanted to go into town with them and have a drink at a real bar? She'd smile politely and decline such offers. Being with Jacob was enough. She wasn't tempted to be intimate with him, yet she enjoyed his company, his self-promoting sense of humor, his friendship. Things were just the way Sylvia Russo wanted them.

Or were they?

She'd stifled all thoughts of Howard and of the Fluke for many months now, but one late April morning, she laid in bed under her blanket listening to rain drumming on the roof and found she could no longer suppress the analysis that was drumming in her brain.

Damn it, I had the aperture open enough. There was enough light pulsing fast enough. The portal in the mainframe worked. The image transferred from the camera to the screen, no problem. It's got to be the program, or the command language.

She threw the blanket off, sat up, and reached for her robe. She looked at the picture of Howard on her nightstand. She picked it up. "I give up, Howard. I'm sorry, but I give up."

She laid it back, face down.

27

"This war, more than any other war in history, is a woman's war." Sylvia had clipped this quote from the last edition of the campus paper. What exactly the American ambassador in London meant, she wasn't sure, but the sentence stuck in Sylvia's brain and needled her. Secretly, she harbored the desire to go back to Tortola, and Virgil, after graduation, but now it was dawning on her there was something else she had to do. It would break Aunt Louise's heart, too. The elderly woman had been so happy to have her back home. She couldn't stop making her stew and soda bread.

Even Jacob had enlisted, though with the guarantee that he wouldn't be sent into combat. The deal was made possible since he'd graduated second in the class, one point below Sylvia's perfect cumulative average. He wound up being shipped to an undisclosed base in New Mexico. The last she heard from him they'd given him the title, Weapons Engineer. That was all he was authorized to divulge.

If Jacob, who didn't seem to have a patriotic bone in his body nor any political leanings one way or the other, could muster the courage to support the war effort, then so could she. Tortola, her future, would have to be put on hold. She signed on with the Women's Army Auxiliary Corps.

In a matter of days she received a letter asking her to report to the downtown recruitment center for an interview and to bring a portfolio of her photographs. She found that request a rather odd one. She'd written "Photography" in the blank space next to "Hobbies." Since a portfolio of her photos didn't exist, she scrambled to assemble what she could in a binder.

"A graduate of Rensselaer Polytechnic? And an avid photographer?" Edward Steichen, the famous fashion photographer——Sylvia recognized him immediately from his photographs in The New Yorker——was sitting behind a small desk by a large window. "So you want to be a WAAC?"

"I want to serve my country, sir." Sylvia stood near the table with her portfolio in her arms feeling slightly apprehensive about sharing its contents with Steichen.

"I feel the same way, Mrs. Russo, that's why I've volunteered to organize a corps of photographers for the Navy. The military needs photos, not only as documentation, but also as, I hesitate to use this word, propaganda. It sounds so negative, but really all our government wants to do is propagate support for our troops. Citizens must be reminded of the sacrifices that many are making in this war in order for us to win the war. If every American is behind the effort, and the troops know that, they'll be more motivated to do some of the difficult things they'll be asked to do." Steichen looked Sylvia up and down skeptically. "How good are you?"

"Well, sir, it's difficult for me to be objective. I like most of what I have here, but in comparison to your work I would categorize it as amateurish."

He took her portfolio from her. "If these are good enough..." His voice trailed off as he studied the photos spread out in front of him. In a matter of minutes he looked up and smiled.

"Good enough? Good doesn't begin to say enough. Mrs. Russo, I am impressed. You've got an eye for composition. The light is right in all but a few. All in all, I'd say, welcome to the Navy." And his eyes went back to a charming photo Sylvia had taken of Jacob in Vermont.

28

The USS Raleigh was an impressive vessel. Sylvia and eight hundred and forty-one other Navy personnel boarded in Brooklyn and set sail in October of 1941, bound for Pearl Harbor. They passed through the Caribbean heading for the Panama Canal. Sylvia, topside, clung to the railing—Tortola! She could see its mountains on the horizon like a black silhouette of a rotund, sleeping giant. But then the cruiser veered west and her sighting of the island might as well have been a mirage.

When the novelty of being carried across the Pacific Ocean aboard a floating world unto itself wore off, Sylvia got down to business. She scheduled portrait session for anyone who wanted to sit for her. In between she wandered around the massive ship snapping candid photos of the inhabitants as they went about their daily routines, polishing and buffing every inch of the vessel, playing cards, smoking cigarettes in the moonlight, vomiting over the side during storms, and lying in their bunks writing letters that wouldn't get sent until they reached Hawaii. But her favorite of all was the shot she'd taken of two nurses, Vanessa Grice and Kate Pazder and their new friend, Seaman Skip Jackson. The women put on red lipstick and let their hair down. They posed on the bow of the ship at sunset, Skip "the thorn between the two roses" as he described it.

How young and beautiful they were. How the photo captured their exuberance. You could see it in their eyes. What awaited them on this grand adventure? This truly was the best time of their young lives.

Sylvia, Vanessa, Kate, and Skip became friends. They were there to help with the war effort, to contribute in some way to the American cause, but being isolated on the Raleigh had turned into more of pleasure cruise than anything for them. The weeks flew by with one gab session after another late at night under the stars.

The last week in November the Raleigh pulled into the harbor and was formally welcomed with a gun salute. Now the real work began and it was over a week before the friends were granted permission to explore the island. The base commander, Captain Will, as everyone called him, lent them his own car so they could explore Oahu.

When they reached the North Shore, they pulled off the road onto the edge of the beach and made their way in the dark through coconut palms and a thicket of hibiscus and bird-of-paradise onto the sand. They sat on a blanket waiting for sunrise. Skip told a few jokes. Their spirits were high. Slowly, a sliver of light lined the horizon. The waves were breaking a good distance off shore, their cap grew luminescent. A warm breeze kicked up and rustled the palms. Then, just as the golden coin of sun emerged as if the ocean were giving up its bounty, a loud boom startled them. Then another. The noise was in the distance, but the earth beneath them shook with each explosion.

"That can't be thunder, can it?" Vanessa was on her feet looking around, trying to locate the direction of the sound.

Sylvia's first thought was that the sky was too clear for thunder, and already there were multiple blasts exploding simultaneously, unnaturally. They were all on their feet looking southwest. Beyond the mountain peaks that sliced through the center of the island, smoke was rising. The sun was fully up behind them now and hot on their backs, but their eyes were riveted on the mass of planes that came into view humming like a swarm of giant hornets. They could see the proliferation of bombs dropping out of them. Ba boom! Ba boom!

Skip drew in a deep breath. "Holy shit..." he whispered, "...we're being attacked."

His words snapped them into action. They ran to the jeep, jumped in, and sped south. Skip pushed the pedal to the floor, and the countryside became a blur. No one said a word. Sylvia silently prayed the Hail Mary over and over.

Kate and Vanessa held hands. They were heading directly into the holocaust. Sylvia was weak with terror and fought back tears. This could be the end for them all, but they could not stop and turn and go in the other direction. No. They couldn't even speak of that. This was, after all, what they'd signed on for.

As they got closer to the harbor, they watched wave after wave of enemy aircraft join the assault.

"Jesus Christ, Jesus Christ." Skip kept saying the same thing over and over. It was clear he was trying like hell to control the car and himself, but the spectacle of destruction in front of him was making it almost impossible. The bombs whistled through the sky, blew up, the explosions deafening. Flames licked at the smoke which had completely filled the sky. Sylvia began to tremble. Try as she did, she couldn't stop herself from shaking.

Just west of Honolulu the road was clogged with vehicles. Panic-stricken, people trying to evacuate had taken up both lanes. There was no way to get around them.

"Damn it, I'll walk." Kate got out and held the door open. "Are you coming? Look, we can't just sit here and wait. They need us. Now!"

Sylvia grabbed her camera and followed Kate, and in a few minutes Skip and Vanessa caught up and they were all running as fast as they could toward Pearl Harbor. By the time they stopped to catch their breath, the planes had disappeared and an eerie silence set in over the flat expanse of land between them and the base.

They walked more cautiously now. A siren pierced the air and whined on for the full half hour it took them to get to the edge of the war zone, for that is what it was. Then unexpectedly and to their horror, the screams and cries of the wounded and dying became audible.

Sylvia instinctively, yet in a state of disbelief, began photographing the carnage. The lens separated her just enough from the blood, the detached limbs, the burnt flesh, the shredded uniforms, the scattered belongings, the flaming ships sinking in the harbor for her to do her job. She was here to document the war, and this is what war was. Shock and awe and grief consumed her, but she opened her aperture and took the evil in. She had to hurry. She had to get as much of it as she could on film before the enemy came back and pulverized everything, including her.

She catalogued the bodies that had somehow remained whole as they were pulled from the water or from the burning hulls of the vessels. Some of the corpses she recognized as guys and girls from the Raleigh. No time for weeping, no time even to pray.

Sylvia spied Vanessa and Kate out of the corner of her eye. They were busy examining more bodies as they were retrieved from the wreckage.

They are checking...for survivors.

Sylvia reached in her pocket and reloaded her camera. She boarded a small rescue craft that attempted to navigate around the debris, but the piers had collapsed, the half-sunk ships were smoldering, and the water itself was aflame. If she didn't get this spectacle on film, no one would believe it.

The enemy never returned; the sky remained quiet.

Once the sun set Sylvia convinced a befuddled officer to allow her to drive into Honolulu to develop the photographs.

"No time should be wasted. I've got to get these to the mainland," she pleaded. He seemed to be in a state of shock as he got in a jeep and drove her himself. He dropped her off at the home of a wedding photographer he had used at his own wedding last month. He kept repeating, "This guy will take care of everything...this guy will take care of everything." He must've said it a hundred times in the two hours it took for them cover the twenty miles.

All night and well into the morning Sylvia and Fred, the wedding photographer, worked side-by-side in the small dark room in Fred's basement. They struggled to rush the processing along. And it was going pretty fast until Sylvia heard Fred gag and cover his mouth. He ran out and she could hear him retching his guts up. She looked over and saw the photo clearing on the line. It was the headless body of Captain Will.

Sylvia began to feel sick to her stomach too. She had to look at the pictures and select which ones to mail to Steichen. No aircraft from the base would be heading to the mainland so she'd have to rely on the post office, and even then who knew when any sort of communication would get through.

The pictures were so nightmarish, she cringed at the sight of them. It was like they'd been staged by some insane Hollywood director. But, unfortunately, what had happened had really happened. Now it was up to her to let the world know the truth, America's finest had made the ultimate sacrifice for their country.

She began organizing the ones she would send into two piles. Fred returned looking peaked and gave her manila envelopes and stamps, and together they walked to the post office to mail one package of pictures to Steichen and the other to the President.

No sense wasting time going through stupid channels, she thought.

29

Three things happen in the Dwyer apartment on December 7, 1941.

In the morning Jake took his first steps. He wasn't a particularly agile child so this accomplishment thrilled Lizzy, who fretted that he might never walk on his own. How he wobbled when he tried, and he was so lazy about trying! If it weren't for the way he talked, she might have thought his brain wasn't right. After all, he had rather surprisingly dropped right out of her onto the floor when she was having contractions and hanging onto the footboard of the bed. But everyone who met him was stunned by his language skills which could only be described as remarkable.

At nineteen months he was able to hold a decent conversation with just about anybody, but he especially liked to talk to his dad. After work and weekends they talked so much Lizzy began feeling a bit left out; and Eddie forgot most of the time that his baby boy was technically still pretty much a baby. Little Jake just seemed to have so many questions about so many odd things. It ate up all of Eddie's time coming up with the right answers.

So Lizzy was relieved when Jake pulled himself up by the sofa and let go and tried to make it across the room. The fact that he only took about three actual steps didn't matter one bit to her. A step was a step.

Right after noon, Lizzy was sitting on the floor trying to convince her boy to take a few more steps when Eddie unexpectedly burst through the door.

"You scared the living daylights out of me, Eddie!" Lizzy was breathless.

"Turn on the radio!" he screamed and ran to the radio and turned it on before Lizzy could get up. "We've been bombed. Pearl Harbor's been bombed! Goddamn Japanese. That does it, Lizzy. I've got to sign-up now."

"Bombed? No, Eddie, it can't be true. It's got to be some radio prank like that 'War of the Worlds' thing."

"Lizzy, it's true!" His voice was strained.

"But you can't go, Eddie. You can't leave us!"

But the announcer was talking and Lizzy could hear that what Eddie said *was* true. Her husband would enlist. He had to, how could he not help fight to save them. Lizzy started crying, and Eddie put his arms around her. He was crying too.

They weren't paying attention to Jake as he wobbled over to them and wrapped his small arms around his father's legs.

"Daddy, don't go. If you do, you will never come back."

30

Fred drove Sylvia as far as he could, and she walked the rest of the way back to the base. In the morning Sylvia was assigned to assist the medical personnel in the care of the injured and in the evacuation of the wounded and the dead; but when she was given a short break, she'd grab her camera and make the rounds taking photos.

The disaster was so massive, so entire that it looked like this was the way this place had always been. Nothing of the old base remained. All was rubble, everything scorched and blackened and unrecognizable.

Sylvia worked tirelessly under Kate's and Vanessa's direction, dressing wounds and wrapping the dead in shrouds. At night they headed out to a makeshift camp in a field beyond the tarmac of the airstrip and passed out from exhaustion.

The United States officially declared war on Japan, deployed an arsenal of aircraft carriers to the region, and immediately stepped up the bombing raids on Tokyo that, up to this point, had been sporadic at best. The escalation of activity in the Pacific arena was paralleled by the huge salvage operation at Pearl Harbor. Hundreds of tenders and ships' crewmen set about refloating vessels, removing weapons, and recovering remains. The base had to be rebuilt, anything worth saving had to be shipped to the mainland for reuse in other vessels.

Days, weeks, months passed in the blink of an eye. On the second anniversary of the bombing, Pearl Harbor became almost fully operational again. When a new commander arrived to oversee the raising of the last viable ship, Sylvia, who'd been reassigned to recording the inventory of construction materials arriving almost daily, was surprised to be ordered to report to his office.

Sylvia arrived in the sweltering Quonset hut to find her new boss seated behind a battered metal desk holding a Life Magazine. He smiled at her and turned the magazine toward her so she could see the cover. On it was an old photograph of hers, the first photograph she'd snapped after the bombing. She'd been on the hill above the harbor. It was a wide angle shot of the half-submerged battleships engulfed in flames.

Sylvia blushed and said nothing. The horrific image rendered her speechless. Was she ashamed? Embarrassed? Yes, she'd been too hasty, too insensitive, taking a photograph like that. But how had Life Magazine gotten it? She'd sent her photos to Steichen, to the White House? Now, here was the most disturbing one circulating around the globe. If the commander was angry, if the President was angry, she could see why. Steichen probably sent the photo out without going through the proper channels. Sylvia stood at attention facing her superior officer, expecting the worst—a formal reprimand.

The man's face, lined and flushed, was moist with sweat, his eyes as unyielding as marbles. He put the magazine down on the desk with the cover facing Sylvia and cleared his throat.

"Russo, this is one hell of a photograph. The President telephoned me regarding it just the other day. He said he'd been meaning to get to you about it a long time ago, but as you can understand, he's been extremely busy with other things."

Now Sylvia broke out in a sweat but did not divert her gaze from her commander. She saw that the magazine was already almost a year old. She steeled herself for what she knew was coming next.

The man continued in a firm voice. "Were it not for that photo, the President believes the citizens of our great nation might not have rallied behind us to the extent that they did. We needed the support of the whole country after the bombing. We needed everyone to support our troops in the fight against Japan. Thanks to you that's what happened. You are a remarkable woman and an asset to the Navy. Even under attack you had the courage to do your job and do it well. Both the President of the United States and I commend you and thank you for your contribution to a great cause."

Sylvia's face turned scarlet. Her commander rose and shook her hand.

As Sylvia turned to leave, she thought of Howard, his belief in the power of the camera, of photography. Now, for the first time, she knew exactly what he meant.

31

Yamato Yoshio, alone in Tokyo for nearly two years, had gotten into the habit of celebrating the attack on Pearl Harbor every night. It had become a ritual for him. He'd pour himself a glass of scotch whiskey—that first night it had been the Dalmore 62, the best scotch whiskey in his collection—and stand at the large window in his office and survey what was left of the skyline of Tokyo. The once sporadic bombings by the hated Americans had become routine and more vicious, the bombs themselves more powerful. Nearly a third of the buildings in the Ginza district alone had been reduced to rubble. The scorched structures left standing looked like the remaining teeth in a rotting mouth. Yes, he had been right to send his family to Hiroshima, his employees to the outskirts of the city, and Masuki, a great distance away to Nara.

At least my wife and children are safe, the prototype safe.

Yes, he'd been lucky. The Noboru Industries building and its precious computer were also still intact, but there had never been any guarantee that this would have been so.

Yoshio raised his glass to his battered city. At least his country had shown the brazen Americans a thing or two at Pearl Harbor.

Why do we not strike again? He wondered. *Put them in their place again so I can send for my family, my employees, my prototype. So I can move forward and regain the money that's been lost.*

The smooth scotch made his tongue and the back of his throat tingle. He took another sip and held it in his mouth before swallowing. As a satisfying warmth spread through him, he held the crystal tumbler up and smiled at the miracle liquid before he put the glass to his lips and downed the rest.

He'd been sleeping on the leather couch in his office, leaving Noboru only to go to the bathhouse two blocks away every other day. He rarely went to his home in the Rappongi Hills. Why bother? No one was there, and being in that house made him long for his wife, the sound of her voice, the softness of her skin, the look of desire in her eyes. He bought rice and fish from the carts that lined the Ginza in the daylight hours. At night everything was blacked out. No one was on the streets. Even tonight, Yoshio had watched from his office window as the last human disappeared into a dark alley.

The plush couch was comfortable, the room quiet, and the scotch had calmed him so it wasn't long before Yoshio drifted off to sleep. In his dream his wife was lying next to him on a tatami mat. She had on a white silk kimono that was loosely tied and one of her breasts was exposed. Yoshio was staring at it, trying to decide if he should wake his wife. He hesitated because he knew she was exhausted from caring for their new baby boy. But her breast was tempting, so swollen with milk it looked as though it might burst. He wanted to touch it, take it in his mouth. How would her milk taste? His curiosity, coupled with his love for her, was driving him mad. He desired her. He desired to discover the life-giving secret of her milk. It alone sustained his son. How can that be? How can the body of one human being keep another alive? Rashly, he sunk his teeth into his own forearm and ripped off a mouthful of his own flesh. Putrid tasting, he spit it….

The whistle of the rocket screamed in his ears. He jolted upright just as it exploded. Through the window he saw the flames rise up a block to the west and spread like a fiery tidal wave toward Noboru. There was the rumble of planes overhead. Another whistle pierced the air. Yoshio jumped up, but when the second blast hit, it shook the building and knocked him off his feet. He crawled to the door and out into the hall. When he got to the steps, a third bomb burst so nearby that he feared the sound of it had deafened him. His head throbbed, and he vomited in the corner before he pulled himself to his feet and ran down the stairs. His heart was pounding. The bombs were coming so fast now the din was constant. Yoshio could barely breathe by the time he got to the heavily reinforced basement, pushed the thick metal door shut, and bolted himself in.

The insulation in the lab and the hum of the mainframe muffled the sounds of the onslaught until the mainframe fell silent. Yoshio collapsed in Masuki's chair by the typewriter his Chairman of Research and Development had been trying to rig up to the computer. He closed his eyes and tried to calm his pounding heart by meditating on the spots behind his lids.

*Why wasn't it...*he pushed the thought away and took a deep cleansing breath. *Stop thinking. Think nothing.* But he couldn't because he was scared and angry. *When would it be over?*

Yoshio was so disheartened he wanted to cry, but even alone, even though this was the worst onslaught thus far, he couldn't let himself breakdown like that. He was a grown man, not a cry baby.

He pushed the typewriter back and put his head down on the desk. It was all such a hateful mess. All he wanted was for this war to end so he could once again be the happy business man he'd been.

Okay, so he'd rarely been a happy business man.

He was a perfectionist and perfection was hard to achieve. He seemed always in a constant state of dissatisfaction with those around him, and with himself. Happy and business were only synonymous in his book when his company was on top and raking in the big money. He knew Kodak was nipping at Noboru's heels, and Leica was always a threat; but if his prototype became a functioning camera that could do what he wanted it to do, the resulting photographs would put what the competition could produce to shame. And if the camera could be hooked up to a computer and actually control the mind of a subject in a photograph, well, though he had his doubts, he would become the richest, most powerful man in the world. It was a longshot, but if he could light a fire under Masuki's ass, maybe, just maybe the genius would finally have a....

A loud boom. The earth shook throwing Yoshio from the chair. For several interminable seconds everything shuddered. Yoshio stopped breathing as he listened to the sound of walls tumbling down above him, his walls, the walls of Noboru.

32

For Masuki Shin being sent to Nara was like being sent to hell. The house Chief Yamato had procured was a rural farmhouse set on a patch of cleared land surrounded by a great forest. The place consisted of a stable, a muddy fenced-in corral, a weed-infested yard, and a ramshackle house that sat on rotting stilts. The stink of livestock permeated the place and made Shin sick to his stomach. When he went outside, he was accosted by mangy sika deer that overran the entire forest and also stunk. He was a sort of Shinto and knew the deer were considered messengers of the gods; but when they surrounded him and nudged him in the direction they wanted him to go and he had to shoo them away, he wasn't at all sure that whatever message they were trying to deliver he wanted to hear.

What a filthy dump, a slum if I ever saw one. Masuki rued what he took to be a demotion by crafty, cruel Yamato. This displacement only verified in his mind his boss's loathing. If it weren't for his superior computer expertise, Shin believed he would've been long gone from Noboru Industries. *Well, the only good thing is that this poor excuse for a habitat makes my humble apartment back in Tokyo look like a mansion.*

The distance from the farm to town was so great that it took Shin, walking at a fast pace, an hour to get to the edge of it. Once he arrived, there wasn't much there for him to do. No fancy Roppongi Hills bar. No pretty young women. No ice-cold drinks. He sat in a local's place, sipped room-temperature sake, and tolerated the ill-bred, small-time hustlers who catered to the temple pilgrims. When he'd drunk enough to make his head spin, he hiked home to face Kenta and his mother. Their wagging tongues made him cover his ears. How they harangued him, lashing him with every mean word in their vast repertoire of complaints.

The temple, though hidden from his view, was another nuisance. Hundreds and thousands of his fellow countrymen scrounged and saved to journey there and pay homage to the enormous bronze Buddha. They littered and peed and defecated everywhere, fouling the air even along the most obscure paths through the forest. And they were noisy! On their way in, their voices swelled with anticipation the closer they were to the temple grounds; and after, having given their burdens up to the gods, Masuki had to endure the sound of their exuberant chatter.

This along with the fact Masuki had no work to occupy his mind—not real work like dressing and hurrying off to Noboru, heading to the laboratory where the new computer had been installed, donning his lab coat, going over the diagrams, tinkering again with the prototype, the keyboard he'd modified from a typewriter, the screen he'd modified from a television that itself had not yet been mass-produced—was driving him to desperation. His work now was only in his mind, his imagination whirring, ideas popping up, but then just as quickly disappearing. He tried to keep a notebook with him and write down whatever brilliant insight occurred to him, but as time dragged on in Nara he became lazy and, instead of fantasizing about the camera, he became obsessed with fantasizing about sex. Even Kenta began to look good to him, if only he could gag her to keep her from talking.

Yes, he could fuck her and fuck her, if he could gag her. Once, he pictured it in his mind. She was sitting at the low table opposite his mother talking rapidly, her voice in such a high pitch it squeaked. She was very animated, her hands gesticulating as rapidly as the words spilled from her lips. He took a black scarf of hers he'd found on her shelf and wound it tight till it became a thick rope. He snuck up behind her and just as she was saying, "...what kind of husband would..." he quickly gagged her, pulled the silk rope taunt, and tied it in a knot at the back of her head. She made some muffled sounds, but no words were possible. His mother screamed in horror.

"Mother, go to your room. Leave my wife to me."

"But what are doing?" his mother hollered.

"What I have to, what I must. She is my wife' I will not hurt her. So leave. Now!"

After his mother hurried from the kitchen, Masuki petted his wife's hair and took her by the shoulders and brought her to her feet. "Kneel down and bend over." He saw the terror in her eyes. "Like I said, I will not hurt you." But he could feel his frustration mounting. Why was she so difficult? Why couldn't she just go along with him? He was done being kind to her. He'd tried, but she was impossible to be kind to. His penis was hard. He was going to fuck her good now. He was done being nice.

It was only a fantasy. Well, for a week or so that was all it was until he came home from town one particularly rainy, bleak afternoon with his head still spinning, and there was his mother and his wife at the table talking. Kenta uttered the exact words in Shin's fantasy, "...what kind of husband would..." and it was like a switch went on his brain. He could not stop himself, and, truthfully, he didn't try.

Afterward, he felt more satisfied with himself and her, then he had been in years. He felt even somewhat tender toward her. She, at first, seemed stunned; but, later, when they lay side by side in the dark, she turned toward him and kissed his cheek.

So what had seemed like hell, now that he'd found such an unexpected and satisfying release, had, at least, become tolerable; and Masuki dreamt up other surprises for his wife, and his mother, whom he seemed to have finally silenced. She rarely spoke in front of him now; and if she did, it was in a whisper. Things went on amicably like this deep in the Temple forest for several months.

On his daily trips into town Masuki continued to learn of the bombings back in Tokyo, of how Japan had retaliated and bombed the hell out of that base in Hawaii. It looked like the Americans had learned a lesson and were backing off. The citizens of Tokyo were adjusting. The sporadic bombing seemed a way of life for them and not at all as dangerous as it had been.

Shin was again becoming antsy to get back to Noboru. He couldn't be certain Yamato hadn't replaced him and was keeping in exile so he wouldn't have to face him. His fears mounted with each day that passed. More and more he believed himself to be an outcast, a nobody, a nothing.

Then one morning when he arrived at his watering hole, he was greeted with the news. The United States had unleashed its revenge on Tokyo. The bombardment the worst ever. One hundred thousand dead! The payback for Pearl Harbor had come and now what? He feared he'd be stuck in Nara till he was an old man...but at least he'd get to be one.

33

How many different war-torn islands and dead bodies could one person be expected to bear witness to? Island by island, body by body, and still Sylvia's tender heart did not toughened up. Quite the opposite.

Whatever ship she happened to be on traveled by night, sometimes through roiling seas. At dawn, when they dropped anchor, the floating debris was her first clue to the extent of the devastation. In a small motor boat she followed its trail it to the beach where the bodies were.

Now she was among them, almost like one of them, almost dead, at least her spirit was. The only sound besides the crashing waves and the screeching of birds was the click of her camera.

After she'd gotten on film what was expected of her—the bloody damaged bodies, the putrid rotting flesh—she'd take a minute to stare out at the horizon and pray for the dead souls. There would be more of the same again, soon, too soon. Somewhere on another island they were getting killed this very instant.

Dear God, make it stop…please.

But it didn't and weeks turned into months and months into years. Sylvia wished she'd never been sent on this assignment. If only she'd been allowed to stay at Pearl Harbor, she'd never have to do this God-forsaken job. She lost track of how many miles she'd covered to capture on film the inhumane aftermath of battle.

And why? Did it really matter to the folks on the other side of the planet who were sitting in their cozy homes having roast beef for dinner? Did the fine, upstanding citizens who glanced at the morning paper and tossed it aside with the shrug of a shoulder or the shake of a head really care? This war was too gruesome, dragging on too long. Yes, she could imagine, these people back in the States really must be getting sick of this stupid war.

Sick? They have no idea what sick is, thought Sylvia.

Every photograph she'd ever taken haunted her. And, though her work had won her critical acclaim, she'd grown to hate what she did, hate that she'd become an integral part of a great destructive machine. She knew her photos had turned into weapons every bit as powerful as guns or bombs. The more graphic they were, the more effective they were. At what? Inspiring support for the troops? She doubted it. What she was really doing was inflaming the passions of the commanders, fueling the vengeance of the orchestrators of the war, provoking the warriors themselves.

When the men in uniform saw the pictures of the dead, it fanned the fire of their revenge. She was an instrument, a puppet, blindly following orders, mindlessly igniting hatred.

Sylvia's misgivings troubled her greatly, but she saw no way out so she kept trying, telling herself, maybe if she could take even more vivid photos of even more disgusting devastation, the men in charge might decide enough was enough and do what it would take to win the war. That she was helping to win the war was a fantasy she indulged in to keep going. It allowed her to focus on the quality of her work, to obsess about the lighting, angles, foreground, background, the golden triangle of the composition.

But the guilt never went too far away. The subjects of her obsessions were dead men. But winning the war would stop the killing. Right? But winning the war required more killing.

There was no way out.

One day, when she could stifle these thoughts no longer, she considered throwing her camera in the sea and running away to somewhere where she would never see a camera or a dead man again.

That night, aboard yet another battleship, Sylvia went on deck at midnight, the sky black as the sea, not a star, the only light coming from the vessel itself.

She watched the foam of the wake a few yards off the stern and did what she seldom allowed herself to do, think about her family and friends.

Howard, Aunt Louise, Momma Russo, Pop Russo, Jacob, Harriet, La Bomba, Virgil. Virgil, there, in the water, in the clear pool between the boulders. His body is so beautiful, so sleek and golden. Oh, he's rolling over. He's smiling up at me!

Thinking of Virgil made her smile, something she seldom did these days.

Sylvia went below and climbed in her bunk, this day no different except she had smiled.

In the morning she went ashore on the next beach and snapped her ghoulish photos.

Back on the ship, she retreated below deck to a windowless room and developed the negatives, magically bringing, as it were, death to life. As usual, she tried not to let her eyes rest too long on one or another of the horrors, wanting to see and not see at the same time. But it registered in her brain, all of it found a place there.

In her cabin she fumbled in the dark for her pill box, took two sleeping pills, and passed out.

But even sleep didn't guarantee a respite from evil.

The same dream! Again! No!

She is trudging across the sand and into the jungle. The air's thick with insects. She's drenched in sweat. Ahead, she sees something white is on the ground. It's a sailor in dress whites, not in combat gear. She runs to him. She gets close. Something is very wrong.

"Please, help me!" He's crying. "Help me! I can't go home to my girlfriend without them. Help me find my legs!"

Blood is spurting out of the stumps where his legs should've been. Frantically, she scans the beach, heads to the underbrush, frantically searches for the sailor's legs. Drops of blood. She follows them into the jungle. There she finds another sailor. He has no arms. Tears stream down his dirty face. His eyes bulge in their bruised sockets.

"Help me! I can't go home to my girlfriend without them..."

Sylvia, jolted awake, her heart pounding. She was awake now for good. She would not fall asleep again, anything not to be in that nightmare again. She got down on her knees, like she did most nights, and begged for forgiveness.

Tell no one...and beg for forgiveness.

Everyone around her already knew war was hell. There was no need to say it. They were all suffering and trying to keep that suffering under a hard shell of supposed courage was all that enabled any of them to endure.

But could Sylvia hold on?

The next morning topside with her camera, she discovered her vessel had joined a massive fleet of American ships off the coast of Okinawa, Japan. It was a brilliant day and the armada looked indestructible in the gleaming sunlight. What a relief to photograph living, breathing crews of sailors, but the impressive display of naval strength only forebode more vigorous killing.

Later, while developing the negatives, there was a knock on the darkroom door. When Sylvia opened it, a sailor handed her a telegraph.

March 6, 1945

Disembark at next destination: Guam

Take first flight to Washington, D.C.

Report to the Admiral of the Navy upon arrival.

34

Aunt Louise and the Russos waited in the cold airport hangar and watched as a gray plane touched down and noisily ground to a halt. Men bundled up in heavy cargo suits pushed the stairs up to the exit hatch. It opened and the travelers deplaned, Sylvia among them.

Her family gathered around her. She had only minutes. No time to talk really, just minutes to hug and hold hands and look into tearful eyes.

Then she was waving to them and blowing kisses. There was a car waiting to rush her to the Pentagon.

"We have to hurry, Mrs. Russo." There was such urgency in her young escort's voice that it rattle her already exhausted nerves.

He pulled the vehicle into an underground garage and led her onto an elevator that went down several levels before opening. A concrete corridor stretched into the distance. Off the corridor were numbered doors. The rest of the day Sylvia spent alone in sleeping-quarters number 23, not sleeping, but wondering why things had been so rushed at the airport. Why couldn't she have spent the day with her relatives if all she was going to do was toss and turn in the windowless bowels of this ugly complex?

Aunt Louise, the Russos, they looked older, worn-out with worry. No, they had not been taking the war for granted. Her heart ached to be with them, sit down to a bowl of soup, a plate of cookies, hear them chatter and laugh, to go back to being the way she was when she was with them. She'd have a chance with them to be herself again.

The next morning Sylvia was showered and dressed before she heard the knock on her door. A different escort. "Please, bring your camera, Mrs. Russo."

She followed him into the elevator. They ascended to the top floor. The hall here was brightly lit, the walls covered in flocked wallpaper. When they reached the double doors at the end, her escort held the rich walnut door for her and Sylvia entered alone.

A nearly bald man with a square jaw and broad shoulders looked up from behind his desk and smiled at Sylvia. She recognized him, the Admiral, the top man in charge of the Pacific theater.

"Ah, Mrs. Russo, come in," he said as he got up, walked around his desk, and shook her hand. "You've done a great service for America, and I am proud of you. All of America is proud of you."

"Thank you, Admiral," Sylvia almost sighed with relief. She'd spent most of the endless hours of travel vacillating between being troubled by the orders to return stateside and being so weary of everything she didn't giving a damn what they wanted from her.

"But now let's get this over with. I'm not one who likes to get my photo taken, but in my position things like this have to be done."

So I guess all I'm here for is take his picture, she thought. *Why didn't they just say so when they told me I was going back?*

Before she could get too upset about the lack of communication, the Admiral ushered her into a small anteroom set up for the photo session. An American flag was hung flat on the wall, an oak chair was angled in front of it, and two large spotlights were aimed at the chair. Sylvia had her trusty Leica with the old lens on it. She took it out of its case and fiddled with the settings.

The Admiral smoothed what hair he had, straightened the jacket of his uniform, and sat down. Sylvia, satisfied with both the lighting and the man's posture, looked through the lens and adjusted it until he came into perfect focus. He was looking directly into the lens, his deep-set eyes hard as stones. Her hands started to shake.

These eyes are windows into the soul of the human being who made all that I have witnessed happen. Him. He is the one who gave the orders.

Sylvia had seen so much through this camera and now she was trying to see what was inside this man, what was it that made him so sure of himself.

Sylvia moved the camera away from her eye in an attempt to steady her hands. She walked over to one of the lights, adjusted it a fraction of an inch. She was stalling, hoping she could regain her composure, hoping she could contain the anger that was welling up inside her. Still trembling, she went to the window, pulled back the thick red satin curtains, and let the sunlight stream into the claustrophobic space.

The Admiral wiggled in his seat and repeated what he'd said before. "Get this over with. I've got a war to fight."

He pulled on the collar of his uniform and craned his neck like a bird listening for the call of another bird. "And you, my dear, have a train to catch. After this last shot, I'm sending you home. Admiral's orders."

Home? Sylvia looked around to make sure he was talking to her. There was no one else in the room. *Home, back to Aunt Louise, back to Trenton.*

It had only been three days since she left the Pacific, could it really be true she would be home by tonight? The Admiral's pronouncement altered her mood entirely. Her concentration was gone, but now more than ever she wanted this to be the best portrait she'd ever taken. She owed that much to this man who was making her deepest wish come true, who was stopping the war, at least for her.

Sylvia took a deep breath and aimed her camera. This time, in her jubilance, she expected to see the hope and the kindness that she knew must be somewhere inside of the man. When she stared into his eyes again, though, her heart turned cold. Was it her imagination? She blinked and looked again. No, she saw something terrible and troubling. And it was real. And it scared the hell out of her.

Hours later, when she arrived in Trenton, she found her aunt and in-laws huddled around the radio in the living room. Aunt Louise and Momma Russo were crying. Aunt Louise looked at Sylvia through her tears. The expression on her face was a mixture of relief and agony.

"Oh my God, Sylvia, thank God you are here and not on the other side of the world. We just destroyed Tokyo. One hundred thousand people are dead!"

35

All of Noboru Industries headquarters had been destroyed in the firebombing except the basement. The building toppled onto the single story structure beside it leaving only a shallow pile of rubble above the metal door. It took Yamato Yoshio two days to push open that door and dig his way through the debris. Exhausted, hungry, but uninjured, he wandered through the unrecognizable streets of Tokyo. The smoke and dust make his eyes sting, and to the West a wall of flame still licked the sky. There were steaming ruins everywhere and dead bodies and body parts. Yoshio stared around in disbelief. Was that someone's head? One hand still holding another hand? Legs, feet, indistinguishable things, muscle, and tangled knots of cartilage were everywhere. And clothes, food, toys, cars, twisted things Yoshio couldn't identify. He choked back tears, his heart keening in grief. The sight of this holocaust, of such evil, was wrenching every last bit of goodness out of him, forever.

When he found what used to be his home in the Rappongi Hills. It, too, had been reduced to dust.

His situation seemed dire, but he consoled himself and staved off despair by looking not at what he had lost, but at what he still had, his expensive computer and his family!

He *would* rebuild, and, eventually, he would make the Americans pay for what they did to his city.

36

Sylvia was crossing Greenwood Avenue on her way to the corner deli. Aunt Louise needed eggs. Taking care of her aunt had become Sylvia's main occupation. She avoided the newspapers and the radio, and if anyone so much as started to talk about the war, she excused herself and went to her room and opened up another book. In the months since she'd been home, she'd plunged into Hardy, committed to reading all his notable works before moving on to Jane Austin, then Trollope, then…Oh, she knew it was escapism, but it calmed her to get lost in her books. But now she was on Dickens and had "Tale of Two Cities" left. She knew it was about the French Revolution. Could she do it? Could she read about war, even a century-old war?

She was pondering these last questions when the street began to fill with people. They were making such noise it echoed off the brick row houses. Windows were thrown open and people leaned out waving flags, towels, aprons, sheets, anything they could get their hands on. Sylvia heard someone yelling, "We bombed 'em! We bombed 'em!"

Someone else hollered, "We dropped the big one on the Japs!"

Another voice screamed, "Guess we showed them!"

And another, "The bomb, the fuckin' atom bomb! We did it!"

The crowd in the streets swelled and spilled into the alleys. Sylvia had to elbow her way through the screaming mass of humanity. Momma Russo was out in front of the restaurant banging a ladle on the bottom of a pot, Pop next to her slamming two pan lids together like cymbals. Didn't they know what dropping the atom bomb really meant? Sylvia had seen what a single gun wound looked like, what damage a hand grenade did, the way a tank could flatten a human body? Why weren't these people crying with grief?

Sylvia fled to her room, locked the door behind her, and slammed all her windows shut, but the wild celebration continued through the night. Undaunted by the August heat and humidity, the war-weary citizens got drunk and danced and sang. The war would surely end now!

For days, Aunt Louise and the Russos kept vigil by the radio waiting for Japan to surrender. By the looks of the photographs of the mushroom cloud on the front page of every paper, there couldn't be much of the enemy country left. Oh, the satisfaction some of the neighbors got from those photographs—Japan had gotten what it deserved. Others, Sylvia hoped were feeling what she was, remorse and fear. What had we done? What monstrous thing had we unleashed? Was destruction of this magnitude really necessary? Did we really need to melt human beings into the concrete of the sidewalks, boil them in rivers and ponds, turned them into ash. Five square miles. The mushroom cloud was that big. Five square miles of life erased. Who would have ordered such an overkill?

Sylvia knew. She'd seen it in the Admiral's eyes.

No surrender came, three days later the United States dropped the second bomb. More statistics, numbers Sylvia found difficult to fathom. She'd seen thousands of dead men, women, and children, but she'd never seen hundreds of thousands, and all at once. The thought of what happened made her ache all over as though she herself were wounded. Though it was the middle of the day, she hid in the corner of her room behind the door, pulled her knees to her chest, lowered her head, and wept.

When it grew dark and the light from the street lamp shone in through the window, she wearily roused herself, took her old Leica and the last notes from Howard, and climbed up the ladder into the attic. She opened her cedar chest and put the camera and notes beneath the blankets. She looked at the boxes of Howard's papers and shook her head.

What a horrible place this world has become. If only Howard had lived long enough, maybe his camera would've been able to make a difference; but if it gets into the hands of the wrong people, and they get it to work, then none of us will escape destruction.

Following a turbulent late summer, the war did end, but not the suffering. A toll had been taken on humanity that would never be mitigated. This Sylvia knew for sure, and how it tormented her.

When winter's fury took hold of Trenton, she attempted to maintain a routine. Shopping, cooking, cleaning, sitting around Momma's kitchen table, listening to the neighborhood gossip, keeping the coffee flowing. Those were her days, and they were at least tolerable. But the nights were becoming impossible for her to get through. Unable to sleep or even lie still, Sylvia began pacing around her room. Feeling too caged in, she eventually went downstairs and walked from the hall toward the front door, into the parlor, straight ahead into the dining room, around the table, into the kitchen, around that table, into the pantry to the back door, where she made an about face and retraced her steps back to the stairs. How many times each night she did this? She lost count, but at some point, exhausted, she'd get under the afghan on the davenport and fall asleep, nightmares at bay for the moment.

One frigid morning after a howling snowstorm, she woke up screaming and slapped her hand over her mouth so hard her lip started bleeding. She hurried up to her room, dressed, put on her coat, hat, and scarf, and headed out the door. The handiwork of the relentless wind surrounded her, drifts as high as the porch railing, turrets of white everywhere. Sylvia trudged down the steps kicking her way through the snow. She went to the corner, turned and trudged back. Over and over again, she followed her own footsteps, head down, eyes riveted on her own backwards footprint.

Don't think. Stop thinking. Don't feel.

But one of her photographs would flash across her mind, then there would be a swirling collage of them in her brain, then the collage would whir and whir, faster and faster into a wheel, and the photos would fly off the wheel, and she would be forced to see them again, one by one.

By the time she got home, her face was raw and chapped from the cold and from her tears. She knew then she had to do something or she'd die from guilt, from heartbreak, from doing nothing.

She recently received offers of employment from several camera companies, newspapers, and studios. She was a famous photographer whether she liked it or not. Even Steichen tried to recruit her. She found the thought of photographing some model in a satin sheath both amusing and ridiculous, but she was flattered by his acknowledgement. One oddball offer had come from a new computer company called Lansing Technologies. No cameras. Now she wondered if she hadn't made a mistake not responding to that letter.

Sylvia hurried back to the house and rummaged through her desk drawer and found the proposal. Seems they'd just installed a mainframe, the first in all of New York, and wanted her as a programmer. The salary was more than generous, and they didn't care if she wore slacks. It said so. The fact that they'd done their homework on her, impressed her. She took the letter, went across the street to Uncle Sal's, and called Lansing Technologies. The secretary who answered put her on hold, but returned to tell her she was to report for work on the first of the month, and said, "Welcome aboard!"

Hope, the feathered thing...

Had it landed lightly in heart? When she found her apartment and was, well, almost feeling normal, it was like she was seeing a small light at the end of a long, dark tunnel.

The second-story place on 83rd and 3rd had a tiny bathroom, a closet-sized bedroom, and a cramped living room with the sink, stove, and old ice box in one corner. Sylvia loved it, though. The warm chestnut woodwork, the three windows that looked out on the street below, the high ceilings, the solitude. And she loved working at Lansing. Since her days of working with Turing, there'd been major advances in the world of computers, but she hadn't lost her knack for picking things up quickly.

Every week the programmers participated in a roundtable discussion about what programs the programmers should be writing. Everyone was supposed to brainstorm about what a computer might be made to do.

Sylvia found these meetings stressful. Her mind was stuck on Howard's prototype and his program that would enable the computer to control the subject of a photograph. She was afraid to say anything about it. A program like Howard's might end up not being a good thing. She didn't want to even think about it, yet that was all she did think about every time she was in one of those sessions.

But, she knew if she wanted to keep her job, she'd better come up with something, anything. Desperate, she began querying total strangers. The girl at the dry cleaners, the mailman, the baker's wife, the kid who walked the brown mutt in the morning, the old men who sat on the bench near the park, it didn't matter. Wherever she was, she asked whoever would talk to her what he or she thought a computer should be able to do. Most of the time she'd have to explain what a computer was, but generally, once the conversation got going, ideas started to flow.

Solve problems, calculations, things like that came first, but then, be a dictionary, speak, sing, keep track of weather, be portable. She was never at a loss for what to say at a meeting again. Eventually, Chief Lansing, himself, assigned her a seat next to his.

"Fascinating idea, Sylvia." He said it all the time now, and it was obvious he was impressed with her.

In less than a year and just before her twenty-sixth birthday, Mr. Lansing put Sylvia in charge of the Department of Research and Development. She had her own office, her own staff, and a hefty raise. She really was surprised and pleased, and almost happy. She'd been so dismal for so long, she wasn't quite sure she knew what being happy felt like. But she was making progress. She embraced the challenge of being part of a company whose goal it was to make the world a better place through new technologies. She believed she could make a difference in the lives of many people if she did her job well. It was this belief that was beginning to silence the horrors of her past.

Late one Saturday afternoon after canvassing several teenagers in the park for ideas, Sylvia went to the movies alone. She was looking forward to clearing her head and mindlessly watching Bogie and Bacall duke it out. She arrived at the theater in time to catch the newsreel. There were the opening credits and, before she could turn away, a montage of war photos, her photos! In rapid succession and to the sound of troops marching and bombs exploding, they flashed before her eyes. She gasped, stunned by the carnage, the recognizable terrors she'd witnessed firsthand.

Oh dear God, the war, again, the whole horrible war.

She fumbled trying to get out of her seat, pull her jacket on, and leave.

Too late. There, on the screen!

"Little Boy"!

"Fat Man"!

The narrator excitedly describing the decibels, ranges, the numbers of victims.

There on the big screen, the blasts, the clouds, the dead.

Head throbbing, Sylvia ran out of the theater and onto the busy sidewalk. She could barely see through her tears. Would the war never end for her...never ever?

She looked around.

No one else seems bother by what we did. What's wrong with me?

God she was sick and tired of the highs and lows. One minute everything was almost okay, the next, she was almost ready to do something terrible to herself.

The vestibule of her apartment building smelled of stale cigarettes which sickened her even more than she already was. She held her breath and hurried toward the door to the stairwell, but damn if there was something in her mailbox. Reluctantly, she went back, opened the box, and took the envelope out. No return address. Indistinguishable postmark. Something vaguely familiar about the handwriting though. She shoved the envelope in her pocket and climbed the stairs to her place.

Later, lying on her bed listlessly watching the lights from the street blink on the ceiling, she imagined killing herself, how she might go about it without too much fuss; but her options all seemed messy and inconvenient, and would it really solve anything to self-destruct? And even if it would end the pain she was feeling now, did she really have it in her to brazenly welcome death, actually make it happen? And weren't there minutes, hours, days, even weeks when she was alright?

The sudden sound of a siren made her heart race, and she whispered a quick Hail Mary for whoever was in trouble. It was a habit of hers. That quick little prayer did something to her, and she was crying again, this time begging God's forgiveness for even thinking what she was thinking. She had to stop the self-pity. There was much to be grateful for. At least she was alive to remember the bad stuff. She had time. So many millions of others didn't.

Okay, she'd go get the envelope and see what was inside. Maybe it'd be good news. She stood by the window and opened it in the light from the streetlamp.

No heading. Only a few sentences:

Dear Sylvia,

Thank you for being my only friend. I always liked you. No, I always loved you. I want you to know the truth because by the time you read this, I will be gone. The bombs. Well, I worked on that project. I helped make them happen.

Your friend,
Jacob C.

PART TWO

1

At dusk, before the cicadas got started, a chirping bat broke the silence and swooped over their heads. Jake Dwyer stood beside Sylvia on the towpath, the air heady with the scent of the wild honeysuckle. A pair of geese flew past, slowed, and skidded feet first into the swollen Delaware River.

"I'm glad you're here," Sylvia said as she looked up at the tall, young man and saw again in the last light of day how beautiful he was. When she'd first interviewed him for an internship at Lansing, she was taken aback by his boyish good-looks. She really did not want such a distraction around; but his resume, though short, was too impressive for her to ignore. He graduated a year ahead of schedule from the most competitive public high school in the city and had completed two semesters at NYU with a perfect cumulative average. Reluctantly, she'd offered him the position, and she'd never once regretted it.

Early in the day, around noon, they'd hiked north along the river from Sylvia's weekend cottage in Stockton, New Jersey, all the way to Bull's Island. Now they were almost back to the path that led to her cottage. The sight of the geese had stopped them and made them look toward the river.

"It's been a nice day," Jake said without taking his eyes off the geese.

"We both needed a break from work, didn't we?" said Sylvia.

"I'd have to agree to that. You've been under plenty of pressure lately." Jake picked up a stone and skipped it across the surface of the water.

"Howard used to do that, but I never could."

"Why didn't he teach you?"

"Oh, back then my husband considered me nothing but a little pest."

"You? A pest?"

"I was just a kid. We both were kids. We'd sneak down to the river, and Howard would show off how good he was at skipping stones."

"I'll teach you now." Jake picked up another stone and handed it to Sylvia. "See hold it sideways and put your index finger over the curve. Now watch." He hurled the stone sideways and it skimmed the surface.

"Three skips! Great!"

"You try." He handed her a flat stone the size of her palm.

She gripped it the way he'd shown her and mimicked his sideways throw, but the stone sunk the minute it hit the water. "I'm hopeless. At least that's what Howard used to tell me." Then, without thinking, Sylvia said, "God, I still miss him. After nearly twenty…Oh hell, don't let me get started."

She kicked at the gravel and fought off the feeling that a hundred years could pass and she'd never get over losing Howard. Maybe, if she'd stayed in Tortola and married Virgil…maybe then she would've been able to forget; but she hadn't, and now Howard's memory was a part of her mission, her daily life, almost her every thought.

"Let's go back and open a bottle of Chianti." She smiled up at Jake.

Jake smiled back. "I agree with popping the cork on the wine, but I don't agree that you are hopeless. Tomorrow, we start at dawn and won't stop until you skip a stone across that river."

"Okay, and I promise I won't say a word about Howard, you must be sick of hearing about Howard."

"Actually, I'm not. I've spent so much time on his project that I feel like he's inside my head. It's weird, tough to explain, but it's like I know what he would be thinking if he were alive."

"Really?"

"Really."

"So what does my dead husband think about me not being able to get his prototype to work? I'll bet he thinks I'm a mess. You have no idea how obsessive he was when it came to his work. He wouldn't let anything or anyone stand in his way."

"Maybe he was like that; but if he were here right now, I think he would say you were doing a great job."

"Thanks for trying to make me feel better, but I'm positive he'd be disappointed," Sylvia said as she turned away from the river.

Jake followed her on the path that led to the rear of her cottage. He sat on back porch steps, untied his boots, and pushed them off one at a time.

"Be right back." Sylvia went past him into the kitchen and flipped on the light over the stove. When she looked back, she caught Jake watching her through the screen door. He'd been doing that a lot lately. It was like he was trying to figure something out about her. Maybe he had ulterior motives for being so attentive. Her money, her position at Lansing, her apartment, her cottage, all she was and all she had, would, of course, be enticing to a young man just starting out. She could make things, big things, happen for someone like Jake Dwyer. She smiled at him and his face lit up.

God, he's gorgeous. She had to admit, the way he looked at her with those eyes the color of corn husks, the same color as Howard's...was that what it was about Jake that made her feel...like a girl again?

She'd seen his birthdate on his application. It jumped out at her because it was the same day and year Howard died, September 23, 1940. So Jake was twenty-three now, the same age Howard was when it'd happened, and she'd been only eighteen.

What in God's name was she thinking inviting Jake to the cottage? He was nearly two decades younger than she was. And she was about to open a bottle of wine and have a drink with him?

Well, there may be a huge difference between them in years, but Jake had proven to be her intellectual equal. More progress had been made on the program for the Fluke in the months since Jake had been at Lansing than in all the time she'd been trying to get it to work. He was patient, persistent, indefatigable. Maybe that was what drew her to him, his mind and the fact that he might be the one to make Howard's dream a reality.

True, Sylvia had thrown herself into other projects at Lansing and had only worked sporadically and in secret on the Fluke. She couldn't entirely give up on Howard's prototype. If the wrong person had gotten his or her hands on it, if it ever became operational, then she needed to have the same technology in order to even the playing field.

When she felt she was on track, she confided in Chief Lansing who gave her his blessing and the funding she needed to move forward. Hiring Jake was a last resort. She'd been stumped, even with a new mainframe. Both Lansing, who had tried to help, and she had run out of steam. Sylvia hated to do it, but she widened the small circle to include the young genius.

The bottom line was, Sylvia needed Jake Dwyer badly and sharing a glass of Chianti wouldn't be the end of the world.

She opened the wine and grabbed the glasses and couldn't stifle her exhilaration. It was fun being around Jake. Before she left the kitchen, she turned off the light and turned on the radio. Tommy Edwards was singing, "...then I'll kiss your lips...."

The yellow chrysanthemums with the fireflies twinkling around them were luminous in the moonlight. Sylvia sat down next to Jake. He took the wine and she held the glasses up while he filled them. He raised his to her and said cheerfully, "A toast to the new leader of Lansing Technologies!"

"Thank you, kindly, but you know how bittersweet this promotion is." She half-heartedly clinked her glass with his.

"You should be proud of yourself," Jake said, "moving up from lab tech to running the whole damn company. You must be the only woman in America, or the world for that matter, running an operation like Lansing."

A cloud had wiped the moon from the sky. Sylvia could no longer see Jake's face clearly, but she felt his breath on her cheek and sensed he was staring at her.

Big deal, sure, she thought, *but it's only because....*

"Look," Sylvia said, "I don't want to talk about it, not yet, anyway."

"Sylvia, come on. I know you've got to be torn up inside. Mr. Lansing was your friend and you cared for him. Of course, you're upset, but Lansing left his legacy to you. He'd want you to be happy about it."

"He would...."

Sylvia fell silent and took a sip of wine. It warmed her insides. Yes, she'd taken over the reins at Lansing. Yes, there'd be no limit now to what she could accomplish, especially with Jake by her side. Then an odd image popped into her head, Jake riding to the interview on a skateboard! She'd watched him from the window of her office. He sailed down 3rd Avenue, his suit jacket flying out behind him like Superman's cape.

"What is it then, Sylvia?" asked Jake. "Are you afraid of moving into the big office, of leaving the lab behind?"

"I wouldn't say I'm afraid, but you can't understand what it feels like to have to make such a big change."

"No, I probably can't. I wouldn't want to leave the lab. I love it down there watching over that bastard of a machine, trying to line up those relays, stroking all those wires into action. Hell, I'd die in a normal office with a phone and a secretary."

"I never wanted any of that either, Jake. Lansing was the one. He could talk me into anything. He was a generous man and that made you want to be generous back. He taught me so much. He was family to me. Losing him, well, is like losing a part of myself."

The moon was out again. Jake leaned over and boldly tucked a strand of hair behind Sylvia's ear. Such a tender gesture. *Not since Virgil,* she thought. And in Jake's eyes she could see the pleasure he was getting from looking at her, touching her.

After his internship, when he'd graduated from NYU, she'd hired him full-time. In the year since he never once disappointed her. He had imagination and patience, the perfect set of twin qualities. With Lansing Technologies, he was on the cutting edge of the computer industry, and how many times had he thanked Sylvia for putting him there. The corporation was ready to install a third generation mainframe. It would be his baby, and she knew he could hardly wait.

"Sylvia." His voice low, like fluttering wings. His breath hot on her neck. "Sylvia, I want you to be happy. Let me help you to be happy."

When she felt his lips on her neck, she stiffened and said, "You're friendship makes me happy, Jake."

But instead of backing off, he put his arm around her and kissed her neck again. He opened his mouth. His hot tongue swirled on her skin.

She pulled back. He wasn't just a friend. He was an employee, her employee. But the song on the radio was still playing, "...and your heart will fly away..." and Jake put his glass down, held her face in his hands, and kissed her cheek. She inhaled his breath, sweet like the wine. She was about to say, we can't do this, but he put his forehead against hers and said, "Don't be afraid. I know what I'm doing."

"But Jake, I'm so much older than…."

He kissed her. The heat of the kiss spread through Sylvia like a fever. His lips, soft and warm. His arms around her. The sensation of his hands on her back made her hesitate. Jake stopped kissing her. "Your age doesn't matter to me, Sylvia. We were meant to be together."

His words fell into a part of her heart that, after Virgil, she'd buried beneath years of work, hours of her life spent on theorems, diagrams, charts, meetings, traveling, taking photographs…. How could anything or anyone ever get to this part of her again?

But her lips felt like they were on fire.

For years, when she was lonely or depressed, Sylvia reached for her camera and lost herself in capturing whatever there was to capture on film. Her whole world revolved around her camera and her company. There was nothing else for her, no one for her. So why now? Why Jake?

His hands were under her shirt, undoing her bra, and she found herself helping him, wriggling out of her clothes, not caring they were on her porch, not caring someone might see.

She laid back. Her body was alive like it used to be with Howard, with Virgil. How wonderful it felt to be wet and hot and know that soon she wouldn't be thinking of anything, soon her body would take over, her mind shut down. Sylvia turned and kissed Jake as passionately as she'd ever kissed anyone. Finally, joyfully, she was ready to give in to Jake Dwyer, in to her own need to have him.

But just when she could feel the sweet release coming, everything else crowded in on her: dead sailors, wounded bodies, war ships, Turing, Jacob, Howard. Dead Howard. Howard. How could she do this? How could she be happy with all of the evilness coming alive, too? It was all there inside her, but right at this moment none of it could hurt her, and there was nothing for her to do, but let it all go.

When it was over, Sylvia stared up into the blackness. She was completely naked and drenched in sweat. Jake was next to her, his heavy arm weighing her down. He'd fallen fast asleep. The odor of their bodies intermingled in the cool night air. Sylvia listened to the sound of the mosquitos buzzing around them and to Jake's heavy breathing.

How can I get him off me? She didn't want to wake him because now remorse had set in; and all she wanted was to go upstairs, take a shower, climb into her soft clean bed, and fall fast asleep. *Alone.* She didn't want to look at him or talk to him or hear the sound of his voice. All she wanted to do was undo what she had done.

2

Chairman Masuki Shin was on the warpath. The first thing he did when he arrived at Noboru Industries was ream out his custodians about what they hadn't done right yesterday and threaten them that it had better be done right today. Today was *the* day! The day of his demonstration. All had to be perfect.

Masuki watched as the poor menial laborers cowed in fear. He knew they knew their jobs dangled from a slender, kiss-ass thread, and the demands on them were like poop rolling downhill. Yamato dumped on Masuki and Masuki dumped on them. Well, it had been good for them to be dealt with so harshly. Out of necessity, they'd become as anal about cleanliness as both Yamato and Masuki were; but why did they always fail to keep the conference room with that ugly white shag rug clean? Granted the thing was almost twenty years old, but it was still so highly prized by Yamato. No, Masuki would show no mercy. Today of all days, that carpet and that room had to be clean.

One brave soldier in the battle of the rug tried to explain to Chairman Masuki that no matter what they did, what type of equipment or products they used, fibers, millions of them, like a minion of specters rising up from hell, worse than cat hair or dog hair or dandruff, shagged free, infiltrated the air, and settled over everything in the room.

Masuki cut him off with a wave of his hand. "No excuses."

So the custodians powered up three giant vacuums and swept the nozzles over all surfaces and each inch of airspace trying to suck up what dust they could.

Masuki, observing their valiant efforts, was momentarily assuaged. It gave him hope that this would not be a disappointing day, that his workers trying to satisfy him was an auspicious omen.

Masuki entered the conference room late and nodded to the four other department chairmen who were already seated and most likely fuming over his apparent rudeness. Masuki paused behind his place at the table, took a deep breath, and bowed ceremoniously to Chief Yamato, who was seated at the far end of the long granite table in an enormous pigskin armchair that made him look like a dwarf. Masuki Shin remained slightly bent over, but lifted his head. A new generation of fibers were doing pirouettes in the bright rays of sunlight, and he had all he could do to keep from going back into the hallway and finding one of his custodians to thrash. Their best effort wasn't at all good enough.

Ignore it. There are more important things right now. He fought to contain his annoyance, to start the meeting and stop worrying about the blasted motes in the air. Someone would pay for that later.

The matter at hand could not be put off another second so he took his seat opposite Yamato and gently adjusted the knot of his tie while surveying the men to either side of him. Such loathsome faces, the features chiseled by fear, hacked by jealousy. Masuki knew their hearts were the hearts of ravenous vultures eager to consume the corpse of his failure. Theirs was a cutthroat world, devour or be devoured; and Masuki was, quite frankly, tired of being devoured, tired of being ridiculed and doubted, tired of being Yamato's lackey.

They are right to fear me, and soon they will have good reason to be jealous, he thought, *because this time I have done it. The prototype works! And that achievement will catapult me up the corporate ladder. When stupid, old Yamato leaves, or dies, it will be me they will have to obey. What a bitter pill for them to swallow. But one they deserve; one I will enjoy forcing down their scrawny throats.*

Yamato, too, was doing his best to appear vacant. His eyes were fixed almost dreamily—Masuki shuddered at the notion—on Masuki's pursed lips. He wasn't fooled. Chief Yamato, when he cared to, could whip an unsuspecting employee into a froth with a glance. Behind those rheumy eyes, the placid dullness of them, Chairman Masuki knew the small man's mind was calculating his own vulnerability. It had been decades since Yamato himself had created Noboru Industries' answer to the Leica. His Shootfire was revolutionary, and its popularity carried

Yamato to the top of the corporate ladder. But since the Shootfire, there'd only been some minor adaptations in the company's product line, not enough to prevent stagnation. Noboru's dominance in the world of camera design depended on someone coming up with something innovative, something spectacular. That person, if he were clever enough, could usurp even the Chief's position.

Chairman Masuki's mouth was dry with anticipation. He swallowed and paused meaningfully for dramatic effect before beginning.

"The Department of Research and Development is pleased to announce the creation of what will become the greatest camera in the world. What you have asked me to do, Mr. Chief, is done. I...I mean, we, my department and I have finally perfected the prototype. It is now fully functional. What it can do—and I will demonstrate it for you in a moment—will astound you."

The four other chairmen simultaneously exhaled. They exchanged furtive glances and fidgeted with their notebooks. The Chief's face bunched up into a churlish smirk. Masuki expected this nonplus reaction. Once again, as far as any of them could tell, he was making the same old, ridiculous claim. How many times in the past almost twenty years had they heard it? Everyone had given up hope long ago that anyone at Noboru, let alone Masuki, would ever make Yamato's dream camera a reality.

Masuki ignored them and continued, "The working name, which I hope the corporation will agree to keep, is the Warrior. I selected this name in honor of the African natives who first inspired the original prototype. To refresh your memories, I will reiterate the history of the prototype."

Their sighs only made Masuki more determined than ever to have his say. *To hell with you feeble-minded, old fools.*

"Two decades ago in the 1940's," Masuki continued, his voice clear as a bell, "a young American scholar named Howard Russo took a class in anthropology. There he learned of the odd reactions Masai tribe members had to the white man's cameras. The women, the children, even the bravest of the warriors were terrified of the small machines. When the anthropologists showed the tribe's people the photographs of themselves, they collapsed in fear thinking the camera had captured their minds and their spirits. The machine made them empty shells, bodies without essence. They wept and cried out, overwhelmed with grief for the part of them that had been stolen by the camera."

Shin could see he was losing their attention. They were all staring down at their distorted reflections in the black granite, most assuredly trying to block out the sound of his voice.

He ignored their insolence, leaned slightly forward, and said more firmly, "We, too, know what fear and madness, what pain and suffering man's inventions can cause. Not long after young Mr. Russo learned of the Masai and set about creating a camera that could capture the essence of its subject, something the United States of America created destroyed much of our beloved country. Which of us will ever be able to forget Nagasaki, Hiroshima?"

Masuki Shin's lower lip quivered. "Listen to me. With the Warrior we will never suffer indignation or defeat like that again."

His plea to their patriotism seemed to fall on deaf ears. Damn it, he knew he was rambling. He hadn't wanted to, but then he thought, *to hell with these men who I know loathe me. I will have my say.* He puffed out his chest and focused on the top of the Chief's balding head.

"Mr. Howard Russo, though an American, was an engineering student at Oxford University during World War II when the bombing over there was just beginning. Photography was his hobby. He rebuilt an old Leica and achieved unprecedented clarity. He wasn't satisfied, though, and came up with the idea of feeding his photographs into the new mainframe computer the university had just installed. He was going to try to use the computer to manipulate the clarity of the photos. He wanted to capture, as I said before, the very essence of his subjects. Fortunately, though, for Noboru Industries—really, gentlemen, for all of us—our Chief, a great visionary, indeed..." Masuki nearly choked on the compliment and had to clear his throat. "...learned from one of his spies, about this radical idea, and he spared no expense to acquire young Russo's nascent prototype."

Masuki paused, and when Yamato looked up, Masuki bowed dramatically. The Chief, in response, fluttered his eyelids as if to say, big deal, I've heard it all before.

This infuriated Chairman Masuki. He clenched his jaw so tightly his teeth hurt, the muscles of his face quivered, but through the thick flesh of his moon-shaped cheeks, his anger was imperceptible.

He wanted to rush ahead and reveal everything, but he swallowed hard and whispered, "The Warrior will make our company the most powerful entity on the planet. With a camera that can take someone's picture and transfer it into a computer where we can control that person, well, as you can see, the possibilities indeed are infinite."

He saw his colleagues exchange glances and his boss wince slightly.

More skepticism or was what he said finally sinking in? He couldn't be sure.

"Think about what this means," he continued. "We will be capable of controlling anyone whose picture we take. Anyone! An impossible dream is now Noboru Industries' reality. With the Warrior we will ride the crest of the wave of an eternal apogee!" Masuki Shin's voice cracked, his armpits and groin dampened. He shifted his weight in his chair. How he wanted to get up, get some air, cool off. He was getting ahead of himself, bragging too much, when he should just get on with the demonstration. He placed his hands in front of him, one atop the other as evenly as he could. Beads of sweat broke out on his forehead. He waited for the Chief's response.

"Alright." Yamato's voice was shrill and impatient. "Get on with it."

"Gladly, sir." Masuki stood up, reached in his breast pocket, and pressed the button on a small device.

The enormous double glass doors, beautifully etched with fire-breathing dragons, opened. Chairman Masuki's assistant, a somewhat homely, young woman entered. She was dressed, as he had so ordered, in a black tailored jacket, crisp white blouse, black pencil skirt, and white gloves. From a distance she looked quite nice, but on closer inspection a certain lack of symmetry in her face was evident. The right side slanted back from her nose further than the left side. Her forehead was short. Her most redeeming feature, her small but well-shaped mouth seemed lost in the large space between her wide nose and long chin. Her hair was pulled back into a knot at the nape of her neck; and, though each strand gleamed like a thread of silk, she didn't have enough of it to keep her pale scalp from peeking through the gaps. She was short, stood only a head taller than the seated Masuki, and looked childlike enough to be his granddaughter.

In her gloved hands she carried a ten by twelve by six inch grey metal case. In the precise moves Masuki had choreographed for her, she lifted the lid of the case, removed a slim rectangle of polished steel, and flipped open a large lens. The camera looked like a dazzling cubistic sculpture, wrought by a genius with an eye for modern restraint. Light glinted off the sides of the compact wonder.

Masuki stared at it as the young woman held it up. How proud he was and of his assistant too! She handled the camera with dexterity and respect, turning it and tilting it so the men could admire it, but not touch it, as she walked around the table and paused by each of them.

Their faces revealed little emotion, but the Chief appeared to be irritated.

The old goat's thinking, once again, all showmanship, no substance, and wondering why he didn't rid of such a blowhard as me years ago. Masuki knew this is what was going through Yamato's mind, but Masuki was so confident this time he ignored the anger bubbling up inside his boss.

"Shall we proceed with the demonstration, Mr. Chief?"

The Chief's mouth turned down into a sad little hill, and he snapped, "Stop wasting our time, you fool, and get on with it."

Masuki grinned at Yamato and motioned for his assistant to hand him the camera. Gingerly he took it, raised it to his eye, and aimed the red lens at the young woman. She stepped back and smiled a closed-mouth smile. Through the viewfinder he could see her lips were trembling. Then they parted to reveal her crooked teeth. He adjusted the aperture until her face came into sharper focus. He pressed a button––click––and held it. The machine emitted a soft whirring sound like a chorus of tiny frogs singing at dusk. The young woman's eyes were riveted on the swirling red lens, on the aperture, on the thin bright undulating waves that snaked hypnotically across the fragile glass opening and turned green and blue. His assistant had told him in the lab that she'd only seen such unusual colors in photographs of the aurora borealis.

Masuki, still compressing the button, observed through the aperture how the hard blackness of her eyes softened. By now she should be in an only slightly altered state, not exactly brain-numb, but something akin to that.

He released the button. The whirring stopped. His assistant blinked and looked dumbly at him. She seemed to be trying to think of what she was supposed to do next. But Shin knew whatever thoughts she had, as soon as they came into her mind, drifted off quickly into some unreachable miasmas.

Relieved and confident, he smiled warmly at her, "Go now."

She turned on his command, her body first, her head following. Slowly, she wobbled through the doorway, her limbs completely out of sync with her torso. Another lucky omen.

"Now, to the laboratory, if you will?" he said as he carefully returned the camera to its case and, carrying it with him, led the way out.

It was a short trip down on the elevator to the basement level containment room where Masuki plugged one end of a cable into the side of the camera and the other into a portal on the side of the massive computer and sat down at the keyboard. The chairmen, the Chief in the center, formed a neat, polite semi-circle behind him.

The young woman's face appeared on the monitor. Concentrating on the task at hand, was a little difficult because Masuki couldn't help noticing how much prettier his young assistant looked on the screen. She appeared more attractive than he ever found her to be in person. A small dimple on her left cheek. He hadn't noticed it before, but now found it quite inviting. Her eyelashes were long. Her skin like white jade. *A pity*, he thought as his hands began to sweat. Memories were rising up inside him. *Not now. Don't think about these things now.*

There had been indiscretions, many of them. He pictured one time when he was on top of her, her face, a cool pond without a ripple. For some reason that had infuriated him. He slapped her and came the minute he saw the tears pooling in her eyes.

Stop it, he thought, *this is no time to think about…*but the intensity of such pleasure was in his head for he had exploded in her, unlike any time before, or, for that matter, since. He remembered her wetness, the way her insides clenched his penis even as her tears flowed down her temples. Inside her he felt bigger, knew she made him bigger than he ever was with anyone else. She was so young, still only a girl, really.

Stop, he told himself again, *now is no time to recall the way such young forbidden fruit, such forbidden things, heightened the thrill, made me insane with passion.* Oh, how this girl had made him resent going home to his wife, with whom all had become so predictable.

It wasn't that he had forced himself on her, not exactly, but the way she squirmed under his weight or tried to extricate herself from between the wall and his body, or the floor and his body, the way she whimpered like she was trying to stifle a scream when he was behind her and in her…*oh, just the thought of….*

He licked his lips, swiped the sleeve of his impeccably tailored suit across his forehead. No time for hesitation, for second-guessing. He typed the command quickly, pushed enter.

It was done.

"We must return to the conference room now," he announced. "We have only a few minutes to wait, and then you will see the miracle the Warrior can perform."

Masuki picked up the camera and walked briskly to the elevator. The entourage slugged along behind him. He knew they were thinking it was all a charade. He was sure the chairmen were hoping Yamato would lash out at him and fire him at last, and Yamato was probably already formulating his tirade.

Meanwhile, though, Shin struggled to hide his excitement. All the decades of work, all the frustrations and failures, the nights spent in the company's sleeping tubes where it was difficult for him to so much as roll over––he'd gotten so fat––would only be sore little parts of his past now. The Chief couldn't help but be impressed with his breakthrough, with his all-consuming loyalty and fierce determination, with his ability to drive himself and his underlings to the brink of exhaustion and not give up. Visions of promotions, bonuses, shares, money danced in his head. He could see himself, very soon, somewhere near, if not at the top, of the Noboru food chain.

3

"It's not my fault business has been slow." Virgil stared at the rough condition of his sandals as he talked out loud to himself. He leaned back in his creaky old office chair and plopped his tired feet atop the piles of paperwork strewn across the desk top. "God damn hurricane, bloody Mother Nature!" he continued.

He didn't usually talk to himself, but he wasn't in the best of moods. Things were not going well for him. The Mercy and the Goodness, two of his small fleet of fishing boats had suffered severe damage. That left the single engine, the Love, available for the season. How was he supposed to make any money when he could only accommodate two fishermen at a time? Harriet had been forced to take a second job at Pusey's Tavern in Road Town to help make ends meet; and, again, they'd postponed plans to get pregnant. Could he approach his brother-in-law for another loan? It was embarrassing, humiliating. He hated having to go to La Bomba because this time some sort of service would be required in return, for sure. Being Harriet's husband just wouldn't cut it anymore.

Christ, he felt like a bloody worm—a small, powerless, slimy, creature who could easily be squished into nothingness. Shit, he was more disgruntled and feeling more pathetic than usual. Yeah, sure, the evil deed he'd done was there, always there, close to the surface. He couldn't stop himself from going over it again and again like running his tongue over the edge of a jagged tooth. Instead of fading with each passing year, the memory of it grew into sharper focus and loomed larger than life itself inside his pounding brain.

"I've tried to make up for things and make a go of it, I really have," he said to the top of his desk as he leaned forward and picked up his framed wedding picture. He even had regrets about his marriage, lesser regrets, but regrets all the same. It wasn't that he didn't find his wife attractive. No, there was not a more beautiful woman on the island. He looked at the photo. *She was beautiful then. She is beautiful now.*

No, Harriet was not the problem. He was. He thought of the party that followed the wedding and lasted long into the night. While Harriet danced with her family and friends in celebration, with such joy, he went out to the water's edge to clear his head. He should have been elated. He was young and embarking on the kind of relationship he thought he wanted, he thought would turn things around. Instead, though, he felt absolutely nothing, and that scared the hell out of him.

A fucking cold stone where a heart should be, he hated himself for being such a zero on his own wedding night. Harriet deserved better than what he was. *I pulled her down into the fucking rut with me. I shouldn't have married her. I should've gone after that bastard Astin and killed him, the bloody liar.*

He had known from the beginning, from that day Sylvia left, there was no hope for him. Damn it, he should've gone after her too and not let her get away.

"Bad karma, really bad karma," Virgil said this as he dug through the desk drawer and found his brown leather pouch. He unzipped it, took out a small pipe, and a rock of hashish, the size of a pebble. He fumbled around in the drawer looking for his lighter, found it, and held it over the pipe on an angle while he flicked it to life and the rock glowed like a small ruby. He inhaled hard and held it until he coughed the smoke out and it filled the space around his head. Had someone walked in on him, they would have thought his face was on fire.

Several hits later, Virgil was ready to make the visit to his brother-in-law. *So what if he knows I'm high? Who the hell cares?*

He grabbed his sunglasses and stuck them on his head to hold his hair back. He stood up and turned to look at himself in the small mirror Harriet had hung by the door. He could see fine lines crisscrossing the once-smooth skin of his face. The whites of his eyes were yellow and webbed with tiny red veins. Wrinkles fanned out from his eyes toward his temples. His nose was sunburnt, his once thick golden curls stringy and dull and tangled with grey.

Forty blasted years old, he thought, *now what?* He made a face that was sarcastic and cruel as he glared at himself. "I hate you, you stupid bastard." He was talking out loud to himself again. "Yeah, you really fucked your life up." He walked out of the door and slammed it hard behind him.

Surprisingly, La Bomba agreed to loan Virgil more money. The only thing he wanted in return was for Virgil to get those boats out on the water before the season started. So after Virgil slept off his morning high, he headed to the marina. He felt better now, even hopeful. He could pay for the parts he needed. The weather was mild. Maybe the tourists would return. He'd heard talk that a cruise ship might start making regular stops in Tortola. That would be big, really big, a steady stream of customers with money in their pockets. He jumped on board the deck of the Mercy, unscrewed the panels beneath the wheel, and began taking the engine apart.

4

As the small group exited the elevator and reentered the conference room, Masuki Shin was thinking about the first time he heard of the prototype. It was back in the early '40s before the bombings began. There had been rumors that the Chief had spies all over the globe. Yamato had enough business savvy to know he had to stay on the cutting edge of technology. Innovate or deteriorate. Where better to uncover the next big thing than on the campuses of the world's great universities? So when the photography exhibition at Oxford, featuring the already highly acclaimed work of engineering student, Howard Russo, was announced, Yamato's man in England was dispatched to investigate.

Even before the doors to Ashmolean Hall opened, Yamato Yoshio was well aware of the skepticism of Russo's professors concerning his hypothesis. Linking a camera to a computer and somehow being able to program the subject of a photograph was an outlandish idea. But not to Yamato. So intrigued was he that he instructed his spy to procure, at any cost, Mr. Russo's modified Leica, and soon the crude prototype arrived at Noboru Industries. It was then that the young man Masuki Shin was given the near-impossible task of making it work.

A better computer had to be created and a better program, and it had to work in tandem with a camera that was like no other. How many times had Chief Yamato been on the brink of firing Masuki and his whole department? It had been a nightmare, but somehow Masuki had survived; and now he was so close to success he found the anticipation unbearable. He was sure the camera and the program were airtight; but, most importantly, he was sure he had chosen the right subject for the demonstration.

He carefully considered which staff member would be the best candidate. He needed someone who was smart, but who would also be susceptible to being controlled. His assistant, Segawa Megumi, he believed, fell into that category. She had one of the most gifted minds he had ever encountered. She had an extremely high aptitude for problem-solving. She knew her way around the giant mainframe, knew how to communicate with it. In fact, she had been instrumental in overcoming some of the most difficult glitches in the current program. Besides Masuki, she was the only other person in the world who might be able to operate it.

But, on the other hand, she quickly and mutely obeyed all of her superiors at Noboru without fail. She, in fact, seldom spoke. Shin could not, at the moment, recall what her voice sounded like. Maybe like the muffled chirping of a wren in a windstorm. She was a blindly loyal, devoted employee whose only purpose in life was to please the company officials, especially, Chairman Masuki, no matter what it took.

And why shouldn't she want to please him? Hadn't he been the one to hire her right after she finished her degree, to pluck her from the masses, mentor her, teach her all he knew? Hadn't he helped her advance to become his first assistant? There were others he might have chosen.

And hadn't he given her pleasure? Did her wet insides lie? True, he'd been forceful, and he'd taken her unawares that first time. To be honest, her repulsion then was almost palpable, but he ignored it. And after, she never once refused his advances, though he thought he sometimes saw dread in her eyes, when he dared to look into them. But, nonetheless, she never openly spurned him.

He knew what was best for her, best for an inexperienced young woman. Yes, young women needed to be controlled, kept in their places. His rough treatment of her had been good for her, and for him, well, for him it had been heaven. Her fragility, the scent of her fear, the moment she relented and subjugated herself to him made him feel as though he had conquered the world.

Yes, she was the one who would enable him to conquer the world now. She wanted the camera to work almost as much as he did. She had a crucial stake in its success.

And though using the camera on Megumi did involve risks,—she could become dumb, brainless, totally mute—the benefits for Masuki outweighed them. She could be made to do things she didn't want to do. She would lose her will to choose. He would be able to control her even more than he did now.

When Shin approached her about being the subject of the demonstration, she bowed profusely, told him in her unobtrusive way she was honored by his decision, and saw it as a great reward for all of the long hours, the endless days she'd devoted to the project. It filled her with gratitude to be recognized, if only secondarily, by the Chief and the other chairmen. It was, most of all, the greatest honor for her to be of service to him, Masuki Shin, her great and beloved mentor.

It was more than she'd ever said at one time to him. Her lowered eyes and flattering words made him swell, and were they not in the lab with others nearby he would have lifted her tight straight skirt, pulled down her hose and her panties, and fucked her. Instead, he put his hands down to hide his excitement and told her that they would demonstrate the mind-control capabilities of the camera in a more complex way than prior experiments. Up to now, they had only tried the camera and program out on mice, and the results, quite honestly, had been erratic.

"Will it hurt?" She'd never been hypnotized before in her life. "I'm a little afraid."

"My dear, it never bothered the mice." Masuki thought it odd that she would worry about mindlessness hurting when she taken such hammerings from him.

"True, they did seem to come out of the trances easily." She seemed to be thinking back. She lowered her head, but boldly kept her eyes on Shin. "I trust you, and hope I perform well so everyone will believe in what we have done...I mean, what *you* have done." She quickly corrected herself, but it was too late. Masuki had heard her.

How dare she try to take half of the credit? The thought flashed through his mind like lightning. And at that moment he finalized his plan. He knew now exactly what he would make her do.

5

Megumi stared down at her folded hands painfully aware of her blunder. She wished she could reach in Chairman Masuki's monkey ears and pull her words out. She didn't like this man, not one bit. That first time she smelled him sneaking up behind her, she thought he was a skunk. She loathed the thought of him touching her just as she felt his cold, clammy hands on her bare arms. She was frightened, and her instinct was to turn and slap him hard across his fat face, spit in his small eyes, and walk away. But resisting him would end her career and put her on the street with other intelligent women who had said no to powerful old lechers.

He turned her around, pushed her to her knees. His penis was out. Engorged as it was, it looked no bigger than her thumb.

"Put it in your mouth," he said.

She fought the urge to bite it off and spit it out.

"Suck on it."

Calm down, she told herself, *just try to get it done. Quickly.*

But Masuki couldn't come. He stepped back and pushed her to the floor. He took off his pants and pulled on his penis to make it hard again. She hoped he would make it squirt, but not on her.

When it didn't, he knelt and tried to pull her skirt down. She helped him because she didn't want it to rip, these uniforms were so expensive. He climbed on her, crushing her back into the cold floor. How heavy he was. Then he pushed himself up so he could angle his penis into her. He thrust so hard her head hammered into the wall.

It was horrible, a nightmarish encounter that, unfortunately, was repeated many times over. But she got wise and found a way to make it happen that didn't result in pain.

Lately, she even tried to think about it differently. At the climax, at that last moment, was it not her body that controlled his? Did she not, if only for a split second, have some kind of power over him? Oh, if only she could control him entirely, make him leave his wife, take that wife's place? If she had to put up with his body, why not have his money, too? How different her insignificant life would be if such a powerful man as Masuki Shin were hers.

6

When the chairmen and the Chief were seated, Masuki nodded toward the double doors. Again, he pushed the button on the remote to open them. Segawa Megumi walked steadily through them. She stared straight ahead, her eyes focused on a spot just above the Chief's head. Both her arms were behind her back as though she were stretching her diaphragm by clasping her hands behind her. She came to a stop at the end of the conference table and smiled a queer, closed-mouthed smile.

Nothing happened for several long minutes. She appeared to be frozen in place when suddenly her eyes widened as though she was witnessing something only she could see, something horrible like an explosion or a flame leaping up at her.

Shin saw what he thought was panic in her eyes and moved slowly toward her whispering, "It's all right, dear; everything is all right."

Megumi's mouth opened. Her lips curled back into a grotesque snarl as though she was trying to scream, but nothing was coming out except her tongue. It shot out at the men then wormed around before she began flicking it in and out between her large, crooked teeth. She stared at Shin for several seconds.

I can't fail now, he thought, *not now, not when I've come this far.*

Just as he felt his impatience rising, Megumi swung her arms quickly into the air above her head.

There it is, he was so relieved he could've cried.

It gleamed and flashed in the sunlight.

There it is.

His loyal assistant clutched the long, gleaming dagger in her delicate hands. She held it aloft and slowly lifted her head and moved her eyes up to it. Her dilated pupils were black bullets, her irises wet brown worlds cradled in the crescent moons of her bulging eyeballs. She took a cavernous breath. The men heard how loudly and deeply she sucked the air, the silence that followed.

Masuki held his breath too. *Do it...do it,* he silently commanded.

Before anyone could move, Segawa Megumi plunged the blade into her left breast.

Magnificent, thought Shin, *absolutely magnificent. It worked!*

He had made his lover kill herself exactly the way Juliet had done in the play he believed to be Shakespeare's best, despite what the critics claimed. *What do critics know? Look at my critics now. Look at their stunned faces.*

There had been an initial small squirt of blood, but now it spurted out of the wound. Masuki Shin couldn't help but wince a little as it splattered all over the place to the rhythm of Megumi's still-beating heart. Then her eyes came alive and searched the ceiling in desperation.

Did she, in fact, know what was going on? Shin pushed the thought away. She choked on the blood that was in her throat. He watched as she tried to swallow, tried to say something that came out as a gurgle. Her head wobbled as though it were a heavy weight her willowy neck was struggling to steady. She arched her back, gasped, stood still for a second as though she were on the edge of a cliff and couldn't look down, couldn't look at what was coming. Then her body slumped.

Before Shin could react, she fell forward in slow motion. The chairmen pushed themselves away from the table in horror. The Chief was out of his seat, pressed against the wall.

Megumi careened into the granite. Her face followed the weight of her torso slamming down hard onto the cold stone. Blood splattered everywhere. Her mouth must have been open because her teeth smashed to smithereens, scattered through the blood across the black expanse of the table, and shivered into place.

Like small stars in the night sky, thought Masuki, *trying to create some new, unknown constellation.*

7

Masuki, Sir Astin, and Chief Yamato walked slowly and ceremoniously through what seemed to be miles of corridors before arriving at Yamato's large library, the walls of which were lined with leather-bound books in rich shades of burgundy, brown, and navy. When they seated themselves around a low coffee table, the Chief turned to Masuki and said, "Shin, your demonstration last week was disturbing and attracted far too much attention from the authorities. For this I am tremendously displeased." He then leaned forward, poured himself a cup of yellow tea from the large silver pot, and slowly brought the gleaming cup to his lips.

In the face of Yamato's rudeness at not offering tea, Masuki lowered his head and stared at the creases in his pants and at his hands and the way the pinstripes were running out of the tips of his fingers. He dare not defend himself. Yamato would hear the worry in his voice. He kept his head down and listened to the fat man, Astin's, lumbered exhalations.

"On the other hand." Yamato's voice now sounded somewhat conciliatory. "You have demonstrated beyond a doubt the perfection and effectiveness of the Warrior. I know that this is the crowning glory of more than twenty years of devotion to this project."

Masuki lifted his eyes to meet Yamato's. Could it be true? Yamato was pleased?

Before Masuki could decipher his boss's real intention, Yamato looked back into his tea cup. Masuki glanced at Astin and wondered why he was there.

Masuki had been anxious enough about this meeting with the Chief without this stranger taking it all in. If anyone had to be there, why not the other department chairmen? Masuki wouldn't have minded if those wolves were there, but not this greasy, slovenly person, Astin.

"The applications of such advanced technology are endless, and the success of Noboru Industries will be secured at least for the next four decades," Yamato quietly declared. "It will be the new century before anyone will have the ability to compete with us. We will be the company that will return Japan to her rightful place of power in the world. For this, I am tremendously pleased, and tremendously grateful." Yamato bowed to Shin; and even though his expression remained rigid and unreadable, the gesture made the blood rush into Masuki's cheeks.

"Now, we must get down to business. What we discuss here is of the strictest confidence. No one is to be told what I am about to tell you. All of the other chairmen in the company have been informed of the failure of the Warrior and the unfortunate, though thoroughly understandable, subsequent suicide of your assistant. Shamed by her failure to perfect the program, she had no recourse but to valiantly take her own life. This is how it has been explained. And, I am sure, this was, indeed, part of your clever plan, Shin, to protect yourself and your primacy at Noboru. Now, we are three of only four people in the world who know the truth about our..."

"And who might the fourth be?" interrupted Astin.

"Sir Astin." Yamato shot him a cutting glance. "Allow me to finish. The Warrior will be sent on its first mission in the United States of America. The first subject to be photographed by the Warrior will be an ordinary person, someone considered a failure, a minor criminal who leads a pathetic life. All of the research has been done. All of the arrangements have been made."

Astin had a quizzical look on his face, and his mouth fell open as though he were going to say something. Instead, he nervously moved his bulky frame around in the plush chair and patted his breast pocket to feel for his cigar.

Yamato ignored his commissary's anxiety, glanced at his manicured nails, and ran his thumb over them to test for rough edges before continuing. "Masuki Shin will be dispatched to the state of Texas with the camera and will be taken to the person I have selected as the subject. At that point he is to capture the subject's image without him being aware of it."

Masuki could feel himself getting hot under his collar. Why was his boss, who'd just congratulated him on his success, talking about him as though he weren't there?

Yamato tented his fingers in the air in front of him and studied their tips. There was long silence. Yamato seemed to be contemplating his next pronouncement, or falling asleep. It was hard for Masuki to tell.

"You, Shin," at last he addressed him directly, "will then bring the camera and the image of the man back to Japan. When you load it onto the mainframe, at that time, I will tell you how you will program…"

"Chief Yamato," Astin interrupted, "I apologize in advance for my utter stupidity, but what are you talking about? I was under the impression that you wanted the Warrior operable so we could make money, all of us, lots of money. That's the only reason I've been in it from the start. The money. The damned bloody money! Now you are saying that you want Mr. Masuki here to photograph some criminal? Some American scoundrel? How is that going to make us any money?"

"Why, Sir Astin, I'm surprised by such an outburst? Aren't you happy with what I pay you now?"

Astin's face flushed, but he didn't utter a word. Perhaps, he'd seen in Yamato's eyes the same arrogance Masuki had.

"Now, Sir Astin, as soon as Masuki completes his part of the mission, you will be required to take the Warrior to Tortola where you are to renew your connections with one of your former associates. That young man Virgil Faultington, I believe you used him before? Well, you can certainly blackmail him with the photos you took of him then. It seems in your younger days you were able to think of everything."

"Why bother with that chap? And Tortola. What is there for us on Tortola?"

"Tortola? Did I say anything about Tortola? You will take him to New York City, and that is all you need to know for now. Soon, I will instruct you further. Until then, I warn you, sir, be happy with what I give you and forget your greedy dreams. Remember, Mr. Astin, money is not the only evidence of success and certainly not the only thing that can give one satisfaction in this world."

At this rebuke Astin decisively reached in his breast pocket and took out his cigar.

"Do you mind?" he said this quickly, but he struck a match and had the thing lit before Yamato could object. Yamato needed him once again and that gave Astin leverage. He clenched the fat cigar between his teeth, puckered his big lips around it, and sucked in deeply. When he exhaled, the smoke created a dark cloud in the space between the men.

"I'd have thought you'd just manufacture the blasted thing and sell it to the right people and get all of the peasants under control and just keep them working and buying, working and buying? Why, there would be no end to the wealth, no end. I don't know what you're up to, Chief, but it doesn't much matter to me as long as the money is right, very right," observed Astin, "but have it your way."

"Oh, I most certainly will, that is, have it my way." Yamato peeked at Astin over his tilted tea cup. He finished sipping and turned to Masuki. "Why the puzzled look, Shin?"

Masuki was unsure how far to go. "Chief, forgive me, but how will what we do ensure the financial success of Noboru Industries?" As distasteful as it was to him, he had to agree with Astin.

The Chief's demeanor shifted like a flash of spring lightning, and Masuki shivered in response to the transformation.

"How dare you ask me 'how' anything? Why you are a complete imbecile when it comes to the larger picture. Masuki Shin, you are so small in your thinking I cannot even explain it to you."

He abruptly stopped himself and shifted gears. He needed Masuki for the programming, "Shin, you stick to the programming at which there is no talent like yours and leave all of the strategy to me. You see, business is a complicated matter. At times it is so distasteful, so very political. But never mind all of this for now. You both are good men and will be generously rewarded for you cooperation, as usual."

Masuki failed to stop himself from frowning. There was that hollow promise again of a generous reward. All these years and still Masuki remained underpaid. True, the company would care for him in his old age. For this he felt grateful, but he couldn't escape the dark thought that now hammered at him like a woodpecker hammering away at his hole in a tree. *I am the only one in the whole company who can make the program work...I am the only one in the whole company who can make the program work....I am the only one....*

When Astin and Masuki had been fed and dismissed to their rooms in a far wing of the mansion, the Chief rang for a snifter of cognac to be brought into the library. He settled himself in front of the fireplace which roared with well-seasoned cherry wood. Handel's Water Music played on his newly installed stereo sound system and the smooth liquor, sent to him by the Emperor, felt like warm velvet in his mouth. Then he was distracted by the sound of his beloved dogs yelping in their high-pitched little barks, happily returning from their late evening run, eagerly seeking him out.

"I'm in here, my little darlings," Yoshio called out to them, anxious to see their sweet furry little faces and have their strong tiny pink tongues lovingly lick his face. "Ah, here you come, my sweets, little Hiro, sweet Shima, darling Naga, and, last but not least, my precious Saki. Ah, it is almost set now. The Americans will pay for what they have done to me and to my family." The four animated dogs trying to jump onto his lap all at once were knocking into one another in their excitement and tumbling around in a flurry of white to their owner's complete and perfect delight.

8

The land beneath the feathery film of passing clouds was a khaki tan that stretched out in humps for miles. Every so often there would be a jagged black wound in the stark landscape that marked a deep gorge or dry river bed. Masuki had been to the United States twice before and on those trips he crossed China, stopped in Moscow, Paris, and London, and had only gone as far west as Manhattan, where he did business with prospective franchisees.

Now, for the first time, he was flying east out of Tokyo over the Pacific. There had been a stopover in Los Angeles, but he'd stayed on the plane. After they took off he enjoyed his view of the San Bernardino's, but since them there'd been nothing to look at out his side of the plane. The American Southwest was a colorless, bleak place.

Masuki was dressed as a tourist in brown pants, a plaid short-sleeve shirt, and a fishing vest. He had the Warrior on his lap, its wide camera strap around his neck. He caressed it with both of his soft, well-manicured hands. He had removed neither his sunglasses nor his blue denim hat for the fourteen hours he'd already been traveling.

The plane was three-quarters full with other Japanese tourists heading for a ten-day tour of the Wild West. They were to land in Dallas and spend the afternoon at a rodeo before checking into an unusual motel on the outskirts of the city where all of the rooms were in giant teepees make of plywood, painted in garish colors, and decorated with huge black bands of Navajo designs. Masuki wouldn't get to see these marvels. The Russian operative would meet him at the airport and drive him to his destination in a burgeoning suburb just south of the airport.

For the first several minutes after the limousine driver turned off the freeway near Duncanville, Shin was struck, first, by the size of the green lawns that stretched from the sidewalks to the tidy front porches of the houses, and then by the size of the houses themselves. The ranchers with were low and long with double, sometimes triple garage doors.

So this is how these spoiled Americans live, he thought as he saw the nice lawn furniture on the side patios and glimpsed through the picture windows the flickering screens of T.V.'s. But soon the neighborhood changed, the houses were smaller and not well-kept.

The silent driver pulled up in front of the worst houses on a street full of shabby houses. A man who looked to be in his twenties hurried out of the house. The man's hair was slicked back and so thin that the shiny freckles on his scalp were visible. His face was full of pockmarks and he hadn't shaved. He bent over to get into the back seat and smiled nervously at Masuki.

"It is nice to finally meet you," said Masuki slowly, trying to enunciate the unfamiliar syllables. "My company and I are very grateful for your assistance in this matter."

"Sure, as long as I get my money, I will be more than happy to get the painting for you," the man said so quickly that Masuki wasn't sure what he'd said. But he had heard the word "painting" and that was not correct.

"It is a scroll," Masuki explained, "not a painting; and it is very old and of great value to the Japanese."

"Sure, whatever you say. It'll be taken care of."

"This word, 'sure'? Does it mean, yes?"

"Yes, that's exactly what it means." And the man started biting his nails.

This turned Masuki's stomach. He didn't like anything about the man who looked dirty and reeked of cigarettes and perspiration. Masuki looked over at the man's arm. Bulging blue veins beneath dark wiry hairs. A few white scars and one nasty-looking scab practically an inch in diameter. The sleeves of his worn and yellowing undershirt were rolled up. That the man hadn't bothered to put on a decent shirt or clean himself up, bothered the hell out of Masuki and made him wish he were back in Tokyo walking through the gleaming halls of Noboru.

Soon this will all be over and this time I better get the generous reward I have been promised, or else.

Or else what? It was hopeless, he conceded, he was tied to the company for life, no matter what.

The driver took them to an empty warehouse off a main street in Dallas. Across from the rear of the warehouse there was a grassy knoll. Even though the governor's motorcade wouldn't be passing through the area until the day after tomorrow, city workers were beginning to unload barricades from a large white van.

Masuki unlocked a door off a narrow alleyway, and the two of them entered the warehouse. The man followed Masuki across the empty expanse of the room and up a staircase to a small abandoned office that overlooked the street where the workers were still busy. Light streamed in through the panes and bounced off the shining metal of the Warrior still hanging from the strap around Masuki's neck.

"Here is a key to a safe-deposit box at the United Bank. In that box is your payment." Masuki reached in one of the large pockets on his vest and retrieved a small key and handed it to the man who eagerly took it and put it in his pant pocket.

"And tonight," Masuki continued, "you will receive your instructions concerning the location of the scroll. Behind you is a rifle that you should leave here for now. I will give you the key to this place when we leave and the rest will be up to you. Don't disappoint us."

"Well, you can bet I'm going to get the money first before I do anything." The man, who was no taller than Masuki, had a dissatisfied look in his small, steely eyes.

"One more thing, my superior insists that I take a photograph of you with the safe deposit box key in your possession as proof that I have carried out my part of the transaction. So if you would be so kind as to move into the light, hold the key up by your face, and look directly into the camera."

There was a pause as the man fumbled in his pocket to retrieve the key.

"That's it...yes, now hold the key up a little more." Masuki saw the man's eyes through the lens staring directly at him as he pressed the button on the side of the Warrior. Two thoughts came to Masuki's mind: first, this would be a perfect image for the program, and second, where had the Russians ever found such a pathetic bum for such a critical mission.

9

Sir Astin, lost in a daze, stared out the small window of the plane. He barely noticed how low the craft was to the green-blue sea before it touched down on the same airstrip Howard's did nearly twenty years ago. Astin was deep in thought. How in bloody hell was he going to get Virgil Faultington off the island before La Bomba discovered that he, Astin, was back?

La Bomba was the only person on the island that Astin didn't have one thing on, and that meant La Bomba was a threat. Astin knew it probably hadn't taken the huge black man long to figure out that the young American, Howard Russo, hadn't committed suicide, nor had he accidentally fallen off the deck. No, La Bomba would have had little trouble figuring out that Astin was somehow behind the murder of the young genius.

However, if all of Astin's orders had been followed to a T and all of the right palms had been properly greased, he should have no problem apprehending that lug-head Faultington and leaving this God-forsaken spit of land in a matter of hours. He patted the case he had handcuffed to his left wrist. He wasn't letting the Warrior out of his sight. Masuki Shin, who Astin thought was an ass, smart but still an ass, had gotten the photo he needed in Texas, transferred it into the computer, and, under orders from Yamato, reluctantly turned the camera over to Astin. If something happened to this blasted camera, Astin's very life would be in jeopardy. Yamato was a ruthless man and his reach long. Everything had to go like clockwork. Yes, he'd planned carefully. Now all he needed was a little luck. He climbed into the back of the jeep, and the young driver took off in a cloud of dust.

By the time Astin got out of the vehicle, he was sweating like a pig in his linen blazer, but he didn't dare take it off. Someone might notice the handcuffs. The jeep sped away, and as Astin crossed the street and headed toward the marina, he reached in his right pocket. His revolver was where it should be.

Astin spotted the peeling hull of the Mercy along the last rickety dock and headed directly towards it. He hurried along, pulled his panama hat down in the front, and avoided eye contact with the numerous people going about their work.

Ah, there he was, stupid, naïve Virgil Faultington in the hull of his rotting boat lighting up a cigarette. Astin picked up his pace, his jowls jiggling as he humped along and finally came up behind Virgil.

"Well, well, look who it is! Fancy, we two meeting up again, Virgil, old chap."

Astin's shadow stretched across the bleached wood of the cabin floor. Virgil turned and looked up.

"Think you're seeing a ghost, don't you?" taunted Astin. "Yeah, a bloody hobgoblin? Or maybe this is all just a terribly bad dream, hey?"

"Oh my God!" Virgil's voice cracked. He leapt onto the dock and charged at Astin. "Get the hell away from...."

But before Virgil reached him, Astin took a photograph from his breast pocket and waved it in front of Virgil's face. "Don't be so hasty, old chap. See what I have here. Just an old bit of evidence, which will remain confidential as long as you cooperate. You see, little buddy, I need you to do something for me… once again, might I add."

Virgil quickly looked at the photo of himself, the yellow bungalow, the deck.

"You fucking devil." Virgil's face was so distorted he looked like he'd lost his mind. "You lied to me and tricked me. I was only a kid."

"Oh, shut up. You were a smart kid who wanted a new boat. So stop whining. You got what you wanted. Now I need you again, and I don't have a lot of time to argue. So shut up and listen while we head to my plane."

"Your plane? I can't just leave. I'm married now. My wife will call the authorities if I go missing."

"She won't be calling anyone because she'll be missing too."

"I will kill you if you've hurt Harriet. I swear I will kill you."

"I haven't hurt her yet. And whether I do or not will depend totally on you."

Astin grabbed Virgil by the upper arm and steered him down the dock. An old silver Chevrolet was waiting. They got in and in minutes were on the other side of the island and pulling up to the airstrip. Another car was already there. Out on the tarmac sat a small sleek jet plane.

"Get out!" shouted Astin as soon as the Chevrolet stopped. As he struggled to get his bulky frame out of the back seat, he hollered to Virgil, "And get any thought of running out of that pretty little head of yours, Faultington. Head to the fucking plane. You heard me."

Virgil walked across the tarmac with Astin on his heels.

The interior of the plane was dark. There were three rows, one seat on each side. Someone was in the last seat on the left.

"Harriet! Jesus Christ!" Virgil screamed.

"Shut up, you pussy!" Astin had his revolver out and jammed it into Virgil's ribs.

"Have they hurt you? Are you alright?" Virgil kept talking. Harriet didn't say a word.

"Didn't I tell you to shut up?" Astin jabbed him again. "You say one more word and I'll shoot her." He motioned with the case which he still grasped firmly in his left hand for Virgil to sit in the first seat. The engines were already revving. Astin tied Virgil's hands to the armrests and took the seat across the small aisle from Virgil. The plane taxied, accelerated, and was airborne.

Astin leaned toward the younger man and yelled over the din from the engines. "How in bloody hell did you ever wind up with such a lovely piece of ass like her, chap? She's too good a flower for the likes of you. Why look at you. You've fallen apart, gone bloody downhill since the last time I laid eyes on you."

Virgil turned. The backs of the seats obscured Harriet from his vision. He turned back to Astin and hollered, "I'm begging you. Please, let Harriet go. She did nothing wrong. She doesn't deserve this and you know it, you old bastard. Tomorrow's our anniversary. Please have a heart, Mr. Astin. Let her go!"

"What do I care about your bloody anniversary? Nothing. But what I do care about is insurance, and that beating heart back there is mine so shut the fuck up, Faultington, and stop begging. It makes you look more pathetic than you already are."

Virgil started trying to yank his arms out from the ropes that held them down and yelling, "Harriet, I'm sorry! I'm sorry! I'm such a sorry bastard. I love you!"

"I thought I told you to shut up," hollered Astin then he slapped Virgil across the face so hard his hand hurt.

10

Large oak leaves blew across the pavement on Bleeker Street as Sylvia and Jake emerged from the Trattoria de Pesce. The air was crisp and they could see their breath puff out ahead of them.

"Looks like autumn is finally here." Jake looked down in the gutter where the leaves had piled up and then over at Sylvia. The wind was whipping through her long dark hair so she gathered it in one fist, pulled it to the side, and secured it beneath her scarf.

In the dim light from the restaurant windows, he admired how luscious Sylvia looked, in spite of the fact that her red lips were clamped shut and her brow furrowed. She'd had another full day, locked up in her office for eight hours and then hurrying off to that photo shoot at the Puck Building. No matter how exhausted she was, Sylvia always had enough energy to take some photos. She rarely talked about it, but her actions spoke louder than her words. She couldn't give up photography. It was in her blood, who she was, her passion. She was always booking locations and models, and disappearing for hours in her private dark room at Lansing. She was doing work on commission too, though, she didn't want it to get around. Jake, in fact, was the only person who knew she'd flown to Washington D.C. for a portrait session with the handsome, young President.

Sylvia had a secret, though. Some project that she wasn't letting Jake in on, and he was getting a little worried about why that was. It had been almost a year since their first night together in Stockton, but their relationship hadn't progressed as quickly as Jake had hoped.

Even now, he thought as he watched her, *she's magnetic, not drop-dead gorgeous like some of the young secretaries at Lansing, but elegant, strong, sure. A fucking rock of a woman. More of a rock than I am.* He couldn't get enough of her. The more she kept him at arm's length, the more he wanted to be with her. He had to admit it, what they had together Sylvia almost totally controlled. Time, date, location, sex or no sex, breakfast or lunch or dinner, a movie or the theater? *Hell, she controls me as much as she controls her company.* But that only turned him on even more.

He kept his efficiency on the upper West Side, but spent many nights, when invited to, at Sylvia's brownstone on Christopher where their incredible sex life played itself out. They got in the habit of closing all the shades and walking around naked. Sylvia suggested they never have sex in the same place two times in a row. They discovered they liked to do it in the kitchen best because sex, they both agreed, was juicier if it involved food or Saran Wrap or counter tops. Most nights they emptied a bottle of Chateau St. Jean and did it at least twice before filling up the Jacuzzi and taking a luxurious bath.

Last month, though, Sylvia added a twist. As soon as Jake got naked, she went into the closet and took out the Fluke.

"I want you to pose for me."

"What? Me? No way."

"Ah, come on, Jake. You'll be great! Look at you, you're so handsome, so well-hung," Sylvia exclaimed with what seemed to Jake like genuine admiration.

"How can I say no now? You always get your way, don't you?"

"Well, not always, but almost always." And she snapped a picture of her naked boyfriend, and the flash lit up the kitchen.

Of course, the photo shoot led to sex and more sex, but then instead of opening the wine and getting in the tub, Sylvia got dressed and called a cab.

"Look, Jake, you relax, make yourself at home. I've got to go to the office. Be back in an hour or so, Sweetie. Open the wine. See you." And she was out the door.

When Jake did finally see the photographs of himself, he wasn't all that happy with them. It wasn't that he didn't look good, because he did. Especially, his tall, lean body. His skin looked flawless. His hair, which he was letting grow a little longer, was shiny and golden. No, everything about him looked good. He was even grinning ear-to-ear in all of them.

So what was it?

He studied each picture carefully. Something about his eyes wasn't just right. They were...vacant...expressionlessness. Something in them was scary and lonely. On several occasions he tried to tell Sylvia about how his eyes in the photographs looked odd. But every time he tried, the words that came out of his mouth didn't make any sense. He sounded to himself like he was talking gibberish. It scared the hell out of him, but Sylvia seemed to understand everything he was saying. He feared he was losing his mind so he stopped trying to talk about the photographs and soon avoided looking at them altogether.

One early Sunday morning, Jake woke up in his own apartment, dressed quickly, and left for Sylvia's townhouse. He knew she had spent most of Saturday at Lansing, and he was thinking that she had said they would take a walk through Central Park before going to late Mass at St. Patrick's. At least this is what he thought he remembered her saying; but when he got to her door and knocked, he couldn't for the life of him remember ever having a conversation about any of it with her. Fear gripped him. *Jesus, am going insane?*

He stood on the stoop and attempted to remember the details of his last conversation with Sylvia; but after a minute he forgot what he was trying to remember, his thoughts drifting up and away, his mind a bubble machine filling with bubbles of thoughts that burst almost as soon as they formed.

Could it be a brain tumor?

He knocked on Sylvia's door again. Then without thinking anything, he opened the door, walked in, and headed up the stairs to the master bedroom. The bathroom door was closed, but he heard water hitting the plastic shower curtain. Slowly he undressed, carefully folding each piece of his clothing as he removed it, carefully making a neat pile of his things on Sylvia's bureau. He knew this was not like him, but he couldn't stop himself from doing it. Why wasn't he just ripping his clothes off and leaving them on the floor like he always did when he was horny and Sylvia was naked?

When he was down to the last garment, he calmly walked to the bathroom and opened the door. The small space was full of steam. Sylvia was in the shower and held the transparent curtain aside for him, saying, "I've been expecting you."

"Did we have a date for this?" he said half-jokingly as he looked down at himself. The sound of her voice, the sight of her body, never failed to arouse him. But, meanwhile, the sound of his own voice was freaking him out. He sounded like a zombie. *Did…we…have…a…date…for…this?* It scared the shit out of him so much so that he froze.

Sylvia laughed and reached out for him. The touch of her hand on his arm made him feel better, and soon he was facing her and the hot water was streaming down his back. She grabbed him and turned him around and rubbed his back with the bar of soap. He could relax now. She was in control now. She would do with him whatever she wanted, and he would mindlessly let her. It wasn't love, real love anyway, for her. He knew this, but it was for him and he would take what little bit of herself she was willing to offer.

With her fingers Sylvia traced his spine down to his coccyx. "You know, young man, I think you are getting really good at reading my mind. Yes, really good."

Sylvia laughed a laugh that sounded to Jake as though it was coming from another planet.

11

When the plane began its descent, it turned west over the ocean and headed inland. Virgil stared at the blanket of many colored trees beneath him. It looked so different from the green landscape of Tortola. Then he noticed the small towns. The roofs of the houses looked like they were made of cardboard.

As the plane rumbled to a stop, Astin untied Virgil's arms, again jabbed the gun in his ribs, and escorted him off the plane. Virgil tried to turn and see Harriet. He wanted to go to her, kiss her, apologize; but Astin was shoving him forward, breathing hoarse orders quietly into his ear, moving him along as though they were attached to each other. Virgil caught a glimpse of a small sign that said Solebury Airport as he was pushed along an empty corridor in an isolated building. Harriet was still on the plane, and Virgil was trying not to panic, trying to think of some way out of what he knew was a very bad situation.

The building appeared to Virgil to be some sort of reception area, but it was completely deserted. Astin shoved him through the door to a men's room. It was large and clean. After a row of urinals, there was a shower stall. A blue suit and white shirt hung on the hook outside it. Neatly folded white underwear was on a chair nearby, and a pair of new wing-tipped shoes sat on the floor.

"Get a shower and make sure you wash that filthy hair. Then get dressed. And don't take fucking forever."

"Look Astin, what's going on here? I've had enough of this."

"Don't get frisky, little man. Remember, your wife is on that plane being watched by my big man."

"I swear, Astin..."

"You'll stop now, if you know what's good for you." Astin raised the revolver and pointed it directly at Virgil's face.

Virgil scowled, turned away, and stripped. He quickly showered, dried off, and dressed without as much as a glance in Astin's direction. He didn't want to screw this up. He knew if he did Harriet would die. He took a deep breath, tried to clear his head, and get a hold of himself. *Keep your big mouth shut, go along, and maybe the fucking gangster will make a mistake....* It was the most Virgil could hope for.

Astin motioned for his captive to head toward the exit. Outside, they got into the back of a black limousine, and an hour later they got out in front of a building on 53rd Street in Manhattan. On the massive wooden door was a brass sign that said "Private Club." By now it was almost midnight and under any other conditions Virgil would have been exhausted, but his adrenalin was pumping from the flight, the drive on the huge highway, the tall buildings, the bright lights. He was jonesing for a cigarette, some hash, anything to calm his nerves, to help him stop worrying about his wife. God damn, he was a screw-up.

"Come on, sir, you can see that I'm going to do whatever it is you ask of me. Just let Harriet go. What if the pilot you left her with does something to her? You have to agree, she doesn't deserve that?" The whole ride into the city Virgil begged for mercy for Harriet, and all Astin kept repeating was, "Shut the hell up, old chap." He must've said it a hundred times, but he didn't hit Virgil over the head with the butt of the revolver, nor did he stop the car and shoot him dead on the side of the road, so Virgil knew Astin needed him, badly.

After Astin rang the buzzer, a man in a tuxedo led them to the rear of the long, narrow room and into a private room where they sat down in a booth in a dark corner. No waiter came, although there were several carrying trays of drinks to other tables.

"Now, this is what is expected of you, Mr. Faultington, so perk up your ears and pay attention." Astin unlocked the handcuff from his wrist and put the camera case on the table between them. He tilted his bald head slightly to one side and pursed his generous lips. "Do you remember Sylvia Russo?

Well, of course you do. How could you possible forget someone you were so fond of, someone you spent so much time with, delightful time with, ferrying her around in your little boat like some princess? Oh, it must have been that guilty conscious of yours that made you fawn over her trying to make her happy. And how could she be happy when her young handsome husband was dead? Murdered by someone, pushed from behind by someone, someone who stood there and watched him plummet to his death. Yes, I am sure you remember your old friend Sylvia, the pretty dark-haired lady whose husband you murdered."

"I didn't...you...."

"Damn it, shut up before I go to a phone and tell my man to shoot your wife." Tiny droplets of spit flew from Astin's mouth. "You are about to run into Mrs. Russo, and when you do, you are to take this camera and convince Mrs. Russo that it is a great camera. Make a date with her to see her tomorrow. It is crucial you are with her tomorrow. Tell her you want to demonstrate the camera. Tell her whatever you have to but make sure you are going to be with her tomorrow." Astin bared his crooked teeth in a devilish grin. "Oh, and have fun, old chap, with your old flame. The lovely, rich lady whom I will have my gun aimed at the entire time." He threw his head back and laughed bizarrely, then he lunged forward and grabbed the lapels of Virgil's suit. "Everything is up to you. You screw up. Everybody dies. You lose this camera. Everybody dies. You get it, you little weasel? Every last body you know dies."

"Whoa, wait a minute, Astin! How am I supposed to get a date with Sylvia when I haven't seen her or talked to her in over twenty years? What in the hell am I supposed to...."

"Stop asking so many damned questions! Put your bloody thinking cap on and be creative for the first time in your screwed-up life. You've had a lot of practice lying, say twenty years worth? So I'd imagine you're pretty good at it." Astin reached over and put the handcuff that was dangling from the case on Virgil's left wrist and clicked it closed.

Virgil stared down at the handcuff and the case like he'd suddenly been attached to a ticking time bomb. "Okay, Astin, look, I know I have to go along with you, but give me something to work with. What's so special about this camera that I've got to have it strapped to me?"

"Oh, that little camera is about to change the world, my boy." He caught the waiter's eye and motioned for him to come to the table. "I'll have a double, your finest vodka, neat. And nothing for my friend here. He has to have a clear head tonight of all nights."

Astin spent the next half hour telling Virgil about Sylvia Russo's career as a famous war photographer and about how she had just taken over as the top executive of Lansing Technologies. Then Astin gave him a few pointers about what to say, and what not to say.

The whole time he had this cocky look on his face that made Virgil want to spit at him.

12

The key to the whole process is in the eyes. Sylvia stared at the photograph of Jake on her screen. *They are the windows to the soul. So much of who he is, or rather of who he was, is in them.* She was about to type another command, but hesitated. *God help me for using him. When it's over, I'll tell him….*

Looking into his eyes once removed like this, made her want to cry; but she fought off her guilt.

MEET ME AT THE PRIVATE CLUB. 8:00 PM

She hit the control button, turned off the screen, locked the door, and left.

She hurried out of Lansing into the fine November drizzle and took a deep breath. Her driver was waiting and he came toward her with an umbrella. She pushed it aside and looked up between the skyscrapers into the thick fog.

Not a single star. Bad luck, Aunt Louise would say. How she missed that woman who had been a mother to her most of her life. If only the woman could have lived long enough to see how successful Sylvia had become, but she hadn't. Momma and Pop Russo were gone too. Uncle Sal was the only one of that generation left. She'd moved him into a very expensive nursing home outside of Lambertville so his kids could visit, and she could, too, when she was in Stockton.

The club was crowded and dimly lit. Sylvia waved to a few of the beautiful people as she walked to the private room in the back and took an empty armchair at the low mahogany bar. The bartender eased a martini into the circle of light from the small Tiffany lamp. Sylvia plucked the toothpick with a large green olive on it from the glass and stared at it.

Only minutes and he'll be here. She was very confident now. All of the trials had been successful. The Fluke, the program, worked. Howard would've been elated. *What good use we could've put it to if he were alive, if he were here with me.*

Sylvia ate the olive, sipped her martini, and checked her watch, 7:50. She leaned back, closed her eyes, and silently prayed a Hail Mary.

"That's Sylvia." She heard a male voice.

"Sylvia? Really?" A different male voice. They both had some sort of British accent. She turned to look at the two men sitting in a dark corner talking loudly. She couldn't make out their faces, so she ignored them assuming they recognized her from the news or a meeting or something or other. She turned back to her drink and took another sip.

"Is it really you, Sylvia?"

This time when Sylvia looked up, she was looking into Virgil Faultington's eyes.

"Virgil? My God, can it be you? What are you doing here?" Sylvia stared up at him in amazement. "I can't believe it. I just can't!" She stood up, hugged him, and touched his cheek.

Virgil hesitated, not knowing what to say next. She was so happy and excited to see him. It made him sick inside not to be honest with her, not to say the hell with everything and confess. But the "everything" was Harriet. He had to pull this off for Harriet. He smiled weakly and took Sylvia's hand.

"It's good to see you too, Sylvia. I'm here on business."

"Please, let me buy you a drink."

Virgil sat in the empty chair next to Sylvia, put the case with the Warrior in it on his lap, and ordered a club soda. At this moment all he could think about was what he should say next. He felt anxious and about to break into a sweat. He studied Sylvia in the half light of the room. She looked superb, rich. Her long dark hair shone like polished ebony. Her lips were the same red as Harriet's geraniums. Her olive skin was light, smooth. Her kohl-rimmed eyes looked like a tigress's. She wore a sedate brown sheath and a long string of pearls. She smelled of gardenias and oranges.

"Sylvia, you look so grown up, so...."

"So mature?"

"No, just all grown-up, but wonderful. Don't get me wrong; you do look wonderful."

"Wonderful? I doubt it. You know me, Virgil, I never gave a damn about how I looked, but now that I'm in the corporate world...well, I have to dress the part," Sylvia smiled at Virgil.

"You were beautiful then, and you are even more beautiful now." He wanted to keep talking like this because it was easy to tell her the truth. Soon he'd be lying his ass off and it would be terrible, so he put it off and said things he shouldn't.

"So what business are you in?" She leaned back and sipped of her drink.

"Me, well, I've just been hired to work for a Japanese camera company. Noboru Industries is just starting their American campaign to bring the latest innovations in camera design and accessories to the States. As luck would have it, I have sample right here." He patted the sleek metal case on his lap.

"How did you ever get involved with a company like Noboru?"

"Well, I was buying and selling classic yachts."

"On Tortola? Wow! Things must have really changed on the island."

Virgil pushed the vision of his decrepit fleet out of his mind. How he wished he could have a drink. That would make the lying so much easier. And he could feel that creep Astin in the shadows staring at the back of his neck.

"Well, yes, they have. One of my clients was on the board of Noboru. That's how I really got involved. He traveled all the way to Tortola to take a look at the stock in my marina, and we hit it off, and a few months later he asked me if I wanted to work for him."

"So, you gave up your cushy life by the sea to sell cameras?"

He could hear the skepticism in her voice. *She always was too smart for her own good*, thought Virgil as he struggled to find a way to turn the conversation in another direction.

"I get to travel all of the time now, and I love to travel. Noboru Industries really takes care of their sales people, and what a product!" He again patted the case. "This is no ordinary camera. This is the future, Sylvia."

"I know how good their cameras are. I'm the proud owner of several." Sylvia checked her watch.

Virgil jumped on the chance to change the subject. "Are you waiting for someone?"

"Yes."

"Well, of course, you would be. I'm sorry, what was I thinking? But before I take off, can I see you tomorrow? Maybe I could demonstrate the Warrior for you. It is our latest prototype, not even in production yet. Lansing Technologies may want to get in on a joint venture with us." Virgil was on his feet, but couldn't leave until he was promised a meeting tomorrow. That's what he'd been told to do, that's what had to be done.

"Virgil, please, you don't have to leave. Jake won't mind me having a drink with an old friend. Stay, please?"

"Jake? I hope he's a nice guy."

"Oh, he is."

"Well, wish I could stay and meet this Jake, but I've got a busy morning tomorrow. How about we meet for lunch?" The pulse in Virgil's temple throbbed and panic circled in his chest like a hungry shark. *Just say yes, just say yes.*

Astin could see everything, probably could read her lips. Disaster was only a phone call away.

God, Sylvia, please don't throw me off. The thought made him stand ramrod straight, the Warrior at his side, his eyes trying to pierce hers into submission.

Sylvia hesitated. *Something's wrong here,* she wondered. *How does Virgil know about Lansing? I never said a word about my company.*

She had the sinking feeling that he was lying to her about something, maybe everything. But why? She stared up at him and saw his tired eyes, his thinning hair, and remembered the golden young man coming toward her, crossing the road in all his golden glory, her Virgil, who stayed up late with her scrubbing the grill, burying the trash, listening to her stories about her dead husband night after night. And here he was right before her eyes, her old friend lying to her. Why? Why was he here? What did he want? She had to find out.

"Virgil, I was just about to suggest that myself. I would love to show you around the city while you're here. That is if you haven't seen everything before. Have you?"

"No, this is actually my first time in New York."

"Really? I would've thought someone who travels the world would've had to pass through the Big Apple at least once before."

"Well, been through the airport a million times, but not the city."

"Are you free all afternoon?"

"I think I can clear my appointments."

Done. Tomorrow I find out what's really going on with Virgil Faultington.

Sylvia could wait till then.

"My place at one." Sylvia stood up quickly, handed Virgil her card, and kissed him on the cheek. His skin was clammy, but she noticed the expensive fabric of his hand-stitched dress shirt, the impeccably knotted silk tie, and that gleaming metal case clutched in his hand.

"One it is, Sylvia, and thanks. I can't believe my incredible luck at running into you."

As she watched Virgil turn and walk toward the front of the club, she knew there was nothing lucky about their encounter. He had a small bald spot on the crown of his head. It made her feel sorry for him. As he moved through the room, she noticed another man hurry out behind him. Just at the exit it looked as though the stranger caught up with Virgil. She was thinking about this as Jake passed them on his way toward her. Her watch read 8:05.

"Heavy traffic," Jake said slowly, very slowly. He bent over and kissed Sylvia on the cheek. He sat in the seat Virgil had left empty. Sylvia smiled weakly at the young man. She was distracted now by her encounter with Virgil. She couldn't stop wondering about him, about how he happened to find her in this city of millions. She didn't mean to ignore Jake, and he was making it harder to by the minute because his hot hand was already working its way up the inside of her thigh.

13

Astin and Virgil emerged from the club, and the howling wind damn near took Virgil's breath away. Astin nudged the younger man and shouted, "Nicely done, old chap. Now let's get some rest."

Virgil spent the night handcuffed along with the Warrior to a bed post in the Plaza Hotel. Fresh clothes, strong coffee, and pastries were delivered to the room in the morning. Astin showered and shaved without making any conversation, then sat outside the bathroom with the door ajar and the revolver in his hand while Virgil did the same.

When Virgil had passed inspection, Astin sat him down at the small breakfast table and laid out the rest of the operations.

"The President of the United States is going to be assassinated."

"Are you kidding me?"

"Shut up and listen, Faultington. I am only going to tell you what you need to know and what your job is. So don't interrupt me again. You got that?"

Virgil was speechless.

"As I said, the President is in Texas, and by this afternoon he will be dead. The White House will be in a panic. The Vice President will be sworn in and flown back to the White House. Your pretty friend Sylvia, the famous photographer will be asked to photograph the new President as quickly as possible. The country will need to see the dignified image of the man so they'll have confidence in him, trust him. Your job is to make sure you go with Mrs. Russo to Washington and that she uses the Warrior to take the President's photograph. There can be no other scenario. None!

When the photo session is over, you are to take the Warrior from Mrs. Russo, leave the White House immediately, and get into the white van that will be at the gate. When you get to the Key Bridge Inn, I'll be waiting for you. Hand over the camera and go on your merry way, back to your wife, back to your old girlfriend, who, by the way, old chap, wouldn't be a bad catch for a loser like you, being that she's running a huge technology company. Anyway, whatever you do, I frankly won't give a damn at that point." Astin grabbed another croissant from the silver tray. "Now, Faultington, if this all goes as planned, I'll throw in a little bonus for you to keep your mouth shut. You know those photos I have of you doing that nasty little thing for me so many years ago? I'll tear them up. Right before your eyes. You'll be free of me forever, free to start over, or go back to whatever pathetic existence you care to."

It was around eleven o'clock when Astin wrapped up his speech to Virgil, and they made their way through the lobby looking like any well-to-do business partners. They walked north along Central Park and stopped in front of a provincial-looking building. Two men dressed in knee-length black overcoats and top hats stood on either side of the large bronze double door. Four cone-shaped evergreens, almost a full foot taller than the doors, grew out of enormous concrete urns and were evenly spaced in front of the facade of the building.

"Go on, chap, and don't try anything stupid. See you in D.C."

Virgil walked away from Astin feeling he was trapped in a bad dream. The President of the United States was going to be assassinated. He knew it was going to happen, and he couldn't do a thing about it. If he did, there was no hope for his wife, probably even Sylvia was in jeopardy now. How could he sacrifice them? It was unthinkable. Every half minute he told himself he should go to the police, tell them, and try to save the President. Then he'd picture Harriet trapped in that plane, the pilot aiming a gun her, pulling the trigger, her brains splattering all over the cabin. No, he couldn't let that happen. *Stay in the moment, gather your wits,* he told himself. How in the hell was he going to get a person as strong-willed as Sylvia to take him with her to the White House? She'd be on official business. And why in the hell would she want to use any camera other than her own? Who thought up this hare-brained scheme? And how in the hell was he going to make it happen? Virgil's head was spinning. He hadn't a clue, but he was caught in the vortex now.

That bastard, that bloody bastard, he thought as he stopped in the doorway between the two doormen and turned to see a mounted policeman pass slowly in front of the building. Virgil waved to the officer. He waved back. The urge to run up to him and spill his guts gripped Virgil, but he didn't. He looked around quickly. He didn't see Astin anywhere, but that didn't mean a thing. He went into the building

The foyer of Sylvia's apartment was bigger than Virgil's whole house in Tortola. A glass round table sat in the middle of it. A huge crystal vase held a dozen spears of white gladiola. A mammoth chrome chandelier hung above the blossoms like a giant squid mid-stroke. Beyond all of this, in the living room was a wall of windows. Three sleek sofas formed a U facing the view of Central Park. Virgil felt as though he'd just climbed up into one hell of a tree house.

"So what do you think?" Sylvia said pointing to the city-scape beyond the windows and the park. "A place like this must be a real shock to your system. So very different from Tortola, isn't it?"

Virgil, of course, was awestruck, but he couldn't let on to Sylvia that he was. He shifted the case holding the Warrior to his other hand. Astin had dispensed with the handcuffs today. He'd have to be handing the camera over. Damn, he was sweating. He walked over to the windows so Sylvia wouldn't see the anxiety in his face. His eyes followed the green treetops to the grey buildings beyond.

"Yes, a shock to my system alright, why I feel like a fish out of water." Virgil let himself take in the view then said, "I have been to a great many cities, you know. It's just that New York is, well, New York. This is a great apartment, Sylvia. It's huge. Four of our little shacks, as you call them, could fit in here. Did you decorate it yourself?"

Virgil knew his attempt at small talk was pathetic, but his brain seemed addled. He turned his back to the wall of glass and scanned the room. The modern furniture seemed to float above the sand-colored shag carpet. The largest television Virgil had ever laid eyes on was built into one side wall. A fireplace ran along the length of the other. Above it hung a poster size photograph of a royal palm.

"I did it in sepia to match the carpet. Is it still there, Virgil?" Sylvia looked at the large photo. "It was the beauty that stood by the jetty just south of La Bomba's Shack. How is he anyway?"

"The tree. No. I think it went down last season. La Bomba? Yes, he's doing well. Getting older hasn't calmed him down one bit. Still has that sign over the shed. Still wants to look at all the young girl's you-know-whats. Still just as crazy, and kind, as ever. Hey, and he still uses your kitchen."

"You mean, our kitchen," Sylvia interrupted.

"Yeah, okay, I guess I was there a lot."

"You were a big help to me."

"But I should've done more." His voice trailed off. He really didn't want to talk about old times. "Hey, tell me about your company? I hear you're in charge now."

"No big deal. I'd rather hear about your camera company. You know how much photography means to me. So tell me more about Noboru Industries? No offense, Virgil, but it just seems unlikely they'd employ someone without some technical background to handle international camera sales. After all, I know for a fact that they've installed their own mainframe. Now that's a very progressive step for a camera company." Sylvia walked toward the seat by the huge television and motioned for Virgil to join her.

They sat down next to each other. Virgil looked at her and thought, *this is Sylvia, get to the point. Maybe she couldn't figure things out years ago, but this is now. She can probably smell a rat a mile away.*

"Virgil, you're frowning. Are you alright?"

"Yes."

"You don't look alright. Can I get you a drink or something?"

"I would love a drink. You have no idea how much I would love a drink. But I won't have one, not until this is over." He put the Warrior down between them.

"Until what is over?"

Virgil hesitated. "Are we alone?'

"Why, of course, we're alone. Who else would be here?"

"Oh, I don't know. Anybody. Maids. Butlers. Are you sure?"

"Yes, look, you can trust me."

"I knew I could before, but now? So much is at stake." Virgil got up quickly and went to the window and looked down at the street, at the tops of people's heads. There was no sign of Astin anywhere; but Virgil couldn't forget what he said about having his gun on Sylvia. Was he bluffing? He thought it over one last time, and then turned back to Sylvia. "I don't want to lie to you anymore. If I tell you the truth, you'll hate me; but if I don't, worse things will happen than that. Everything depends on you, Sylvia."

"What are you saying, Virgil?"

"We could all die, you, me, Harriet."

"Harriet?"

"He's got her. He's holding her hostage in some airport in New Jersey."

"Who's holding her hostage? Where? Slow down, start from the beginning," Sylvia got up and walked toward Virgil.

"No, get the hell away from the window." He grabbed her by the arms and pushed her back into the chair.

"Please, stay away from those windows. His name is Astin. I don't know if you remember him or ever even saw him. He lived in Tortola, worked for the British government. Just before the war he left to become some kind of consultant for Noboru Industries. I hadn't seen him in twenty years when two days ago he shows up with a gun and kidnaps Harriet and me, and flies us here."

"Why would he want you and Harriet?"

"She's my wife and ..."

"Your wife?" Sylvia's surprise was evident.

"Yes, my wife. But, Sylvia, Astin has something on me."

Sylvia felt faint, and, though Virgil kept talking, she stopped listening. *Virgil married Harriet? This guy Astin has something bad on Virgil?*

As he spoke, she watched his mouth move, his eyes blink, and remembered him swimming just beneath the surface of the water, his hands by his sides, his whole body undulating through the water like a large, exotic, beautiful fish. So beautiful, and so innocent.

14

Back in the lab, Masuki was soothed by the steady hum of the mainframe. To him it was the sound of superiority. He, and only he, knew how to harness the artificial brain, and he was grateful to be alone with this magnificent machine. The photo of the knucklehead from Texas had uploaded beautifully. This would all go smoothly. Masuki could feel it in his fingertips. He sat down in front of the blank screen and waited for Yamato.

"Chairman Masuki, you can begin as soon as Miss Tasho joins you." The voice came across the intercom. The Chief was in the glass enclosed anteroom watching him.

"Sir, I don't need an assistant. I would prefer to complete the task alone." Struggling to hide his frustration, Masuki stared ahead at the blank screen.

"Shin, your preference means nothing to me. Tasho must learn how the program works, and this will be the perfect demonstration, will it not?"

Masuki turned. His boss flashed him a toothy smile.

"As you see fit." Masuki bowed slightly and turned back. He knew what the old man was up to. No way did Yamato want him to be the only one who knew how to use the program.

Tasho, followed by Yamato, entered the lab. Tasho sat next to Masuki. Yamato stood directly behind Shin where he could watch his every move. Not saying a word, Masuki quickly flipped several switches. When the grimy American's image popped up on the screen, he bent over the keys of the typewriter and went to work. His fingers flew like the wind. There was no way the young woman could learn the code.

Did the Chief really think him stupid enough not to recognize this attempt to make him obsolete?

"Slow down!" Yamato shouted at the back of Shin's head.

Reluctantly he obeyed. It was okay, though. Those few final strokes were meaningless without what preceded it.

The die was cast.

Tasho, with a baffled look on her face, bowed to the men and left.

The Chief said nothing, turned, and took a private elevator to the penthouse suite.

Masuki turned off the monitor and surveyed the immaculate environment. He looked at the Warrior and held it up to the light to admire, once again, the flawless craftsmanship. It was like looking at his whole life. Yes, he was mostly satisfied with all he had accomplished, that is, up to these last few moments.

Subterfuge, he thought, *I should have expected it. Yamato, always ten steps ahead. Already he tries to replace me. Me, who has done everything for him.*

He looked up at his reflection in the glass. What he saw frightened him. He was a pale and haggard ghost of his former self.

And now the blood of an American President will be on my hands. Not that Shin didn't hate the Americans. No one who lived through the bombings could forgive the Americans, but they had helped his country to rebuild. The very building he was in would not have been possible without the money the United States poured into Japan. Yamato had been one of the first to apply for foreign aid to rebuild his company.

As Masuki put the Warrior in its case, memories tugged at him. He returned from Nara long after most of the rubble had been cleared away so he'd never really seen firsthand the extent of the damage the city and the company had endured, but Yamato Yoshio had. Yes, old Yoshio knew more than he, Masuki, knew. And Masuki had to admit, by sending Masuki away to Nara, Yamato had guaranteed nothing would happen to the prototype, to Shin, his wife, and his mother.

He tapped the desktop. He should feel at least some gratitude toward his boss, who had to swallow his pride and taken money from the hated Americans so that Noboru Industries could be rebuilt. If Yamato hadn't done that, Masuki would have had to start over somewhere else, and at his age, even then it would not have been easy.

Though they had never spoken of it, Shin knew the first atom bomb had claimed all of Yoshio's beloved family. The United States had in seconds erased everything Yamato loved and lived for, except his company. How Shin wanted to feel sorry for him! How Shin wished he could be Yoshio's comrade in avenging those horrific injustices...but this game of revenge Yamato Yoshio was playing was a dangerous game that could cost Noboru Industries everything.

No, Yamato has gone too far. Twenty years have passed and his stupid plotting could ruin us all!

And Masuki could see once again what little regard Yamato had for him, even after all these years.

He celebrates alone, not so much as a drop of beer for me. Me, who has done everything.... No, he will always be the way he is. He will always only worry about himself. He may have been different before, but now he is...unbearable.

Instead of focusing on a marketing plan for the Warrior or selling it to the highest bidder, Yamato is hell-bent on destroying our old destroyers. Instead of making us the wealthiest entity on earth, he is going to screw it up just to satisfy his thirst for America's blood.

The more Masuki thought things through, the angrier he became. It was true. Yamato was going to send him out to pasture like some weak, useless, old horse.

"I'm not obsolete, Yamato is! The senile old bastard!" Masuki shouted at the top of his lungs, but he was in the well-insulated lab so no one heard him.

Oh, why hadn't he faked the command? If anyone ever found out about the Warrior before Noboru could capitalize on it, well, it would ruin everything. He had the chance to undermine Yamato, to guarantee the security of the Warrior, and he'd let it slip by. Why hadn't he programmed the ungainly American to go buy an ice cream cone?

15

"The plan is for you to use this camera," Virgil said as he handed Sylvia the case. She took it from him, opened it, and examined the Warrior.

"Use it for what?" Sylvia looked from the camera to Virgil.

"For the official photograph you will be asked to take of the new President immediately after he is sworn in."

"Virgil, what in God's name are you talking about? New President? Virgil, I'm sorry, but I am not following you. Quite frankly, you are not making one ounce of sense." Sylvia put the camera back in the case and stood up to face her old friend.

"Astin told me that the President is in Texas today, and that he's going to be assassinated. Oh, I know it all sounds crazy. You probably think I am crazy. I couldn't blame you, but Sylvia, I swear to God I am only telling you what Astin has told me. After the Vice President is sworn in as the new President, you will be called down to Washington to photograph him. Astin insists you use that camera." Virgil pointed at the Warrior. "For whatever reason, I have no idea."

Sylvia went over to the television and turned it on. "I spent the morning alone in the dark room. I haven't heard any news all day."

The static faded, the screen came into focus. Walter Cronkite was in the newsroom. "We've just gotten confirmation. As we have been reporting, the President has been shot. The shooting took place along the route of the motorcade in Dallas, Texas. We have no information, as yet, about the...."

"Damn!" Virgil sank into a chair, lowered his head, and ran his fingers through his thinning hair. "Goddamn it! I should've done something. I should've stopped that bastard, Astin, a long time ago."

"What do mean 'stopped him'?" Sylvia looked at Virgil, and it struck her that he had known this atrocity was going to happen and did nothing to stop it!

"From the moment I met him I knew he was nothing but a piece of shit! Damn him!" Virgil shouted at the television. He was up and pacing back and forth in front of it.

Frightened, Sylvia picked up the camera and looked through the lens.

Virgil went to the window and screamed, "Go ahead, you old bastard, shoot me! I'm such a fool. An idiot. Just shoot me and get it fucking over with!"

In the background Cronkite kept repeating something about the severity of the President's wounds.

Sylvia was trying desperately to remember details, minute details from Howard's original notes. The Fluke had been altered in so many ways from what would've been Howard's prototype that she wasn't sure about the camera she now held in her hands. She aimed it toward the wall of windows where Virgil was standing to get more light into the lens. Gently, she compressed the button on the side of the camera and as the aperture opened, she saw exactly what she suspected she might see.

Noboru Industries must have had the prototype and perfected the program, too. In her mind things started falling into place: Howard's death, his missing camera, Noboru's increasing interest in computer technology, the shooting, the official photograph that would have to be taken for the news agencies. Was Virgil just a pawn in all of this or did he know more?

"Virgil, calm down," said Sylvia. "We've got to make some sense of this mess. This is so much bigger than the both of us, but I'm beginning to sense there is a master plan. But I don't see why Astin went through you to get to me. He could've used someone right here in New York, somcone like Jake, or one of my employees."

Virgil sat back down. His once handsome face furrowed.

"God, I don't want to tell you," he said in a hoarse whisper. "He's had me over a barrel for years."

"Virgil, just tell me." Sylvia was running out of patience. She needed to hear the truth no matter how horrific it turned out to be.

Virgil stared into the space between them and said, "I killed your husband. I pushed your husband off that deck."

"No!" Sylvia backed away. "I don't believe you!"

Virgil straightened himself and looked at her. "I killed Howard Russo. Me. I killed him."

Virgil's words rippled through her like a shock wave. Her stalwart desire to believe Virgil, to believe in him, in all things good and true, had just been shaken to its core. Yes, all the joy in her heart she'd worked so hard to restore since the war was crumbling. She steeled herself for the next revelation and said, "Please, tell me why? Why did you do such a terrible thing?"

Virgil looked away, rubbed his hands together as though they were cold as ice. "It's no excuse, but Astin convinced me Howard was a Nazi spy. Astin said, 'They think they can fool us by sending an American, but don't be fooled, chap, that man is a bloody Nazi.'"

Tears welled up in Virgil's eyes, but he continued, "Sylvia, I know how ludicrous it sounds now, but Astin swore that Howard was an engineering genius who was working on a bomb that would destroy the United States and the whole Caribbean with it. Astin was a powerful man on the island. He'd been good to me, very good to me, so I didn't have any reason not to believe him. Hell, I thought I was serving my country, doing a great thing by getting rid of such an evil person. I had no idea what a fucking snake Astin was. My father had even worked for Astin, and my father loved the bastard. But I swear, Sylvia, as soon as I met you and heard you talk about your Howard, I knew Astin had used me. By that time he was gone, and I didn't have the nerve to tell anyone. I was only a kid, a stupid fucker of a kid. But that's no..."

He buried his face in his hands. "I am so sorry. I know you can't forgive me; but for God's sake, Sylvia, help me save Harriet. When it's over, I'll turn myself in. I promise."

The afternoon sunlight streamed in through the wall of windows. The television screen flickered. Numb, Sylvia stared at the big screen. The flag atop the Capitol Building was slowly being lowered to half-mast.

16

Masuki knocked lightly on the door of the penthouse. When no one came, he tried the knob. It turned easily. Quietly, he entered the room. The back of the Chief's remarkably small head formed a silhouette against the lit television screen. An announcer from the Tokyo National News Service had interrupted normal programming to keep the public informed about the developing story in the United States. Masuki half-heard the commentary, but he knew what had happened. The President of the United States had been fatally wounded during a motorcade through Dallas.

"It's me, Chief Yamato, Masuki Shin."

The Chief didn't turn his head, but grumbled, "You woke me up you fool. Oh, and good that you did. Look, the news I've been waiting for. At last, revenge!" Yamato stood up, picked up his tumbler of scotch and raised the glass to the screen. "Why are you here, Masuki? Everything is going according to plan. And how did you get into the private elevator, anyway? You need a code."

"You forget, your Excellency...."

"Your Excellency, come now, Shin, I am not royalty."

"But, your Excellency, you are royalty to me, to us, to everyone at Noboru. We depend on you, on your judgement. Why we are mere serfs, you are our master," Shin said as he walked slowly forward and bowed lowly before Yamato.

Yamato waved his hand at Masuki in a sign of dismissal. "Stop your nonsense. Be quiet now and watch your handiwork. Again, Shin, you have not failed me."

His voice was soft, his words kind, but they rang hollow for Masuki, who wanted to say aloud, no, it is you who have failed me.

Masuki walked over to his long-time superior and stood next to him.

Yamato's eyes were glued to the screen. "See, there he is. The man whose mind the Warrior controls. He is like a wild animal, trapped, bewildered. The authorities want answers, but the poor creature has no idea why he has done what he has. To the world he is an assassin, a murderer; but to me, to us, to Japan, he is a hero, a martyr for our cause."

Masuki whispered, "And what cause would that…."

The Chief, not listening, interrupted, "Now tomorrow, I want you to teach Tasho everything, how to use the camera, how to program it, how to connect to the computer. She is a bright young woman, and it is vital that we have someone else who knows everything. After all, what if something should happen to you? Look at the risk we took sending you to America. So many things could've gone wrong."

Yamato bent down, picked up the crystal decanter of scotch, and refilled his tumbler, offering not a drop to Masuki, who watched as the old man took a sip of the expensive liquor. How parched Shin's mouth suddenly felt.

"And you know, Shin, you are not getting any younger. I need to arm the next generation with your knowledge, in case, well, like I said, something happens to you."

At Yoshio's words, dark anger welled-up inside of Masuki.

There it is! The truth! He plans on getting rid of me, if he doesn't ruin the company first!

Masuki felt a sharp pain in his chest then a hot flutter that spread up into his neck and down the length of his arms to his fists which he clenched automatically. He looked quickly at the screen just in time to see the hopelessly dumbfounded countenance of the criminal he had photographed only days ago. Slowly he turned to face Yamato.

"My thinking is lucid now. I no longer sleepwalk. People like that vagrant on the screen, like my lovely assistant Megumi, like the young American President may be expendable to you, but I, oh Great One, am not!"

"Shin!" The Chief cried out, his voice high and shrill, like a girl's.

Masuki's hands were around his throat. "Go ahead and scream. Scream your stupid head off. No one can hear you!"

Masuki almost wished that all the chairmen were there, that all of them could hear Chief Executive Yamato beg like a baby for his life.

It was several minutes before Masuki knew that he had succeeded in killing the man, who was stubborn to the last. How Shin's hands ached from trying to choke the life out of that scrawny body. Frustrated by Yamato's gurgling refusal to be strangled to death, Masuki had grabbed the beautiful decanter by its neck, smashed it against the top of the coffee table, and slit his boss's throat.

Masuki dropped what was left of the decanter into the puddle of blood and spilt scotch that was expanding on the white, shag rug, the exact kind of rug that covered the conference room floor. He almost laughed to himself at the irony.

Good god, thought Masuki, *the stupid old man put it everywhere.*

He went over and shut off the annoying television.

17

The passenger cabin of the small plane was sweltering inside even though it was almost the end of November. Outside the small window Harriet watched the wind plucking the last leaves from the trees and scattering them in the air like bats at dusk. She watched as Astin shoved Virgil into a car and sped away down a narrow gravel road.

Hours ago back on Tortola, Astin had stopped her on her way home from work, jammed a revolver in her ribs, and told her it would be in her and her husband's best interest to quietly come with him. Now she sat strapped in her seat with both arms tied to the arm rests. She stared after the vehicle and watched the leaves get lost in the air. She was frightened, but she trusted Virgil to come back for her. He hadn't always been the best husband, but she knew he would look after her. She took several deep breaths and tried to push aside her trepidation.

Suddenly the pilot emerged from the cockpit and smiled at her.

"Excuse me, but where are we? I've never seen a place this barren before." Harriet's natural tendency toward pleasant conversation seemed to fall on deaf ears. The man stared at her blankly.

Slowly, he uttered what seemed for him impossibly difficult words, "I can no talk."

With the engine off, the cabin was heating up quickly. He unlocked the heavy exit door and pulled it inward. A gust of cool air rushed past him, and Harriet took a deep breath.

"Do you know what's going to happen to me?" asked Harriet, hoping she could make friends with this man who was a pilot and maybe not really involved with that British man with the gun. But the pilot stood in the opening and didn't acknowledge her question in any way.

He was short and stocky and his muscles strained against his one piece flight suit. He turned and faced Harriet. In the dim interior his eyes looked like small black slits in his skin. His cheekbones were high and angular, his brows jet black and arched. His thin lips were tightly closed.

"I can no talk," he repeated this in the same flat tone.

"Maybe you would untie me, please, sir? These ropes are hurting my arms. I promise I won't do anything wrong."

To Harriet's surprise, he walked to her seat, bent over, and untied one arm then the other. They were numb and ached. Her hands were heavy as stones. Harriet tried to shake some feeling back into them. The wind and dampness had made the space chilly. She hugged herself and pressed her hands under her arms to stop from shivering.

"Do you know how long we'll be here?"

The pilot stood right in front of her, boldly staring down at her. Harriet started to get a little nervous. She wished he'd stop staring at her and go back to the front of the plane so she could run the hell away from him. But his eyes were open wider now and boring into her. They moved from her face to her body.

Nervous, Harriet said, "It's very cloudy outside, mister. Don't you think it might rain?"

His head turned toward the door, and Harriet noticed how flat his face was. She couldn't help being a little fascinated. Rarely did she see anyone so exotic looking on Tortola. It was one thing to look at photographs in books and magazines of Asians, it was quite another to see one in the flesh and blood. Curiosity began to supplant Harriet's initial fear. She felt rather calm, suddenly, as though, for the moment her whole world was this cabin and everything depended on this strange and alien man, who she was quite sure would eventually help her. After all, isn't that what one stranger did for another?

"So where are you from?" Maybe he would like to try to talk about himself.

He said nothing, but his eyes again went from her face to her body. He was looking down at her thin blouse.

"Oh, I know I'm not dressed properly for such weather as this." She hugged herself more tightly, smiled up at him. "You look young to be flying a plane. How long have you been flying?"

He took a deep breath and seemed about to try to say something.

Good, she was getting to him. She leaned forward and said, "I've never been on a plane before...."

He mumbled something, then suddenly pushed her back into the seat. Hard. Harriet was stunned. His hands were on her shoulders. She struggled to free herself, but the pressure of his hands was too much for her. Frightened, she pummelled him with her fists. He let go of her shoulders, grabbed both her hands, and pressed them into her groin. His mouth went to her neck and he bit into it. Harriet screamed. He covered her mouth with his, all the while still pressing down on her arms. She started thrashing wildly about. He pulled her hands up from her groin and shoved them against her breasts as he jammed one knee into her lap and bent over and took her lower lip between his teeth. Blood ran down his chin and over Harriet's blouse.

She screamed, "Help!"

Someone had to hear her.

He started laughing at her. He had taken both of her hands in one of his and was ripping the front of her blouse open with the other.

"Stop!" she begged, and he slapped her across the face.

Harriet stopped fighting, stopped moving.

Be silent. Give in. If she didn't, she knew he would kill her.

He lifted his head from her bare chest and stared at her. He seemed surprised that she'd stopped fighting him. He said several sentences in a sing-song language. She understood nothing. He had both her hands stretched out to either side of her torso so he could suck on her breasts. He tucked his head down again and started to bite her nipple. Harriet wanted to cry out in pain, but she prayed for the strength to let him do whatever he wanted, as long as he didn't kill her. She started to hum a beautiful unnamed island tune. He stopped again and looked sharply into her eyes. She forced herself to smile at him. He tilted his head like a dog trying to figure out what his master wanted him to do. His grip slackened for a second.

How Harriet had the courage, she would never be able to say, but she lunged forward with all of her strength and found his ear with her teeth and bit down as hard as she could until she tore away his flesh and spit it at him. He yelped like the dog he was, then laughed.

He stepped back.

My God, he's going to kill me now, was all she could think.

He was bleeding and it was dripping down over his pilot suit. He touched his ear and as he took his eyes from her for an instant to look at the blood on his hand, Harriet sprang at him and knocked him to the floor. She straddled his body and tried to pin his arms under her knees. She had no weapon but her hands, so she clawed furiously at his eyes. She felt one nail sink into soft flesh. He screamed in agony as she kept clawing at the eye until she ripped it open. He freed his arms from beneath her knees and both of his hands went to protect his eyes, but Harriet started biting the backs of his hands while still attacking his eyes. Her nails broke and her fingers ached, but she didn't stop. His face was a bloody ball, but she was afraid to stop. When he grab one of her wrists, she reached back and took off one of her thick-heeled shoes and started pounding the heel into the top of his head.

It seemed to take forever, but at one point she realized his body was limp beneath her. Still she didn't trust he wouldn't attack her again. She held the shoe high above his head ready for the next strike. She listened. The only sound was the wind. She crawled off his lifeless body and down the ladder of the plane and walked toward the deserted building.

18

As the train sped southward, Virgil, next to the window, stared straight ahead. Sylvia observed his chiseled profile against the blur of the foliage, the clanking wheels bringing to mind the hundreds of trains used to transport the thousands of victims to the awful places, the Auschwitzes and Dachaus.

So he thought he was saving people from the Nazis....

Her anger, somewhat mollified by pity and understanding, she almost reached over to touch him. Beyond the letters Howard had sent her describing the bombings in England, the smoldering buildings, the dead and injured, she had her own arsenal of haunting remembrances. War was a hell that continued to suck its victims into the inferno long after the last treaty was signed.

No, if it hadn't been Virgil, this man, Astin, would have found some other innocent, young man to lie to, to twist around his little finger, and use to do his dirty work.

"I'll go along with Astin's plan," Sylvia said, "but only until we know Harriet is out of danger."

Virgil turned to her, a look of relief on his face. "Thank you, Sylvia, from the bottom of my heart."

"You don't have to thank me. I loved Harriet too." And she had loved the beautiful, happy girl. Sylvia would never forget the sound of Harriet's laughter, how it pulled the sorrow right out of Sylvia's broken heart. She'd do what she could to make sure Harriet was safe.

When they got to the station, the white van Sylvia had requested was in the lot with the keys in the ignition. She drove to the Smithsonian Mall, let Virgil out, and told him to wait on a bench opposite the Museum of Natural History. She then drove to the White House.

The guards escorted Sylvia to a small room in the basement, an exact replica of the Oval Office. Sylvia took Astin's camera from its case, attached it to a tripod, and set it in front of the mahogany desk behind which the new President would sit for his official portrait. She took the Fluke from its case and set it on a chair by the lights.

Sylvia nodded politely, as the tall, broad man entered the makeshift studio and shook her hand.

"I am so sorry about all that has happened, sir," Sylvia whispered.

"Thank you, Mrs. Russo. It has been a shock, an extraordinary ordeal for all of us. Now shall we get this bit of business out of the way as quickly as possible?"

"Certainly, Mr. President. I'll do my best."

She adjusted the spotlights and snapped several shots with the Warrior on the tripod, but the distance between the camera and the President was too great for her to capture him completely. She thought for a second about purposely not getting the close-up needed in order for the President to be programed, but Harriet's life was on the line. She better get the right shot with both cameras. Hurriedly, Sylvia unscrewed the camera from the tripod, approached the desk, and leaned in toward the President. She looked through the opened aperture. The man's eyes were riveted on the opening.

Click.

Done.

"Just want to do the same shot with my back up, sir. It'll only take one minute more." She put the Warrior down, grabbed the Fluke, and returned to the same spot.

Yes, good...he's looking right into the aperture.

Click.

"We're done here, sir."

Virgil, waiting on the bench in the wicked wind, rubbed his hands together and blew his hot breath into them. His eyes kept going back to the massive petrified tree trunk laying on its side atop a marble pedestal next to the museum stairs. How strange, a tree could turn to stone. On Tortola a tree just rotted away.

Which tree was he like?

Both. His heart had turned to stone, and his soul had rotted away long ago.

He was grateful to Sylvia for trying to help him save Harriet, but he knew her forgiveness was too much to ask for. And Harriet, when she learned the truth, would have nothing to do with him either. This much he was sure of, and it depressed the hell out of him. He was about to get up, cross the narrow street, and touch the petrified wood when Sylvia pulled up in the van.

He climbed in. "How did it go? Did you get what we needed?"

"Yes, everything's alright so far." Sylvia seemed calm and in control.

"We just have to get the camera back to Astin in one piece, then the bastard better let Harriet go. I hope you did whatever he wanted you to do. You know the bastard is going to check out everything." Virgil's voice was panicked.

"I'm sure he will," said Sylvia.

Sylvia's stomach was in a knot. What in the name of God should she do, turn the brain of the President of the United States over to some foreign power?

She'd perfected the Fluke, fulfilled Howard's vision. Jake was living proof. He was powerless to go against her programming. She couldn't believe it herself at first, but after the third experiment, she couldn't refute the evidence. She had succeeded.

Until two days ago, her plan was to move slowly and methodically. Her priority: Keep the Fluke a secret while figuring out the best way to use it to do good and fight evil.

Sylvia parked the van in the circular driveway in front of the Key Bridge Inn. She grabbed Virgil by the shoulder. "Don't give Astin the camera until he tells you about Harriet, until he can prove to you she's okay. He's not stupid enough to kill you in the center of Washington, D.C. Remember that."

"I don't care if he kills me as long as Harriet's alive."

"Just hold onto that camera, hold it up in front of you like it's a shield, and he won't touch you."

Virgil got out, entered the lobby, went to the desk, and asked for Astin's room number. He took the elevator to the fifth floor. Astin answered Virgil's knock by pulling the door open a crack to see who was there. When Virgil held the case up, Astin unhinged the chain and let him in.

"Fine job, old chap, I hope you got rid of your old girlfriend. We don't need her tagging along looking for another reunion with your wife. I'll take that now so I can examine it and make sure you've got what we need." His lips curled into a crooked grin as he reached for the Warrior.

Virgil jerked the case away from his outstretched hand. "Where in the hell is my wife? You're not getting this thing until I see she's alive and unharmed."

"Why she's waiting for you, of course. I had my man transfer her to another plane and fly her down here to a closer airport, only minutes away, for your convenience. Nothing to worry about now. Just hand over the goods and off we go. Hurry now, I've got to get back to New Jersey, get a flight back to Tokyo, or my people will begin to hit the panic button." He reached again for the case.

"I'll give it to you when I see my wife."

"Have it your way for now, Virgil; but you'll see I'm on the up and up." Astin said this cooly, but Virgil saw the man's eyes narrow and his bottom lip quiver.

They took the elevator down and were picked up out front by a cab.

Sylvia slowly edged the van out into the traffic, one car behind the cab. She tried not to think too far ahead. The traffic was at peak volume, and the cab was shifting lanes. Then they were on the Beltway, and the cab picked up speed, still cutting in and out of lanes. Her hands were tight on the steering wheel. Then the cab accelerated down an exit ramp and headed west on a suburban road. She nearly blew past the exit, but careened across two lanes just in time to get behind the cab as it made a left into the service entry to Cumberland County Airport.

Sylvia drove past and turned into the airport's main entrance. She could see the cab across the tarmac as it pulled up next to a plane. She was a football field away so she circled the parking lot and pulled into a spot where some other vehicles were parked. She reached into her equipment bag, unzipped an interior pocket, and took out a utility knife. She got out of the van and headed toward the plane, where she hoped Harriet was.

As Astin and Virgil got out of the cab, she saw that Virgil still had the case. *Good*, she thought, *he did what I said*.

Virgil stopped and turned to Astin. Sylvia's heart froze. What in the hell was he doing?

Virgil started yelling. Only fragments of what he was hollering reached her.

"Not the same…what the fuck are…kill you…."

She started to run toward them, but it was like she was running through mud and couldn't get anywhere fast enough. Astin's back was to Sylvia, but she saw the gun in Astin's hand. It was pointed at Virgil's throat. Sylvia stopped in her tracks and held her breath. If Astin saw her, he'd shoot for sure.

Don't go off…gun…don't go off!

Astin's other hand was on the case. He yanked it from Virgil's grip. Then the short fat man was running back to the cab. Virgil and Sylvia started toward it, but Astin was in it and it was swerving around them and speeding away.

They stood there watching it for a split second, before Virgil turned, climbed the plane's ladder, and disappeared through the open doorway.

"Virgil!" Sylvia screamed. "Is she there?"

Virgil appeared in the doorway. His face was drained of color. He shook his head. "No." He shook his head again and hollered, "Sylvia, what in the hell I am going to do now? What in the hell did that bastard do with my wife?"

"Virgil, this is important. Do you have any idea where Astin was headed? Think."

He grabbed the hair near his temples and pulled on it. "Back to the place we landed when we flew in from Tortola. New Jersey. He said he had to catch a flight to Tokyo from New Jersey. He must be going back to that airport. It was a small airstrip. In the middle of nowhere. Oh shit, there was a sign. Oh shit, I can't remember."

"For Christ sake, try!"

He closed his eyes and inhaled. "Solebury. It said Solebury Airport!"

Sylvia and Virgil ran to the Cumberland County terminal and pounded on the door marked Airport Security. It seemed like an eternity before someone opened it. Sylvia handed over her identification and hurriedly explained that she needed to have the thief who stole her expensive camera with the photographs of the new President in it apprehended. He was on his way to a small airport in a place called Solebury, New Jersey.

19

Masuki Shin went to the control panel by the elevator and locked it. At last, he had Yamato's penthouse retreat to himself. He surveyed the massive room, the walls of windows, and the twinkling lights of Tokyo below. This was where he belonged. If he'd been in charge, Noboru Industries would be closing the most lucrative deal in the history of the camera industry, not meddling in an eye for an eye, a tooth for a tooth nonsense. No, he'd have seen to it that his camera, the Warrior, would have made him and every other poor fool at Noboru rich beyond their wildest dreams.

He walked past his boss's dead body to the bar and surveyed his options. The oldest and best of Yamato's collection of scotch was behind a locked glass door. Masuki picked up a heavy chrome stool, slammed it into the glass, and watched as it webbed and crumbled. He brushed some of the slivers out of the way with his bloody paw and retrieved what looked to him like the oldest bottle of the bunch. The label was in English and made little sense to him. He was too heady with joy to focus and translate that stupid alphabet. What difference did it make? If Yamato Yoshio bothered to lock it up in his own penthouse, well, that was enough assurance that Masuki couldn't make a wrong choice. He opened it, put the bottle to his lips, and took a sip.

Whew! Smooth wasn't the word! Whatever else he'd ever drunk was gutrot in comparison. He put the bottle to his lips again, took a long drink, and savoured the warmth as it went down his throat and happiness welled up inside him. He took the bottle into the bathroom and stripped off his blood splattered clothes. Another slug of the scotch and he felt light as a feather. He sat on the toilet and watched as the marble soaking tub filled with steaming hot water. When it was full, he gingerly lowered himself into it.

Ah! There was nothing like a bath to revitalize oneself.

He poured salts and oils from blown glass vessels into the tub and put his head back on one of Yamato's thick, fluffy towels. As he drank again from the bottle, the image of his hands around Yoshio's throat came to him.

Had he done it? Had he done what he'd imagined doing many times before? Or was he dreaming all of this, the penthouse, the fight, the scotch, his penis growing longer in the sudsy hot water.

He sat up and turned and looked into the main room. He could see Yoshio's bald spot, the thinning silver hair, and, sinking into the rug, his blood.

It happened. I am here and he is there. Dead.

He leaned back again, drank more, and found himself beneath the foam. He thought of his wife, of their time in Nara when she submitted to him, when she let him tie her down and…now he was hard, bigger than he'd ever been. This was going to be the best.

Yes, yes, the best.

He saw Megumi's eyes, the knife poised in the air, in her own hands. He saw himself on top of her, fucking her on top of the conference room table even though she was already dead. He yanked on himself with one hand. In the other he held the bottle and tilted it so Yamato's expensive liquor poured into his open mouth.

He was a god, the god of the world, finally on top of everything.

He was coming.

Yes.

The golden scotch was flowing. He was in ecstasy.

Come. Come.

The liquor flowing.

And as he came, he gasped. And the gasp made him choke on his saliva. He tried to take a breath, but only coughed and began vomiting. The vomit caught in his throat. The taste of the scotch whiskey came back up, gagging him. He tried like hell to catch his breath, scream for help, catch his...breath, scream, but nothing came out. He was choking now, choking to death, and no one was there to save him, and then to his utter surprise he silently slipped beneath the surface of the water.

20

Sylvia, stunned by all that had taken place, avoided going down into the computer lab. She kept to herself in her office on the top floor of Lansing Technologies and did her best to get lost in the business of running her company, without the Fluke. For the time being, she was once again done with Howard's dream. Too much had gone wrong. Too much more could go wrong. She needed time to sort it all out. She locked The Fluke in the safe next to the Warrior after she'd processed the best of the shots she'd taken of the new President, and tried not to think about either of those cameras.

Sir Astin had been caught red-handed by the New Jersey State Police and taken into custody. Once they returned the camera to Sylvia, she dropped the theft charges so the evil man could be extradited to Tortola and charged with kidnapping and orchestrating the death of Howard Russo. It was a cut-and-dry case, thanks to incriminating photographs and documents found in the safe at Noboru Industries.

The new, youthful Chief Executive, the first woman ever in a position of authority in the history of the company, Rin Tasho seemed eager to cooperate completely with the authorities. The scandalous murder-suicide of the former Chief Executive, Yamato Yoshio, and Chairman of Research and Development, Masuki Shin, had opened the door for her to rapidly ascend the corporate ladder, but it had also been disruptive and bad for business. She was anxious to put the whole debacle behind her and the company.

Virgil, too, faced charges as an accomplice, but his lawyer was sure he wouldn't have to serve any time. He was cooperating fully, and he had been only a juvenile at the time.

Harriet had fought valiantly to save herself. Despite her excruciating pain, she made her way to the main road before she collapsed. A man saw her crumpled body by the ditch, slammed on his breaks, picked her up, laid her in his back seat, and rushed her to a hospital. She was so severely beaten that no one questioned the veracity of her story when they found the dead pilot.

Poor Harriet was shocked to learn the truth about what had happened to Sylvia's husband on Tortola. Would she ever be able to forgive Virgil, not for having been tricked by Sir Astin, but for not confessing it to her sooner? What happened to her that cold day in November in a place completely foreign to her, might have been avoided if Virgil had only told her.

In the transcript of his trial, Astin is quoted as saying, "I tell you, chaps, that lady photographer is the one responsible for the death of your President. I tell you, on my word, she is the criminal. She invented the damn camera. It is a weapon. It can capture your mind, control your will. She is a liar, too. That camera belonged to Noboru Industries. Can't you bloody see, she must have been in with those crazy Japs at Noboru. One of them took the camera to Dallas and took a picture of that poor man. They programmed him to kill your President! And then that Mrs. Russo stole the camera from me and used it to take a photograph of the new President just so she could program him and control his mind. I stole the camera back from her old boyfriend, Virgil Faultington, to save your bloody country. I tell you. I am the victim. I'm telling the truth. She is lying. They are all lying."

No one was listening. And when asked, the Chief of Police exclaimed, "I've never seen nor heard of such a preposterous thing."

Everyone on Tortola had all they could do to keep La Bomba from tearing Astin apart limb by limb at the trial. Two people he loved were this greedy devil's victims. La Bomba had known that Astin had a hand in the death of Sylvia's husband. He also had a strong suspicion that Virgil was somehow innocently involved, and that is why he never said anything to Sylvia those many years ago. But now that he knew the truth, that this devil had scared the boy into killing someone, well, nothing the authorities did would be enough. And his beloved sister raped because of this piece of dirt! There was no punishment that the government could impose that would be enough. La Bomba was the one now who dreamt of revenge. No, La Bomba would see to it. Astin would know not the minute, nor the hour, but the payback would come. And it would come with a fury.

21

It was a steamy Saturday morning in July, months after everything had been resolved in Tortola. Sylvia, though she was loathe to go down into the lab, couldn't put off what she knew she had to do. With some trepidation, she unlocked the door and stared at the new Nova mainframe, Jake's baby. She had to admit she was impressed with its design, much more compact than the old computer. She walked in, went to the safe, and took out the two cases. She laid them side by side on the desk, opened them both, and studied the two cameras.

I guess right about now I would be considered the most powerful woman…no, person, on the planet. God, Howard, am I up to handling the responsibility?

She thought for a moment about her life's journey thus far. Though her marriage to Howard had been cut short, those moments with him were dearest to her, and even now she yearned for him. What if they'd had the chance to…? Oh, it was useless to dwell on the what ifs. She picked up the Warrior, carried it to the monitor desk, and plugged the umbilical cord into its receptor. She might as well start learning about the nuances of her latest acquisition.

It took only a few minutes for Sylvia to work through the idiosyncrasies of the program. She hit a sequence of keys, and the President of the United States was looking through the screen directly at her, like he was in the same room, like she could touch his face if she wanted to. Once she overcame the feeling that he might somehow be able to see her, which she knew was impossible, she stared deeply into his eyes.

"Are you going to do horrible things and hurt many people, or are you going to end hatred and violence once and for all?" she asked the face on the screen. Even if he could have revealed to her his deepest, darkest tendencies, it was a useless question. This man was flawed just like the rest of the human race, capable of being perfectly good one minute and entirely terrible the next. The fact that he was the President of the United States, though, raised the stakes. She'd seen firsthand how the weaknesses, prejudices, and mistakes of those in power could have catastrophic repercussions. This man's finger would be the one on the button. Click...a war, a battle, a bomb.

So Sylvia, though she knew what she was about to do could backfire, proceeded. Slowly, deliberately, she typed the command: NEGOTIATION IS PREFERABLE TO ANNIHILATION.

Enough for now. She unplugged the cord, put the Warrior back in its case, and returned both cameras to the safe.

As she turned to leave, she walked smack into Jake.

He blocked her way out.

"Aren't you going to ask me what I was doing?" she said, though she had no intention of actually telling him. She flashed him a Cheshire grin and teased, "Well, if you must know, nothing earth shattering, just some unfinished business."

"I think we have some unfinished business too." He said as kept his eyes on her, reached behind, and locked the door.

"Not here, not now, Jake."

"Yes, here, and yes, now...Sylvie."

"Sylvie? You never called me Sylvie before."

"I've never been this proud of you."

"What are you saying?"

"That I love you. I always have, always will. And I know exactly what you were doing."

She looked into his eyes, unusual yellow eyes, hickory leaves in autumn, or the color of corn husks...

"It can't be," she whispered.

"Yes," said the handsome, young man. "It can be."

"Is that really you in there?"

Jake didn't answer, Howard did. "Are you surprised?"

Sylvia was speechless. Now that it had happened, she realized she'd hoped all along that it would. And, perhaps, she had even inadvertently orchestrated it.

Something inside Sylvia clicked.

And her true love, Howard Russo, went in for the kill.

Made in the USA
Charleston, SC
26 July 2016